UNDER THE DATE PALM

G.C. BLOODMAN

Contents

Dedicated to God

Chapter One

The echoes of recited passages slowly drift into a satisfying silence. As I begin rising, my feet sink heavily into the soft, richly-designed rugs uniformly spread across the spacious floor. I feel the stickiness of my flesh, soaked by the suffocating presence of purpose pressing upon me. My cousin Noor stands next to me, in another row, behind the imam. A flush of contentment squeezes through his rugged war-torn face. It's been three years since I've seen him last, when he denounced me, accusing me of not following true Islam. He looks older now and more beaten down. I'm just glad to see his heart's still beating.

With their foreheads no longer greeting the floor, the men slowly begin vacating the mosque. Following suit, I slip on my brown leather sandals settled behind me, while quickly scanning the soldier-like crowd for Noor's face. I recognize a few of the faces, some old, ravaged and creased with scars from the merciless battles in life, to those as young and fresh as an unreachable mountain spring, all gathering together for the same duty, fajr, but Noor's nowhere to be found. I carefully merge with the others, maneuvering myself through the courtyard. In the immense openness men are huddled together entrenched in serious conversation, while others are swarming the streets, waking the city from its nightly slumber.

Most days, I'm one of those willing to engage in meaningful conversation hoping to be enlightened by some wise words; however, I often leave disappointed. And despite my intellect telling me I should be involved in something more productive, a part of me needs these exchanges. Yearns for them. Today is different though. I have much to prepare for.

As I follow the worn cobblestone path in front of me, it leads me to the streets flowing with abundant life. It is early, before the heat has grown ferocious, where in the faded half-lit sky the ghost of a crescent moon can still be admired. Heading north on Tahlia street, private businesses, shopping malls and restaurants decorate the street on either side. Fake palm trees lining the center median offering little islands of life below the eclipsing skyscrapers. Passing by me are Pakistanis, Indians and Saudi women accompanied by their male relatives, while navigating with their gleaming eyes through niqabs. My destination, the next door on my right.

It's a small shop, deserted from the view at a distance, squished between a coffee shop and a clothing store revealing its relaxed atmosphere. Many Saudis' come here to enjoy the privacy offered when conversations are at the utmost important. Inside, I survey the tables determining whether my guest has arrived yet. As usual it is relatively quiet with only a few older men seated far off in a corner table as well as a pair of men, one young, seated next to the windows conversing between the sipping of tea. Aware of my visitor's absence, I instinctively direct my eyes to the table of choice. The same one I've been sitting at since I was a boy, stationed below the massive glass wall staring right into the heart of Riyadh. Lightly strolling over to it, I mindfully position myself to face the entrance.

"Can I get you anything?" I hear coming from behind me in broken English.

Glancing over my shoulder a small Filipino man approaches me with chocolate brown eyes set in a round pudgy face. His black shirt snuggles tightly against a slender frame. His recognition of me enhancing the warm presence already exuded.

"Yes, a glass of orange juice," I answer, watching him trod off until disappearing into the back.

Bits and pieces of a business deal invade my ears from the two men across from me. The younger one seeking a favor of some kind, no doubt paying for it. As without wasta (connections) one will get nowhere in Riyadh.

The fresh glass of orange juice is gently placed before me. Without wasting any time, I bring the full glass to my lips. The cold, sweet, citrus taste satisfies the dryness invading my mouth, slowly allowing my body to relax, to drift into daydreams, while peering through the glass at the daily living of Saudi's. I remember walking these streets as a young boy clinging onto my mother's black abaya opposite my sister with my uncle Kamal accompanying us everywhere, approving of nearly every request my mother presented. She raised us by herself with my father merely acting as judge, imposing discipline and rules, while offering no real relationship. She was informed, not long after giving birth to me, that resulting from an internal complication involving an injured uterus, she was incapable of conceiving again. This news ripped something out from deep within her soul. She blamed herself, strapping this burden upon her back through life.

This may be partly why the unconditional love she showered upon my sister and I was magnified beyond what was typically observed among other mothers. She faced many struggles because of it, unleashing a fierce determination to be different and accomplish all she set her mind to. This led her to graduating from King Saud University, studying abroad at Johns Hopkins School of Medicine, then becoming a prominent physician at King Faisal Specialist Hospital and Research Center, one of the top women's clinics in Riyadh. She not only gave me the love and comfort of a mother, but provided me with an intellectual and independent perspective in life requiring me to wrestle with questions in my own mind, which stands in opposition to normal Saudi thinking.

Her beauty is striking, constantly mesmerizing friends and family with her high cheekbones reflecting off her luring golden eyes conveying the gentleness of a butterfly; shiny, oil black hair flowing naturally over her slender shoulders, leaving her mocha skin glowing brighter. But what made her presence was a rare confidence, a fighter-like spirit creating a special aura that lured you in.

Sadly enough, I'm unable to count the times that beauty was swiftly struck down by the meaty hands of my father. Deep down he despised her for not being able to bear any more sons for him along with her independent nature, challenging the boundaries in Saudi life. From that first time I tried to protect her, I became a sponge soaking up the aftermath from his outbursts of fury. He once told me, after I endured a ravaging, leaving me in a bloody helplessness, that everything about me reminded him of her.

Apart from his anger, my father has always been an exceptional source of knowledge regarding Islamic history and tradition. The endless hours of the deepest gray eyes you only see in the clouds of a thunder storm reciting surahs and stories of Muhammad's life have ingrained themselves in my memory forever. His intimidating, thick, six-foot three frame captured the attention of most when he entered a room, not only from his genuine handsomeness, but from the unique demeanor he carries, the kind that makes you feel obligated to listen when he speaks and believe every word that comes out of his mouth. As a sheikh, these characteristics serve him well. Although financially he provides for us, his physical presence is nonexistent. Any spare time left from speaking sermons on television or recording videos for the internet is spent on debating with other religious men or with one of his other two wives he married after my mother.

I was instructed early on by my father, Imam and teachers to hate kafir (unbelievers) and to never question the beliefs or traditions instilled in me. Otherwise, I would bring aa'r (shame) upon myself and my family. Appearance to family, tribe and country is most important. And if by chance a confusing question arises, I am directed to my father first, then an imam, but I've always saved my mother's advice for last, as her answers force me to contemplate in the deepest of ways.

"Umar," I hear, echoing through my ears, waking me back to the present.

Slightly shifting to my right, my eyes fall on Nayef. Staring down on me with those lost black eyes always makes me feel a little uneasy. Uncomfortable to say the least.

"Marhaba, akhi, khaif halak (Hey, my brother, how are you)?" he says, extending his arms.

"Bakhair (Fine)," I respond, receiving his embrace and kiss.

"Listen, we are counting on you to deliver today," he says almost angrily from his bare, round face comfortably parked under his shemagh.

"Don't disappoint us."

"Have I yet?" I answer without hesitating picturing the performance required.

I'm ready, the pressure always falling on me, as if I'm the only one out there treading the grass. I'm accustomed to it now. Everyone expects perfection, yet they themselves fall short without a word.

"I know this game is important to you. That you're hoping to be recognized and signed by a professional club abroad, but afterwards some of us are getting an istirahat (guest house). Sheikh Mohammed bin Ismail Khan will be speaking on some controversial contemporary issues and temptations faced in the kingdom. I want you to be there."

I refresh my mouth with a sip of juice.

"I don't know if I'll be able to make it. I've already made prior arrangements," I say sternly, an image of my mother and I appearing in my mind below the date palm, secluded from the draining action of the city, enjoying the peace and quiet it provides.

"Well, if something comes up and you can make it, give me a call," he says with a touch of disappointment in his voice.

"I will."

"We better get going if we plan on arriving on time."

We make our way to his white Toyota. Patiently entering the endless rush of traffic, we head north on King Fahad Bin Abdul Aziz Road. I can feel the adrenaline beginning to manifest itself within the pit of my stomach, the same as the first time I touched a ball at eight years old when my uncle Kamal kicked it into my feet challenging me to get by him. I failed over and over again, but the competitive nature surging through my bones left me yearning for more, to be better than him. After that, countless days were spent recruiting players to play pick-up games at a moment's notice. With soccer in my life, I had no spare time. Fathers brought their sons and young daughters to the games enjoying the full ninety minutes, except my father. He's never seen me play. Never wanted to, only criticizing me for not following his path in becoming a sheikh. Watching the traces of the streets flash by, I suddenly realize we've taken a sharp left heading away from the field.

"Where are we going?" I ask curiously.

I need to pick something up first," he mutters without averting his eyes from the traffic ahead.

Something inside yearns to ask what's so important, but I relent, not wanting to intrude, allowing the silence to fill the air. Soon we pull into his driveway. I slowly climb out of the seat following him to the door, while watching his face for any objection. Once inside, he briskly walks through the kitchen, as I wait in the sitting room. His two sons are on the floor next to each other eating Ma'amoul. They briefly acknowledge their father's presence when passing by, sensing his urgency from the determined expression on his face. It feels as only a few seconds disappear before I hear Nayef shouting followed by a couple deep thuds. It is that distinct sound when flesh collides against flesh. My heart begins pounding with nervousness. With fear. Boom. Another one, this time ending with a groaning. A familiar groaning heard when one is left suffering, wishing to escape only alive. The doorway leading to the noise is out of sight, about ten paces straight ahead and to the right. Thoughts relentlessly eating away at my mind. Should I check it out? Who else is in there? Is Nayef in trouble? This is not my home though. Not my business. A quick movement activates my peripheral. Shooting over my shoulder on my left little Ali stands staring fearfully in the direction of the disturbance. What is he thinking? Is he going to investigate? I can't risk him getting hurt. Against the overwhelming feeling in my gut screaming not to go, I force my feet forward, until standing a few feet outside the door. Its slightly cracked open, Rana's face lying split and bloody, just inside the room. For a long moment I have the strong urge to rush in and help her regardless of any consequences. But I have to obey. It's unlawful for me to interfere.

Suddenly a firm grip latches onto the crevice in the back of my leg. Thrusting my head down to find the intrusion, my eyes fall on Ali. Trembling in fear with horror ripping through his body, I reach down shoving his face into my thigh to shield the trauma. A low mumble draws my attention back to Rana. She's staring directly at me, paralyzed on the floor. Helplessness tragically escaping from her eyes, yet a glimmer of hope is present in the midst of it.

Her lips begin moving. "I'm so......y," she mutters unrecognizable.

Struggling to take another breath, she tries again. "I'm sorry," she utters, clearly enough for me to understand this time. Instantly, after the words battle their way out, Nayef appears behind her. We uncomfortably lock eyes for a moment, then the door slams shut. He's going to kill her, isn't he? The surge of countless scenarios is overwhelming. Ali's head pushing against my hand wakes me from the brief daze I fell into. I must have been suffocating him not even realizing it. He's scared, confused, only knowing his mother lies half dead on the floor. Gently I turn him around leading him back to his brother still seated on the floor holding a frightened look on his face. He can feel the danger. The death lurking near. Why am I involved in this? Can I escape, erase this entire event from my memory? I can't leave her. Leave her limp body spread across the floor. Leave the boys so vulnerable and innocent.

The familiar clicking sound of a door opening cuts through the thick air. Nayef appears carrying a cold, heartless expression etched across his face with a thobe splattered in blood. Stopping a few feet in front of me, he says nothing, a statue locking onto my gaze. Each passed second causes my defenses to heighten. I search his face for a clue, but am unable to collect anything, only that cold gaze of his. An uneasy feeling begins rising from deep within my gut. Something's wrong. Without averting his eyes or making the slightest movement, words fall from his lips.

"Your mother's an infidel. She's … apostatized."

The world goes mute. Stunned, confused, I attempt to hold some of the oxygen instantly forced from my chest, to hold my composure, but a strong dizziness sets in leaving me unable to concentrate on a single thought or even take a breath. What's happening? Willing myself to fight against such an accusation, Nayef's blurred face slowly begins coming back into focus. Is it true? Rana must have known about it. I need to know. I must know.

"How do you know this?" I demand, sifting through the countless possibilities.

His silence wanes on me, then in a deep, cold tone he breaks in, "Rana wasn't expecting us to be here. When entering the room, she was surprised, fumbling with some papers trying to conceal them. She knew she was caught. She hesitated when I asked her to turn them over, then refused. I knocked her to the floor, pillaging the papers from the purse she stuffed them in. After reading them, I soon realized it was Christian material. I asked her if she believed what was written;

He studies me for a moment

she said no. Then I asked how she got them. She told me a foreigner gave them to her. I sensed she was lying to me as her gaze retreated from mine to the floor. This is when I forced her to tell the truth. She held on for a while though, maybe would have given her life. It made sense when I heard the answer: your mother gave them to her."

"This can't be true." Not my mother. I haven't noticed anything strange or different with her. Maybe I really haven't been paying that close of attention. My sister wouldn't lie about this would she? The pressure weighs on me. I need to know if this is indeed the truth.

"I called your father," he says firmly. "There was no answer."

I instantly think of his actions when he hears about this. My mother will surely endure a fate worse than Rana's. Unless I get to her first.

"I need you to take me to my house." I demand, with a fearless tone.

He studies me for a moment, then without hesitation, replies, "Let's go."

As I purposefully walk to the car a piece of my heart longs to help Rana. To make sure she's alive, safe. However, I reason from her looks she will survive, will persevere while Nayef's with me. Weaving through the crowded maze of streets, my mind racing, not a word spoken, we finally arrive at my house. I impatiently scan for my father's black Chevy Tahoe. A sigh of relief softly eases one layer of tension shaking my body when I see an empty parkway.

Door open, my body rebels against getting out. Not until we make an agreement.

I turn to Nayef. "This is between us; the family doesn't need to know anything," I command.

"I give you my word," he responds sincerely.

Quivering to the door in nervousness, I consider what questions to ask, find myself stalling, not wanting to confront her, greatly fearing the truth and in some way wishing it didn't exist right now. What if she has rejected Allah? Converted? Death is her fate. I must convince her otherwise if this is true. And I must do it before my father arrives.

Chapter Two

I close the door behind me instinctively. My thoughts somewhere else, far off into the barren mountains of golden sand sleeping comfortably below the glistening lemon rays. The calm air doesn't help relax the racing of my pulse, as I begin forcing my legs towards the room where the computer resides. Every Sunday morning she is there, reading articles, watching videos or researching new breakthroughs in medicine. Reaching the doorway, I intend to stop, gather myself, then enter, but my feet refuse to halt. Turning the corner, there she is, sitting so peacefully at the laptop, just as I anticipated. My feet conveniently stop now, stuck in position, eyes locked on her. A flurry of anger is recruited to cover the screaming fear. She couldn't have apostatized; I try convincing myself. She's the one who taught me most of what I know about Islam. She has been devout and faithful in ways I admire, inspiring me to live a life as obedient as hers.

"Allah, let this not be true," I mumble to myself.

Noticing me out of the corner of her eye, she turns, directing her attention to me. No doubt she can feel the tension emanating from me. My tongue acts on its own volition, beginning to ask questions.

"Awmy (mother), have you heard what happened to Rana?"

"No, I haven't heard anything," she answers, worry clearly lacing her voice.

"Why, what happened?"

I don't delay. "Nayef found some papers in her purse. Some Christian writings. She said some foreigner handed them to her. He asked her to read them, to reply back with her thoughts. She said she disagreed with everything," I explain, watching her very closely, to read each expression.

"Is she okay?"

I look down, grieved and heartbroken, but at the same time satisfied over the beating she endured rather than death.

"She's...alive."

Raising my head to meet her gaze, I discover two deep wells on the verge of overflowing. Such an image is more than familiar to me. Enough water has flowed from those two golden fountains to fill a sea. And I always found myself drowning in the middle of it. This time though, my role has changed. I'm here to find out if she has betrayed Allah. Betrayed me. However, am I ready to hear the answer?

She breaks the silence. "Umar, I have something to tell you."

As the last word escapes her mouth, a body enters the room from behind me brushing against my arm on the way by. Grabbing her arm with no intentions of letting go, he forces her off the chair, dragging her into the bedroom. That same helpless feeling washes over me again, from when I was a young boy. I dreaded this would happen. My only chance of knowing her thoughts, her heart, crumbling before my eyes in the most swift and decisive manner. If she confesses to a conversion, her fate is sealed. I may lose the opportunity of ever speaking with her again. If he doesn't kill her first for the sake of his honor, the family's honor, then the government will surely do it for us.

Hurrying to the door, I press my ear tightly against the seam of it. I can hear his voice carrying that deathly tone I've heard a thousand times before.

"Did you give Rana the blasphemous writings?"

Not a word, only the rapid beating in my chest. Then, a calm, soft voice penetrates the eerie silence. This is the moment I've been waiting for. The moment of truth. The answer carrying such profound implications. My skin tensely anticipating the words, pressing tighter to the room.

"Yes, I did."

Immediately there is a loud thud felt through the door, leaving behind a whimpering.

"It can't be. Not you. Who has deceived you? Tell me you don't believe them. Tell me Allah is your only God," he demands, his voice trembling with a murderous anger I've never experienced before.

Deep within the halls of my soul I can hear an echo of death welcoming her words. Beyond shaken, I solely concentrate all of my attention to her answer. Envisioning her standing there, arrayed in her beautifully colored abaya, holding that famous undefeated expression on her face, yet not without that special love and tenderness I've only witnessed in her alone.

"Allah is not my God, Jesus Christ is my Lord and Savior," she finally confesses fearlessly.

All of the air is sucked from the room. My mind is not ready to believe what she said. How can she deny Allah? My awmy? My flesh and blood? She must have been tempted or tricked into this false belief. I must talk to her. Convince her to confess this sin. To turn back to Allah.

A sudden flurry of blows erupts from the room, shaking me from my thoughts. Rana's face flashes before my eyes all over again, this time with the one woman I care most about, facing the probability of losing her life, except she has defied Islam and accepts such blasphemous writings. The longer I ponder this unforgivable sin the more anger drives me.

She deserves whatever punishment comes upon her; I try convincing myself. She's an infidel now.

"You will not bring such aa'r upon this family. These ideas you have are haraam (forbidden). You have been deceived believing in these evil lies. And you will reject them," he demands, picturing him holding handfuls of her hair, pulling her battered face to meet his. . . . .

"I will never denounce Jesus," her words echo unapologetically, followed by another blow, but this time a body slumps to the floor.

"Get up. Put this on."

Still standing, the door supporting all of me, I hold my breath trying not to move an inch in fear of missing the slightest whisper. What is he telling her to put on? What's his plan? Suddenly the door opens, throwing me off balance, falling forward a couple steps before catching myself. His face fixes on mine the moment I look up. He doesn't say a word, only stares at me with disgust, then swiftly pushes my mother past me. I urgently search her face to find something, anything, but am blinded by the black engulfing all of her.

Where is he taking her? To the police? Wherever it is I can't follow.

Feeling confused, unsure of what to do, body numb, thoughts in battle, I allow myself the rare comfort of the chair behind me. However, there's one thought that refuses to leave, so I begin attempting to decipher this loneliest one spiraling through my mind: convince her to repent. Yet, the complexity involved is more of a forced action void of any reason. There exists one though more logical, safe: wait until he returns. If she's already dead, then justice has been swift. If she's still alive, then Allah is showing patience.

A ring bursting from my thobe startles me, breaking my concentration. It's Kamal.

"Hello."

"Umar, where are you?" he asks emphatically.

"At home."

"The game is about to start; we're waiting on you."

"I can't make it. You're going to have to play without me," I say bluntly, nothing equaling the importance of the present situation.

"What's wrong?"

I sit in silence for some time, debating on whether to tell him or not.

"Umar, what has happened," he asks in a calm, yet concerned tone.

"Khaly, mother has...apostatized."

I expected the quietness, the delayed response. "Where's Ahmad?"

"He left with her not long ago. I don't know where he was taking her. What do you think?"

"To turn her in," he says. "He's going to the police, if he hasn't killed her already. I have to go. I'll call you soon, all right?"

I sit, phone in hand, retracing the events that flashed by too fast to capture all they contained. All I can do is wait. Wait on the future. If he turned her in, she will only be given a couple of days to repent and revert to Islam before she's gone.

How long has she believed in Jesus? I can't recall the last time I've seen her pray, but I haven't been paying much attention either. Have I been so consumed with my life to such an extent that I haven't noticed anything different? Maybe I could have prevented this if I was spending more time with her? She's made the choice though, to turn her back on Islam, on her family, on me. She's betrayed all of us.

Before I realize it my father's walking through the door, death dripping from his tense face. His piercing gray eyes searching me like a predator at the point of attack.

"How long have you known?" he calmly inquires.

The question offends me. Suspicion chasing his words, as if I was involved with her from the beginning. An apostate as well. I instantly feel the small fragile section of my heart reserved for him quickly shriveling, replaced by a surge of rage swelling up inside.

"Nayef told me just like he told you," I respond, definitely.

There's an awkward stalemate of glances before he goes on. "Yes, he told me everything. Rana should never have accepted the material from your mother. Her defiance has cost her greatly, as you well know."

Her bloody face aggressively flashes through my mind. Why did she accept them? I shift forward, bringing my gaze to the floor below, hoping to end the conversation. He stands for a few moments, then walks toward the bedroom. Inside the doorway he stops and without turning says, "On Tuesday we're going to Deera Square; be prepared." He slams the door shut behind him.

He answers the most important question. She's now waiting in a cell for a private trial with only one way out: reject Jesus as God and revert to Islam. Should I try to see her? Would I be able to control my flurry of emotions? I reach over and close the browser on the laptop. I will take it with me to check for anything later. It's better I find anything incriminating than him.

I wonder what he's doing in there? How long he plans on staying? I push myself to my feet, head to my room through the hall, flop down on my bed, exhaling a deep breath of restrained pressure. For the first time my muscles relax in the solemn quietness. Free from anticipation, however, the thoughts refuse to rest. Still yelling at me.

Why does he seem so unaffected by what's to come? It's almost as if he's been waiting for such a fate to come to pass. Maybe he's hiding the pain beneath that pristine image he must maintain? Too hard to tell. And I can really care less. He's never loved me. The only one who loved me has betrayed me, leaving me surrounded by solitude. If she of all people did this, what does that mean for everyone else in my life? Everyone I've confided in? Trusted?

I continue lying on my bed for hours, endlessly confronting question after question with no answers, until the courage in me finally reaches its threshold.

Gripping phone in hand, I dial Tariq, one of the few people I trust right now, who holds any standing.

"Hello?" Tariq's distinct voice.

"Marhaba akhi."

"Umar, waish halak.?"

"Are you busy right now?"

"No, why?"

"I need a favor," I ask.

"I'll be right over," he says without question. I'm not surprised by his willingness.

The house is still quiet as I make my way to the front door making sure all of my movements are carefully calculated, not wanting my father to be aware of my whereabouts. Passing his black SUV parked inside the wall, I casually travel outside of view, then wait. Hopefully he's gone when I return. Tariq's gray Toyota Tundra turns the corner and comes to a stop next to me. His gentle smile greets me when I open the door.

"Is everything okay?" he asks, genuinely concerned.

Tariq and I can never pass as brothers even though we share the same father. He took more of our father's rusty brown skin, hung on broad shoulders and a sunken face that looked as if a shadow was permanently cast upon it, while I look through the same shimmering golden eyes as my mother, accentuated with sharp, poignant features on a creamy caramel skin.

The love my heart possesses for him is as if he was my mother's own. He lived only a few miles south of me with his mother and three sisters. I've never spent much time at his place because it would mean running into my father, so we generally spent our time scouting any open pickup games being played around Riyadh. If none were found, we would spend the sun's hours playing one-on-one. This time together created a brotherly bond between us, meaningful in many ways. We both shared the same passion in life: to play on the biggest stage in front of millions for a professional club abroad and be selected to play for our country in the world cup. This is the dream we've both tirelessly pursued since we can remember.

"I'll tell you about it another time. I need you to take me to the police headquarters," I say, watching his reaction.

His eyes stay on me for a few seconds, shift to the active street ahead through the windshield for a moment, then back.

"All right," he says, pulling away from the curb.

The city's life penetrates the windows on the drive. It's all dull to me. Just noise dancing around the mission as meaningless filler. No justifiable reason for words in such abnormal circumstances. Tariq recognizes it, respects it. Traces of the suffocating streets seemed faster than usual though. My nerves begin stabbing me everywhere. What if they allow me to see her? What will I say? The distractions of the unknown mount endlessly. Out of sheer will I temporarily force them out to somewhere far away, welcoming the emptiness in place of it.

Green and white police cruisers are scattered across the vast parking lot. Sliding in between two of them, the stop jolts my needed courage into action. Avoiding the expected exchange with Tariq, I step out, lingering for only a moment, "I'll be right back."

That all too familiar feeling of the unexpected swarms me as I close in on the entrance. Reaching the glass doors, an officer pushes his way through eyeing me down as I pass by him, catching the door on my way in.

The building is massive with a sleek layout. Men are spread out everywhere. Some docile, huddled behind their respective stations eyes fixed on computer screens, others casually walking about, papers in hand, heading down long hallways aligned with offices for those in authority. To my right, behind a four-foot-high counter, sit two officers engulfed in conversation. Stepping up to it alerts the closest one. He is skinny, staring intently at me with eyes too dark to call brown. A patchy black beard rests on his narrow face, the creased tan uniform granting him the power his manner exudes.

"Do you need something?" he asks, with traces of annoyance.

"Yes, I've come to see a woman who was brought here earlier today. Her name is Aisha Abdullah Al-Sindi," I say, sure that my father brought her here.

He leans forward, pecks away at the keyboard and after a minute or so slowly rests back into his black leather chair, whispering something into the ear of the short, heartless looking man next to him, pride rippling through his puffed-up chest. Words are exchanged before returning to me.

"No one's authorized to see her."

"Why?" I inquire, confused.

"That's all I can tell you," he responds, coldly.

I'm flooded with a blend of anger and relief. Angry because I am denied access to seeing her, possibly my only opportunity to meet with her. Relief because I don't have to. Have I come so far as to make her a stranger? But, why the denial? I give the men a final glance of submission, then push my way through the door greeting the warm breeze attacking my face. I question her presence there, the officers' truthfulness, all of it. There's nothing I can do now.

I quickly take my place back in the seat next to Tariq, offering not even the slightest acknowledgement, instead stare out the window through the dissipating sunburst rays. I accept defeat.

"Can you take me home?" I request. I don't tell him on the short ride home. I'm not ready yet. He obliges without question.

When we arrive, an empty driveway brings me relief. I need the time alone. To think. I tell Tariq thanks for the help, then swiftly find myself pulling my keffiyeh and sandals off inside my bedroom, closing my eyes until I drift into a sea of endless paths.

Chapter Three

I awake late, around ten o'clock, missing the muezzin's call to morning prayer. Springing up, grabbing a prayer rug, I go to perform wudu (ablution). Unrolling the tight rug, I gently spread it out, facing Ka'ba, then perform fajr. When finished, I make my way into the kitchen, looking to satisfy my stomach's pleas. I spot a bowl of dates resting on the counter. Tossing one in my mouth, the sweet chewiness coats my tongue with pleasure the second I puncture its outer skin. I quickly pop another one in my mouth, then another, adding to my body's much needed energy. There is no longer a full breakfast waiting for me in the mornings: fresh bread with labneh and zaatar, ful medames, hummus, dahl, jam, halawa, falafel, shakshouka, yellow tea with mint or coffee. From now on I will be fending for myself. While waiting for the water to boil for tea, I rip a piece of bread from the chunk that lays next to the now empty bowl of dates. Leaning my back against the counter, chewing on the dense unleavened bread, I can no longer ignore the thoughts of my mother lying dead, in Chop Chop Square awaiting my invitation. According to my father, this is the final day for her to repent. Tomorrow I will be standing at his side, witnessing the judgment enacted upon her and all who have committed a sin worthy of death. Will she repent? This is a question only Allah can answer and for him alone to know for now.

I begin pondering last night. Tariq. The station. The corruption dripping from the officers' badges. No doubt my father's hand was deeply involved, if not orchestrating it. An unusual reminder of him spending unexpected time in the bedroom sparks my interest. I enter the bedroom to find nothing but nakedness. The mattress is laying sideways. I'm not shocked. I expected it. Suddenly a sharp distinct ring startles me. I check my phone only to find no notification of the caller. The second ring comes; it's not mine. Somewhere, there's another phone in the room. That's what he was looking for. Sweeping the room with my eyes, it could only be in one place. I wait for it, the echo comes again, coming from below. I quickly transition to my knees, anxiously lifting the mattress. Nothing. I take position and lift the wood frame. There it is. A black iPhone. She must have stuffed it here last night during the confrontation. But why here? She must have known he would find it eventually, especially if people are calling it. Maybe she was hoping someone else would find it. Possibly me. Why would I not hand it over to my father though?

"What are you doing in here?" My father's voice closing in from behind. All in one motion when turning to stand up, I slip the phone in my thobe while simultaneously pulling mine out.

"I was hoping to find my Qur'an I let her use a long time ago, but you must have taken it with everything else," I explain convincingly as possible.

Even though he absorbs my response, his eyes are too interested in my phone.

"Can I see it," he asks, hand outreached.

I hand it over. He taps the screen a couple of times, expression immovable, then gives it back satisfied with whatever he was searching for.

"Yeah, I probably have your Qur'an mixed with the rest of the things. I will try to set it aside for you."

I follow him back to the kitchen where Tariq's presence surprises me. Growing up, my father always favored Tariq whenever we all spent time together. The undivided attention he gave Tariq along with the handfuls of cash, only fed my caged anger and bitterness towards my father. It pushed me further into solitude, wanting to make my own name in life instead of following his. Some resentment has existed towards Tariq for welcoming all of it when he had to have known the way I was being treated, the ways it affected me. I've always questioned whether that was his way of getting back at me for getting all the praise in being the better soccer player.

Tariq hands me a plate, holding a piece of Baklava. "I thought you might like this."

He knows. It's the reason why he would bring me this, knowing she's not here to cook me anything. "What do they want?" I wonder, tracking their every move. They both turn to face me, a look of preparation to deliver some news. My father opens first.

"I came to tell you that you must be out of the house by the end of this month. You can stay with Tariq if you like or find your own place, it's your choice."

I knew this was coming, but I didn't expect it so soon.

He doesn't wait for a reply before he walks out. He's probably on his way to upload another video or fulfill a request to share his advice on some disputed subject in Islam. He's never cared about me. We haven't discussed anything about what happened, besides his interrogation-like tactics when questioning me. But I'm confident he has revealed everything to Tariq by now. Maybe it's better that we remain distant, surface conversation only.

"You better eat something," Tariq advises.

"Why?" I ask.

"You don't remember, we have a game in two hours. The same man who attended yesterday's game is in Riyadh for one more day. He mentioned wanting to see you play in person to Kamal. This is an opportunity you can't afford to pass up. If anyone can get you signed to a top club, it's him. You impress him and you'll be enjoying the gondola rides in the majestic canals of Italy."

What he's saying holds true in many ways. This could be my opportunity to get signed. But, do I feel up to playing with so much on my mind? He's asking because he needs me. Without me he won't shine. I scoop a piece of Baklava, shoving it in my mouth, confident it will be useful when starving for energy. I finish the entire piece without a word to Tariq. The silence is rather unusual for him, especially before a game. This actually confirms my strong intuition of his knowledge about her apostasy. We always discussed most things openly, yet there will always remain the secrets, those kept hidden in an unseen realm, unwilling to be set free. With neither one of us daring to cross this threshold without a clear invitation. My mother is now living in this realm. A part of me feels a deeper respect for him for not entering into a place he knew was forbidden without causing dishonor upon himself and the family. And for this reason alone, I will allow him to visit just this once.

I intensely glare at him in order to attract his attention. He feels it, looks up.

"I still can't believe it," I say in disbelief, slumping my chin upon my chest.

"Believe what?" he asks, as if he doesn't know.

"You know."

The silence ensues, then he softly says, "We are not to try and make sense of it. It will eat us alive from the inside out my brother."

"When did you find out?"

"Last night, after father dropped off some of A'isha's things." He takes a brief pause. "You know you don't have to find a place for yourself. I expect you to stay with me."

"I haven't made a decision yet. I still need some time to think about it," I say.

My mind is still clouded. Every time I focus on something it is bullied aside by the images and thoughts I refuse to face. Tariq is still looking at me. Studying me. "What do you think about leaving a little early? To get into that game mindset?" he suggests.

"All right," I say, aware of what soccer does for me, the escape it offers. Escape from the restraints life so tightly wraps around us. When gliding along the field, entrenched in a competitive face-off, striving for victory is all that's important. There is nothing in comparison.

"I'll meet you in the car. I need to change really quick," I say, setting the empty plate on the counter. Tariq heads to the front door, while I break away to my room.

Holding both phones in my hands, I decide to take hers with me; I don't trust my father. The recruiters on my mind now, as I slide into Tariq's Tundra. This could be my opportunity to escape this situation, to start fresh somewhere else.

We arrive at the facility early as planned. In no time we are dressed down and warming up on the field, about thirty minutes until game time. I'm more anxious than usual to play, to distract myself from the chaos. The all too familiar nervous, shaking sensation begins sifting through my body.

Eagerly leaving the locker room and stepping onto the fresh-cut grass, there lingers a welcoming for me, a peacefulness. This day, this game, is the most important one of my life. The consequences are insurmountable. All of my talents have to be displayed. No room for error.

Tariq's headed in my direction, halfway doing a warm up drill.

"You ready?" he asks, his eyes reflecting that ruthless vigor you only see in competition.

"You know I'm ready," I answer.

Tariq is the other striker opposite me. His long legs enable him to cover distances faster than most. However, his one weakness is his failure to perform under pressure. When the game is on the line and we need a playmaker, especially one to get by the defender during these most critical moments, he is nowhere to be found. We continue warming up with the rest of the team, preparing ourselves for what's to come. The once empty seats encircling us are now filled with spectators.

Their presence alone transforms the game, creating the pressure, the energy. Everything we feed off. Aware that in this environment, under these conditions, if one rises to the occasion, they will be elevated to a position of praise and recognition inside the Kingdom. These ninety minutes defines who we are on the field, even off it.

Our coach finally calls us in. He's short, slenderly built with the coarsest voice. It is rumored when he played, he would showcase some of the tightest ball control around, something to be admired, but his lack of speed prevented him from going pro. Other personal reasons are really said to be the cause. I've never asked him. None of my business.

After team discussion and traditional pregame ceremony, everyone takes their positions on the field. Each one of us has studied our roles, our responsibilities. There is much discipline that must be maintained in order to play at this level and achieve victory on such a stage. All we have to do is relax, stick to our strengths, while attacking their weaknesses.

Abdullah stands before the coin toss. We receive the ball and defend the south. The significance of the game finally hits me. I'm personally dedicating this game to Kamal and for my mother's repentance. The ball is placed in the circle - time to show what I can do. The screech of the whistle echoes throughout the stadium.

Chapter Four

The ball quickly makes it into their possession, after Abdullah's pass is intercepted, methodically passing it around. They want to establish the tempo of the game, to attack on their terms. Hami is their star striker. He has exceptional ball control and a very strong leg. He suddenly receives a long pass perfectly in stride, streaming down the center of the field. Abdias is trailing a few steps behind, unable to match Hami's speed. As Abdullah comes to help, Hami fakes right then explodes by him on the left-hand side, creating just enough room to take a shot on the goal. His left leg releases, sending the ball whizzing toward the top corner of the goal. I watch helplessly, hoping it's high. This will not be a good way to start off. Bang! It collides with the cross bar, ricocheting wide right where we gain possession. Too close! We must slow down. Focus! The game continues in similar fashion, with them dominating in time of possession, shots on goal and shot attempts, not one tasting the net though. With our defense deteriorating through fatigue and opportunities to score dwindling, closing in on the ninetieth minute, we must take some risks, make ourselves vulnerable in order to create an advantage. Hami makes another calculated move, stealing the ball from Tariq, then taking an unexpected shot at the goal from deep. Khan snatches it out of the air, then kicks it far into the center of the field where a rustling takes place, allowing a header to put it into Tariq's control again. This time he evades one defender, creating an opportunity for me, as my defender is drawn toward him. Diving down the middle of the field, to help set something up, he sends me a swift pass, then speeds down the left sideline a couple of paces ahead of the defender in pursuit. His long strides give him the space needed to receive a leading lob pass. I fake a quick pass inside, freezing the defender for a split second. It's all I need to aggressively push the ball past him, forcing the next two men to attack. The moment they reach me in one agile motion, my right leg thrusts back and forward, launching the ball flying into the air, dropping smoothly in front of him. He follows the edge of the sideline until almost reaching the corner when, flicking his eyes up to me v-lining to the goal from the center, sends the ball toward the goal. I carefully watch the ball's curving path after his foot strikes it. Instinctively, I move myself into the ideal offensive position. Measuring from years of experience being the go-to guy, I discreetly extend my right forearm just enough to create some space from my opponent's body riding my side, jockeying for position. I look to the goalie, back to the ball in the sky. What happens next unfolds in slow motion.

The spin on the ball gives it the perfect angle escaping the defender's head beside me, as we both leap into the air. Lowering my head for impact, it contacts my head for only a moment, precisely where I expected it would, before directing it toward the upper right corner of the goal. By the time I glance up, all I see is the white and green ball, the goalie's hands stretching out as far as physically possible to deflect it, yet coming up inches short, as it rockets by him, ripping into the net.

"Gooo...al!" is screamed throughout the stadium. Some ecstatic, cheering, others silenced in disbelief.

My team instantly swarms me with embraces and pats of praise. Waves of excitement, pleasure, gratification rush through my body. This game, my performance, the winning goal means more than all my others combined. For the slightest moment the urge to find her and Kamal in the crowd is felt. How proud they must be. Happy for me. But it quickly collapses under the memory of yesterday. Only Kamal is watching this time. There is less than a minute remaining with no stoppage time. All we need to do is play defense, get possession and run the timeout. Victory awaits our grasp.

They begin passing the ball around in great urgency, feeling the last minute dwindle in what seems like eternity, when finally, hoping to create an opening, a chance to tie it comes. We pursue the ball diligently when a last prayerful pass arches its way into the pack huddled near the goal. Everyone's scuffling for position, then jump at the same time. Abdullah's head reaches the ball first clearing it out to the sideline as the time ends, the whistle blows - victory! Some of the pressure that has nestled its way into my head is finally released. I've accomplished what I came here for: perform at the highest possible level, in front of the Italian scout watching from somewhere inside the swarms of soccer fans. Now my signing rests solely in his hands. Whether or not he feels my skills and talent are impressive enough to play for his club or another, I'm content, but an unknown tightness still resides in the pit of my stomach. It causes me to begin lightly trotting to the bench. Through the players crossing my path on the way, I catch Kamal's gaze. He's standing right next to my water and towel concealing the phone. I know I should have left it inside. With my paranoia aroused, I approach him suspiciously for some strange reason.

"You played very well, Umar!" he says, his face revealing a slight hint of approval. He loves soccer. It shows in his eyes when he completely submerges himself entirely into each game, passionately rooting for one team or particular player for ninety minutes plus. During these times you can almost catch a softness about him. This same passion he devoted to me growing up, always advising me how to prevent mistakes, to make my weaknesses my strengths. He pushes me harder than anyone else, always saying, "You have a gift to be great, but you alone must be the one yearning to obtain it." This is why he remains an inspiration to me in many ways.

Looking at him with a gratified expression, I say, "I hope it was good enough to get recognized." I take a few steps to my left, reach down grabbing my towel off the seat, where it is sitting next to my teammates. The hard plastic casing of the phone is resisting the tight grip of my palm wanting to slip out. I don't expect him to mention her, since he never called me back last night, but avoided it I'm sure for his own reasons. And I'm not going to bring it up here at this place.

"That first shot you took at the goal, where the goalie was able to get a hand on it, deflecting it out of bounds, was lacking power because your left leg wasn't fully planted allowing you to dig deep from the hips. The accuracy was precise, but it should have been a goal. We will be addressing this issue in the coming weeks ahead," he critiques.

I can see his mind calculating new training techniques already, always viewing me as his sole responsibility, his mission. Because of this, I bring meaning to his life, giving him something worthy to distract from facing the torturing enemies clawing their way out from his darkened past. I've always submitted to this role, knowing it comforts him in some unknown way.

As he finishes touching on the pivotal plays of the game, Tariq comes alongside me, joy beaming from his face.

"We should probably make our way to the locker room. I think coach is waiting to say something to everyone."

We excuse ourselves from Kamal, joining the team. Coach has never been one of many words; short and to the point is how he likes it. He motions with his hand; silence scales the room.

"You played hard today. All ninety minutes. This is why we never stop pressuring and grinding our opponents down. They were a worthy team, but we prevailed because we desired it more. I'm proud of you guys. One step closer to the championship."

The streets are congested, streaming with people leaving the game. This is the biggest turnout we've ever had. Giving it my all out there for these people that they might find enjoyment, satisfaction with the entertainment we provide is an important element.

During the entire drive home, Tariq can't stop replaying, out loud, his perfect pass along with every second leading up to it. It is nice to have my thoughts focused on soccer, but my heart keeps intruding regardless. Her time is running out. When we pull up to the house, I step out, making sure the phone is safely secured in my keffiyeh. Before I open the door, words escape from his lips.

"My mother's cooking tonight. You're coming over. We'll eat and review the game."

The invitation is enticing, especially since I won't have to cook something myself or go out to eat. I'm not sure though, if I want to be around my father tonight.

"I'll give you a call later. Maybe being alone is what I need most right now," I say.

His head lowers in slight disappointment.

"Give me a call when you're ready. I'll be waiting," he says, a smile protruding.

I close the car door, then enter the house eagerly anticipating inspecting my mother's phone. Sitting down in the front room at the computer, I unwrap the keffiyeh, plopping the phone from out of it. After turning it on, I see one missed call from earlier. Pressing the phone icon, the caller is exposed. Should I call? What do I say? I take a second to decide, then press the last missed call. Each ring jolts my nerves. Different scenarios of how the conversation might go fills my thoughts. Disturbs me.

"Hello?" A woman answers in English carrying the slightest hint of a Russian accent.

"Who am I speaking to?" I ask, as formal and friendly as possible.

Click...

She knows something's wrong, a man calling from this phone. I begin searching my memory for any foreigners my mother had contact with...at work! I remember seeing some foreign women walking to their cars in the parking lot when Kamal and I were waiting to pick her up one day. What am I expecting to find out if I find her? It's not going to change anything is it? Looking back at the screen, I tap the email icon, scanning the list. All of them are work related besides some general conversation with relatives. Lastly, I check her photos. The first one is of her and I resting against a beautiful sunset emitting the brightest shades of carmine, a touch of peach, highlighted with canary yellow. An unexpected warmth rushes through my body that I swiftly strike down. Anger begins bubbling again. I scroll through about a dozen more of her with me and Rana and some with other women in the family, all but the last two which are of two foreign women with her at work. I swipe the power button, then shove the phone inside my thobe.

Realizing I'm still sweating from the game, a shower will be quite fitting. The warm water running down my back begins loosening up the tight muscles in my body bringing with it a sense of drowsiness. I'm still undecided on what to do. Should I take Tariq up on his offer of enjoying a celebratory dinner, while risking my father's company or do I cook something myself hoping for the best? Well, the risk better be worth it. I tell Tariq the good news.

"All right, come pick me up."

"I'll be right over. I knew you would make the right decision," he says, excitedly.

He arrives in no time, still talking about the game and the possible signing all the way to his house. He sets up the laptop, playing the video of the game. We spend some time together analyzing the entire game, every detail, critiquing ourselves in the most transparent ways. It is one of the few things capable of drawing my complete attention. Suddenly the focus is disrupted by the opening of the front door. Both of us glance over to find our father entering. I guess this is his night to stay here.

After our greetings, Tariq invites him to watch the last five minutes of the game with us. He takes his post standing behind us, motionless, eyes fixed on the small screen between us, until it ends.

"An exceptional pass you made, Tariq. There was no room for error; you placed it perfectly where only Umar could get it," he says, attempting to sound interested, while at the same time dismissing my game-winning goal.

"They are the best team right now. We haven't beat them in the last three meetings. How gratifying it was to finally achieve victory," Tariq says.

My father changes the subject, bringing up how many Saudi's are becoming corrupt, falling away from true Islam. He could care less about soccer. Dissatisfaction sweeps his face, especially for me, as he doesn't allow his gaze to shift to me once. No praise. No acknowledgment. This has always left me with doubts about my choices in life even though we have never been close, except when his hands are harming my mother and me. I still long for his love, his acceptance.

I take a piece of kunafa off the tray next to us, taking it all in one bite. The creamy cheese melting with the sugary lemon bread layers my tongue with richness. I wash it down with a hot cup of mint tea. We all relax, eat sweets, drink tea and coffee while joining in conversation or rather, listen to advice from our father on proper Islamic living, nodding in agreement. It's a rare occasion to have us all together in one house, spending time with one another.

A hard knock on the sitting room door comes. Dinner's ready. We follow our father through the doorway, face first into delicious waves of shawarma, fresh bread, rice and vegetables wafting from the sheet spread across the floor. We kneel down around it and each begin taking our share. I don't say much, listen while slowly savoring each bite. We finish late. Fatigue setting in from playing, causing my eyelids to close without my permission. Not wanting to be disrespectful, I stand, saying my goodbye.

"I should be going. I need to get some sleep."

I lead the way, Tariq behind me, when at the opening of the door, I hear my father's voice.

"I'll be there sometime after morning prayer." I give a slight nod of acknowledgment. Tariq insists on driving me home, finally conceding to my persistent desire to walk. I need the freshness of the air to uncloud the storm formulating inside. It will also give me some time to mentally prepare for tomorrow, if that's even possible.

Moving along at a comfortable pace, the cool air collides against my body as dusk nears. The continuous ten feet plus concrete and steel walls facing each other furthers my solitude, as I make my way through a maze devoid of life, except for the white lights trickling upon the street, calming me. Yet, in all this division and seclusion from the outside, it will all come crashing down tomorrow if there comes no repentance. Everyone will know. My house is in sight when my phone startles the silence. Kamal. If anyone has knowledge of the current situation it will be him.

"Marhaba, khaly (uncle) khaif halak."

"Bakhair. I've received word that Aisha is being held at the Alsulaimanya Police Station on Prince McHari Bin Abdulaziz Street. But the order has been given for no visits. Paid for most likely. For what, I don't know. Regardless, she's refusing to change her mind. And...I don't think she will. You know better than I, when she's convinced of something, there's no changing it. However, she did change her views from Islam. If I hear of any changes, I'll give you a call. Otherwise, I'll see you tomorrow. If you need anything at all, call. Don't think too much," he says, expressing a kind of understanding of what's taking place.

"Thanks, khaly. I'll see you tomorrow," I say, knowing deep down his words bear the truth. She won't change her mind. She's made her decision, will die because of it. Reaching the big steel door, I pull it open, slide inside the courtyard, into the house. I go straight to my room, undress, then slowly allow my head to sink back onto the soft, feathered pillow. Instantly my eyes shut, feeling the relentless force ushering them into the oncoming blackness.

A man's deep voice awakens me, "God is most great. I testify that there is no god but God. God is most great. I testify that there is no god but God. Hurry to prayer. Hurry to salvation. Prayer is better than sleep."

It takes a few seconds for my conscious to realize it's the muezzin calling out from the nearest mosque. In no time my sandals are tightly on my feet already crossing the courtyard. Returning from fajr, I struggle with the reality...today's the day - Friday. Can I go back to sleep to wake up finding this all a dream? He won't allow it. Expecting my father anytime. The growling of my stomach drives me to the kitchen, playing with the idea whether to satisfy it or not. But, as I move from the dates to bread, my appetite vanishes. Quickly recognizing the pangs are from something else. Nerves. I make a cup of coffee instead. Opening up YouTube, I bring up one of my father's sermons. In another window I download a soccer match between Real Madrid and Chelsea. As I listen to my father, I'm reminded of how much of a hypocrite he is. His sermons are filled with strict adherence to Islam and Shariah law, yet he himself strays from it in many subtle ways. Most Saudi's do now. I'm disappointed by it. Angry, which has warranted the bitterness. I can taste it seeping into my mouth sometimes. I impatiently minimize his sermon, giving my full attention to the game. I love watching them play. Their discipline, skill, passion to play, always inspires me to be on the field competing, winning. When the match ends with Real Madrid claiming victory, I realize how I'm oblivious to much of my surroundings. The soft, warming orange rays of light begin diving through the windows at me. I welcome them as usual, but today they seem duller, lifeless. While soaking up this quiet, calm moment, I'm overtaken by a distinct idea telling me to call her, to tell her of what's to come this morning. In my room, I open up her messages, matching the number I called earlier, finding it second from the top. Without pondering what to say, my fingers go to work: Important! Deera Square eight AM. I stop, finger hovering over the send button, doubt beginning to infiltrate its way deeper into my thinking, before realizing this may be her only opportunity to witness the consequences of what apostasy brings.

If she is the one who tempted my mother to question Islam or even contributed to it, then this may pierce her heart in such a dreadful way it will prevent her from attempting to convert others, knowing death awaits them.

Send.

Tucking the phone away, I make my way to the sitting room where I can greet my father when he arrives. While waiting, I carefully gather the Qur'an off the old faded brown table and flip it to surah 58:22.

"There wilt not find any people who believe in Allah and the Last Day, loving those who oppose Allah and His Messenger, even though they were their fathers or their sons or their brothers or their kindred."

I need the encouragement because my chest is feeling pain thinking of her. She has broken the law - sinned - and now must face her punishment. Judgment will be carried out by faithful Muslims. The love I once felt for her, we shared with each other, has been destroyed, tampered with. Loyalty is for Allah alone. I continue reading for what seems like hours when my father walks in, exuding a briskness like in one of Arabia's cool winter nights. His face says it all: the time has come. Time to watch justice implemented against my mother, the one who conceived me. He doesn't say anything. He doesn't have to. I stand, returning the Qur'an to its place, then follow him into his black SUV. I wonder who else from the family is going? Rana and Nayef? Tariq? Kamal? And who all knows about it?

I heard about Deera Square "Chop Chop Square" growing up. Everyone has in Riyadh. But, I have yet to personally witness a beheading. I never had to, my family and I strictly follow the law, especially with my father being a sheikh. He is constantly speaking to the family about Islam and how to be a faithful Muslim. Now, my first experience will be to watch my own mother killed.

Just as I anticipated, the drive is quiet. I sit, staring into the life of a new day in the desert city, hoping my father will say something. Anything. I would even be willing to hear some of his council right now. At such a critical time, any kind of human emotional understanding and connection would offer some comfort. But nothing. Not even the slightest glance. I accept it. Keeping my eyes and mind on the Saudis and foreigners riddling about the streets. After a short time, my view is eclipsed by the tan mountainous structures, as we pull up to the collection of vehicles off Al Imam Turki Bin Abdullah Street. Perfectly aligned date palms shadow the wood benches reaching down one side of the perimeter, while others offer life before the archways leading outside the square. Shops and mosques decorate the interior along with the religious police headquarters. The buildings were designed by the hands of skilled craftsmen. One can wander in the immense openness of the square. This is where she will die. About fifty people gather together inside the great square. Suddenly, I'm stuck, pinned to my seat, unable to open the door, time moving on without me. Meeting my familiar friend adrenaline, who's with me before every game, except here, he's brought company, a stranger to me. Sickness is his gift to me. The warm blood leaves my face, chasing after something dwelling deeper inside me. What is happening to me?

The slam of the door shakes me just enough to distract my attention from this foreign invasion within me. My father peers at me through the windshield with a look of confusion mixed with an unspoken order to follow suit. Acting from a greater fear of him, my hand automatically opens the door. By the time I catch up with him we are approaching the crowd. It is after noon. The blinding beams of yellow light are pouring down on us. The air is different. Thicker. Suffocating. My father walks through the crowd, stopping in the front. He's been here before. Too comfortable not to. The administration of justice would no doubt draw his presence. I curiously check his expression after forcing my way to his side. His eyes intensely focus straight ahead, glazed over, impatiently waiting for the prisoners' arrival. What's he thinking about? Does his heart feel the slightest grief? I will never know. His conduct is what's most important to him right now. His image. I allow my eyes to drift over the men and women standing patiently behind us. Moving from one expressionless face to another, none are recognizable. Some are hidden behind the bodies of others, requiring my changing of position. Something catches my eye. Something familiar, causing pressure to rise in my body. Nayef. His stern face is staring off into the distance of the Square. Where is Rana? Standing some feet to his right, a female in niqab, has her head to the stones below. It's her. He's forced her to come, to watch her own mother die, a reminder of the punishment for apostasy. Sadness falls upon me. I love her so much, hoping she wouldn't have to witness this; however, I agree to it in a way, find security in it. It will push her farther away from any inclination of converting. This would only magnify the loss if she was to die also. I quickly dismiss the idea, refusing to confront a life without both of them. Suddenly each face is more alert, slowly tightening every muscle in anticipation. In some rest smiles of gratification. I can see the reflection walking across their eyes. Turning forward, the figures move toward the designated position, where a drain is resting in the stone for the gallons of blood spilled. The police and officials each calculating their responsibilities, making sure the area is cleared and everything is in order.

The two women are barefoot, draped with long white garments and blindfolded with a white cloth as they are being escorted by a stout, meticulous officer. Handcuffs restricting their wrists' movement to behind their backs. Without hesitation, I recognize her soft, distinct gate. The square is silent. All eyes are intently attracted to these two prisoners, eagerly watching, as they slowly reach the last piece of earth their feet will taste of. The soldier gives orders the moment they stop. I'm unable to make them out, not because I'm not close enough, but refuse to pry my eyes away from her. I now notice the new figure behind them, as they carefully kneel, surrendering their knees to the stone below, the officer binding their hands to their feet with cord. Gazes continue to be transfixed in our direction. They know who's here. Why we're here. A voice inside is struggling to claw its way out, to scream out the word I've said millions of times to her growing up. Mother! My body refuses to, too fearful of the consequences, the shame that would be etched into me. All I can do is watch. Does she know I'm here? She has to. Why would I miss it?

Suddenly her lips begin moving, saying something. The woman on her side responds. I can't make it out. What would they be saying to each other? The officer is disturbed by it, spitting out a word that leaves her silent, but only after they seem to say what was needed.

The executioner steps forward with a paper in hand. His heartless face is shaded by his keffiyeh as his long white thobe, tightly secured by a thick black leather belt, holds death in its sheath on his side. As he begins reading, I have become even more preoccupied, giving all my attention to watching my mother's every move. If only I could look into her eyes, she may revert to Islam. She would do it for me, wouldn't she? Invading in and out of my consciousness are the executioner's words: "Apostasy...Adultery," he says, reading the execution order.

It's brief. Everyone now knows the crimes being punished by death.

Afterwards, he reaches across his body, gripping his right hand firmly around the metal handle. In one smooth motion the shiny blade is unsheathed, awakened from its sleep. One cannot help studying this chosen weapon about to end two lives. He begins inspecting the long blade. Shaking off this distraction, I redirect my focus back onto her, knowing time is almost up.

I begin crying out to Allah. "Why are you allowing this to happen? Why are you taking her from me? Oh, Allah, in your great mercies save her. Change her heart. Bring her back to the truth, for she has been deceived. It cannot be her fault."

My quivering lips want to burst out, break the silent square. A feeling of great pressure mounts behind my eyes, forcing them to fill with liquid. It takes all my effort to resist this attack. But, the second I regain control, after countless blinking attempts, a violent shaking erupts inside of me, ignited by the steps and positioning of the executioner behind her. Continuing to dig my gaze into her, all I hope for now, all there is time for, is to grant me a final memory with her. Everything around me disappears. Her and I are all who exist right now, just as before when I found her bloody, lying spread out across the bed motionless. The grunts and moans piercing through the walls into my room. Besides the crying, there was a ripping inside. Something continuing to manifest itself into a chamber of loneliness, anger and longing. Intently listening for the closing of the door, signaling the absence of my father, I instinctively rushed to her side in unmistakable panic, tears gushing from my eyes, shaking her while softly whimpering in her ear, "Wake up, wake up amy (mother). Please wake up!"

Then suddenly, I'm no longer fixed on her eyelids, but a golden treasure shining brightly up at me. A rush of comfort, of peace overtakes me, relief from the thought of losing her without her acknowledgment. In that one look my life was reaffirmed. It remained the only answer I ever needed growing up because of what it revealed. And now, once again, I cherish it. Cherish the look worth a thousand words.

Her head finally moves, slightly upwards. In the next second, I feel as if we lock eyes through the blindfold. She's staring straight at me. It's as if she has known I've been here in this exact place the entire time waiting patiently for this precise moment to present itself, when I was ready. My heart is melting, yet is calmest it's been since waking this morning. She doesn't have to see me to know my request. I plead with every emotion from my being. All I'm able to find is that overflowing love I grew to know so well. Her chest expands, taking a deep breath. Relaxing. Submitting.

"No. No, Amy! You can't! Don't give up."

The barricade is about to break. Anger is present, physically urging me to rescue her. Then I notice it. It's been there within her all this time. Something new. This is why I've been unable to recognize it at first when seeking an answer. Peace. A peace that's mysterious to me. Processing this, the officer gives the signal initiating the purpose of this gathering.

Without retreating, I watch the sheen of the blade carefully meet her neck with a tap. I expect her body to lose all strength, to collapse in fear, but there is rather a firmness flourishing through the body of what's to come. She's content with her fate. The blade draws up high, pausing, as the culmination of my life comes to this very moment in time. Can I stay here, where time ceases? Just her and I, living one more moment where I can see with eyes open? This wish is quickly washed away, in one thrust, on its way down, severing every human tissue and bone, reverberating the muffling of an unexpected breeze. A vivid crimson stream accompanies the head splashing against the smooth stone below, finding the escape in the holes of the drain. The body is frozen for a moment, instinctively trying to survive, to calculate the damage for healing, then slumps forward, crashing to the tan square floor with a thud of reality, of death.

I'm paralyzed, unable to function, except to stare unblinking in disbelief at her headless body. She's gone, the only one who loved me unconditionally, teaching me how to navigate through life's unexpected troubles and difficulties. Her warm presence and gentle touch is forever a memory. Now, she's a small piece of firewood in hell. And I did nothing to help her, to convince her to repent, to revert to Islam. Still unable to remove my eyes from the carnage, something is holding me here, forcing me to soak up the image inch by inch, second by second, until every detail is known, logged forever.

Movement in the midst of my vision draws me to investigate. The head halts after a wet thud and slight roll. For a split second, I think my mind is playing tricks on me, that the tragedy has replayed over again for my suffering. No, this is the other woman's head. Finally shifting my attention away from this tragic justice to the thickly bearded officer, I hear his deep voice over the loudspeaker begin listing their crimes: apostasy, adultery...the words slipping in and out of my numbness. As I study this soldier positioned near the executioner who's wiping the blood off his sword on the corpse before inserting it back into its scabbard, then slowly raising his hands in the air, wiping them together, it's finished. The officers and officials depart from the square faster than they arrived. And all those who came as spectators, witnesses, follow suit, their expressions carrying pride, proud of the justice implemented on crimes broken against Allah and the law.

I feel the heat again seeping into my body, hear the progressive distant footsteps chattering behind me, see the tan, stone arch resting high above an entryway, conscious again of where I'm at. Rana instantly comes to mind, but when I turn to find her, Nayef has vanished. And before I have a chance to search the dispersing crowd, my father's figure stands before me, still as a palm, eyes locked onto me. I automatically decipher his body language, telling me to hurry, but I catch something uncharacteristic although familiar in him. I can't quite place it though. Then, it hits me. It is the same look he showed when returning after apprehending my mother, when he came back alone to question me. He's studying me again. In a steadfast manner, I leave the lifeless corpses behind, moving right for him. As I pass by, I can feel his gaze follow me, but I refuse to acknowledge it, to deviate from my course.

When I reach the SUV, the last of the onlookers have disappeared. I get in, close the door, my father trailing seconds behind me. Without exchanging any words, we pull away. Anxiously looking back to the scene of death, longing to capture one last image and take it from our final meeting, where I felt I saw her for who she had become, without secrecy, without deception, spiritually naked. One lone man stands with hose in hand, spraying clean the bloody stone. I wonder how many times he's done this? How many gallons of blood has been washed away?

By the time we arrive at home, I'm mentally exhausted. Partly from keeping such strict composure for his intrusive eyes. When he leaves the engine running, I know he's not staying. But before I get out, the first words escape from his mouth resentfully.

"Are you all right?"

I feel wounded by the grief of losing her, but satisfied by the judgment exacted upon her for such betrayal, for an unforgivable crime she refused to repent of. What's he really asking? According to him there should be nothing but satisfaction for such treachery. Without question he's looking to exploit any weakness in me. Sadness. Grief. Sorrow.

"I'm relieved justice has finally been administered, because every second she lived as a renegade infidel kept feeding the fury stirring inside of me," I answer with a fixed gaze.

For the first time in my life, I could see his face slowly relax into satisfaction. The kind I only recognized on other fathers faces after their son achieves some great impossible feat. A rush of honor, pride, acceptance, splinters through me, acceptance in a way that's new to me, that I've actually done something worthy of his approval. A part of me doesn't want to let go of this moment, let down all my defenses and wrap my arms around his neck. However, it only takes seconds before disgust awakens inside. The old familiar feeling I've forever harbored for him that will die with me.

"Always remember son, you will not find any people who believe in Allah and the Last day, loving those who oppose Allah and his messenger, even though they were their fathers or their sons or their brothers or their kindred," he says, with a flush of dignity making him look even more lifeless.

"Ma'a salama," I say, stepping out, holding the door with one hand.

"Yallabye," he returns through the closing door.

His words continue resonating with me once inside. The feelings so naturally wanting to be relieved to find peace somewhere, are being defeated by those words. So, I submit, inviting them to subdue my mind and body. But it lasts only so long until the constant images ravaging me break through, dropping me to my knees in the sitting room as the waters burst from my face. I feel so alone. Lost. Lost without her. What was she going to tell me? How did I not recognize her behavior sooner? How long was she converted for? Could I have prevented this if I would have focused on spending more time with her these last couple years? Never ending questions, guilt, regrets and what if's take turns flogging me to utter fatigue.

Chapter Five

The tense air touches all the white in my eyes when the sound echoes through the day room. I don't move, just lay in the sleeplessness overcoming me all night long, while beads of sweat drizzle off my face into a darkened wetness below.

It was a night of defeat, resulting in me becoming a prisoner of my own mind's fierce determination to pursue a realm of unanswerable questions and scenarios, with my eyes restless, darting around the room studying the vague shapes reflecting only a fraction of moonlight invading through the lone window on the eastern wall. Trying so hard to forget about her, to place her far away in the past, then abandon her. However, she refuses to leave. Keeps finding her way back to not only controlling my thoughts, but aggressively squeezing every known emotion from my heart unconsciously dictating my life. I finally muster up enough energy to roll over, reach out into the dense pile of clothing bundled up next to me, fumbling around until the phone nestles comfortably in my palm. As the glowing rectangle inches closer to my face, the caller becomes known: Rana. Desperately wanting to hear her voice, I answer.

"Hello?"

"Hey, akhi, how are you?"

"I'm okay. How are you?"

Silence holds my ear for a moment, broken by the muffled sobs she's attempting to restrain.

"I...I'm not doing so well," she responds, trembling, not concealing it from me because that would mean breaking our pact of truthfulness.

"What's wrong?"

"Can you...come over. I need to talk to you?"

"I'll be right over," I say, hanging up.

The first thing coming to mind is the square, the figure draped in black hovering beside Nayef. She saw everything didn't she? Even if she didn't watch it, I know Nayef would have described it in vivid detail. The last thing he wants is for Rana to apostatize, to bring humiliation, disgrace, shame upon him. I agree with him. Such an event would be catastrophic for this family. But what if this is her planned confession to me? Such a question opens with it an opportunity for redemption, to avoid defeat once again. Recognizing the complexities, I hastily reach the white Corolla, igniting the engine without hesitation, invading the early morning streets quickly filling with company.

Upon my arrival, a secret set of black eyes are watching my every move from behind the twelve-foot-high steel door. The height at which the eyes rest convinces me it's Rana. As she yanks open the heavy door, my focus turns to her, scanning from head to toe, expecting to find even the slightest clue as to why she called me over. I feel like a stranger here for the first time. Usually noticing the cracks splintering through the concrete walls, the low growl of the steel sliding open defiantly, the small concrete courtyard inside, spotless compared to the streets outside, the small, but warm feeling in the sitting room.

Stepping into the courtyard, Nayef's car is missing, as I expected. She would never have called me over otherwise. By the time the thud from the door reaches me, she's passing by, entering the house. I push after her not knowing what to expect. But something stops me under the doorway, like hands tugging on my shoulders, trying to tell me something. Then it fiercely hits me. The screams, Ali, the door, her bloody face pleading for her life, Nayef standing there, then boom, shut out. Helpless. The little piece of me calling out to take action, but vetoed by the commander of Islam.

Suddenly, I see myself, bloodied hands staring down upon her ravaged body below, she then slowly turns her head, gazing up at me saying something. I couldn't quite make out the words, her lips are moving, but...

"What are you saying," I scream.

Her eyes glazing over, losing their vitality, their hope, then an endless red waterfall flows from her mouth leaving a drowning gurgle.

"You are guilty. You have shed this blood," a deep voice rings out.

"No! I'm innocent. I have done no wrong." I see the blade unsheathing, raising up high.

"No!" I try to yell, but there is no sound.

A firm grip wraps around my forearm and instantly releases me from the daydream. The images were vivid, real; it takes me a second and some deep breaths to shake it off, to eventually connect the hand still holding onto me with the face bearing a deeply concerned expression.

"Are you okay?"

"I'm fine," I mutter, my mind still a little fuzzy.

I heed the tug on my arm, step inside, find a chair settled near a fresh bowl of dates, pots of coffee and tea and a pair of spotless white cups. She gently seats herself next to me, grabs the coffee filling the two cups, turns to me. Why is she still wearing a niqab? I wait a few minutes for her to begin, to reveal the reason for my needed presence, but nothing ensues, so I quickly take hold of her niqab, pulling it free, exposing not only brown flesh, more than that. It stuns me, disgusts me, angers me. The split flesh cradles the swollen mound forcing her right eye to a sliver of vision. Purple blending with blackish-blue tracks litters the rest of her exposed skin reaching the bulging top lip still mushy, staining her once white smile with bloody residue. The sight causes bile to drive its way further north up my throat.

Softness, tenderness, vulnerability, are unveiled in her eyes and downcast expression. This is what she dreaded might happen...rivers begin flowing nonstop, conjuring up that inner childhood feeling I experienced every time I watched them fall from her swollen cheeks. After the many times she was hit for nothing other than apparently breaking some law unrelated to the situation, she then would intentionally break it realizing the pain was coming regardless. I would run to her, wrap my arms around her trembling frame, slowly rubbing her back as her face sought solace against my chest. It was during these times of affliction that our hearts connected, found comfort and warmth with each other in the midst of the storm. I developed a weakness for her suffering, her grief, her being hurt. And at the first sight of those wells filling up, until they could hold back no longer, exploding effortlessly onto the flushed terrain below, my heart was injected with a compassion forever.

"He...forced me to go...to watch it," she utters through sobbing.

I shift my attention from the damage above to her shaking hands unable to find rest. At a sudden loss for words, I stabilize her hands between mine. She invites the safe touch, leaning in closer, peering into my soul a little deeper. There's something else. Something bigger yet to come. All blood abandons my face, rushing to its destination. This is what she has called me here for.

A confession? No such words better escape her mouth.

"How did you do it," she questions, with the curiosity of an innocent child, "standing close, seeing every detail and not showing even the faintest twinge of despair, of sorrow?"

She was watching me the entire time. At least long enough to study my reaction.

I consider this question for a minute. "She broke the law. Denied Allah, our almighty god, refusing to repent and revert to Islam. She betrayed us, akhti. Lied to us, while living a secret life. For how long? Do you not think this has not brought shame upon our family even after her death? This is how I stood so close to her without any remorse."

"Do you really believe all of this? This was still our mother! Is it so easily forgotten what we meant to her? How much she loved us no matter what we did, sacrificing more than we know, so we may experience a life better than hers? Where was everyone else when we were growing up? She's the one who provided us with the principles and values in life outside of Islam," says Rana, in disbelief mixed with a touch of anger.

"All of that...now she's spending eternity in hell," I recant.

Her head drops. Another round of tears, then slowly ascending, staring into my eyes once again.

"Tell me the truth, when the blade was above her neck, a breath from coming down ending her life, in that precise moment, what was in your heart?" she asks, as a final request.

The mere reminder of it in such unequivocal detail takes me captive, drawing me back to Chop Chop Square. I can see her again. Try with all my might to escape, but some part of me, a part it seems I have lost control of, won't allow it. I can feel the panic take hold, the confusion, the hopelessness, the guilt, an arising urgency to help her, to cry, yet through it all, ultimately witnessing her loss of life. Snapping back to consciousness, she is still intently staring at me, waiting. Holding back the haunting emotions, I tell her what she needs to hear.

"Anger. That's all there was. Anger at her betrayal, at her leaving you and me motherless, at her sin against Allah. She was given many chances to repent, to come back to Islam, but held immovable in her defiant ways. How can I love her for this? Possess any sympathy. We lost our mother the moment she chose Jesus Christ as her God."

The tears don't slow down her face, nor does her gaze falter from mine. As if there may be the slightest reason for her to agree with my conclusion. However, I'm beginning to feel uncomfortable, questioning what exactly she is doing? Thinking?

"Listen, it's time for you to move past this," I say softly.

"I know," she says, leaning back, then peering out the window.

Unsure on whether this is a good time to ask her, I do it anyway, without warning, needing to satisfy my curiosity.

"Did she ever say anything to you about who gave her those papers or where she got them?"

"No, all she said was to read them then tell her what I thought. That's all. Why?"

"I am only curious about how she got them," I say.

We both welcome the silence now. I casually take hold of the pot of coffee she prepared, refilling the two cups. Handing her one, I sip from the other, enjoying the rich flavor between our occasional eye contact, feeling burdened the deeper the purple becomes.

"Are you going to be okay?" I ask, being the one to break the silence. "I'm always here for you, you know that right?"

"I know," she says with soft, muddy brown eyes.

I want to stay longer, to talk, to offer my presence, my heart, but I need to be alone. I sit my empty cup on the table, make it to the door then stop. My body refuses to leave without telling her.

"I love you, akhti," I say without turning around preventing her from seeing the grief consuming my face.

Her words echo back to me before I step out. "Love you...."

I'm relying on these streets to consume these last couple of hours. My gut tells me the truth about the materials. However, the more important question is: did she believe me?

One week later, after Fajr, I'm taking my usual peaceful walk home, contemplating whether or not I should move in with my father or get my own apartment? There's something about these lone walks where the crisp dawn air burns my lungs with every deep inhale, how the brightest blue above opens up the world to me, how the feeling of the energy in the city, with every waking soul pouring into it, revitalizes me. This is when my head clears. Not right now though. My senses alert me of an enclosing danger. The low growling comes upon me almost stealthily. I one-eighty, searching the intruder nearby, to discover a shiny black BMW riding my left. Inside, Noor rolls the window down, leaning halfway into the passenger seat peering up at me.

"Marhaba akhi, khaif halak (Hey, brother, how are you)? It's been a while," he says.

"Bakhair (fine). Good to see you," I say surprised, not only in seeing him again, but him speaking to me.

"Where are you headed?"

"Home."

"Get in, I will take you the rest of the way, so we can catch up."

A hint of caution settles upon me, as I open the door and carefully descend into the firm, black leather.

"What's it been, three years the last time I saw you?" he asks, as we pull away.

"It's been a long time," I answer.

"Do you know why I left? To liberate Muslims. Our country is becoming more corrupt by the infidels' influences. I wanted to stand up to this infiltration of Western ideology, to do good for Muslims by fighting for our freedom, fighting against the Christians, Jews and Muslims who show sympathy towards them. The words of the Qur'an kept repeating through my mind, 'Take not for friends' unbelievers rather than believers.' We can see how their beliefs and values are penetrating Saudi Arabia. Causing Saudi's to apostatize and intermix with infidels. I could no longer watch this happen. For we will all have to answer to Allah one day as to why we allowed it, why we never fought for Islam. On that day I can say I did."

I carefully listen, as he continues.

"I first traveled to Syria for three months of training on everything from tactical operations with an array of firearms to anti-aircraft weaponry, explosives and mines. After Syria, I fought in Iraq and Afghanistan until I was captured and sent back here as a prisoner. The government wanted me to complete their rehabilitation program in order to be released, so I did everything they wanted me to do. Everything externally was changed in their eyes, but they could not see inside the heart; they were unable to steal the one thing that gave my life meaning, to strip away that special something I discovered about myself when fighting. They think this new car, a good job, a wife, will prevent me from joining again, to obey man while disobeying Allah. So comes the reason behind me finding you. But, before I share that, last time we saw each other do you remember what I said to you?"

"I remember every word," I say, as if it happened yesterday, still feeling the anger, the doubts, the shame that burns within. "You told me I was not following true Islam, that you refused to talk to me or be around me."

"That's correct. And I said it to you because we are family, because we were living the same life, until someone told me the same words waking me up. That was my turning point. Now, let me ask you, was that your turning point or have you been continuing to sin against Allah by not truly following his ways?"

The question doesn't take me by surprise. I anticipated something of this nature to come up. Yet, I'm not fully prepared for it. For the guilt, the shame of calling myself a Muslim, the disappointment of following the Qur'an only partially. The proposition of lying escapes my thoughts, as we pull up to the white wall guarding my home. I can't even recruit enough confidence to look at him when finally, I answer in a short, shameful tone.

"I know of no turning point yet for me."

The car comes to a stop, he reaches into his thobe pocket pulling out a wad of riyals, then he grabs my right hand, stuffs them into my palm enclosing my fingers tightly around it into a fist. When I look up from the transfer, he leans in closer, demanding my full attention before he utters his last words to me.

"Your time of being a faithful Muslim, one who truly follows the whole Qur'an, one who walks in all the ways of the Prophet Muhammad, can be now. Time becomes your enemy as an infidel. It will leave you just as it left Aisha."

He releases my hand, resuming his original driving position. Before opening the door to step out, I shove the riyals into my pocket. As I watch him pull away, disappearing behind the distant corner, my thoughts keep me here on the dirty street, pondering his words, his invitation, eventually forcing my feet to move.

Inside, I find the closest chair to help me relax some while I sort through the depth of his words. Pulling the riyals from my pocket, rolling them back and forth in my hand questioning the underlying motivation for the gift. Unfolding the bundle, a small script flutters to the floor. As I pick it up, I discover a single phone number scribbled in black ink. Must be his invitation to a new life. I count the money, then toss them both on the table. Eight thousand riyals, a phone number and uncertainty. One particular thing he said won't leave me, keeps replaying over and over again in my mind. Why will time no longer be with me as an infidel? Her face, her body, her apostasy, I think of the Christians who deceived her, who fed her lies, ending up sacrificing her life for it. This is what he means. Apostasy until death. Revenge begins revealing itself to me toward those who did this. Ideas, possibilities, of how to prevent this from happening again. Suddenly, it all converges into one rational solution: to find whoever converted her and take their life for her life.

Chapter Six

"Way to push yourself. In this limited window of pain and suffering is where you have the opportunity to obtain what the rest of them never will. The package only the elite possess," says Kamal, wearing a look of satisfaction on his face, as he watches from nearby, standing authoritatively.

I wipe the beads of sweat culminating on my forehead, throwing them into the grass below, exhausted intellectually and physically, but rejuvenated at the same time. The heat is blazing as always, without escape. My eyes are drawn to the green field in its lushness, surrounded by the distant lifeless desert.

"Have you heard anything?" I ask, still scanning the field.

"Nothing. It will come in time, just keep focused on refining your skills."

Maybe I have been fooling myself all this time thinking soccer is my purpose, what I'm supposed to be doing in life. I think of Noor, his words, the money, a door being opened for me. It would crush Kamal. Even if he didn't show any disappointment, any weakness, I know it would hurt him in ways I'm entirely unaware of. I turn to face him, finding emotionless eyes studying the field alongside mine.

I remember those eyes, that concentration. He was approving my mother's requests, making the critical decisions on her behalf as her guardian during many circumstances. He bent the boundaries more for her than I have known any man to do. The special love he had for her was definitely apparent, setting the example for me and Rana. His thick, muscular shoulders squared off the short, stocky build he was dealt in life. His dark, cold brown eyes looked to stab their way into your innermost secrets. The five-day shadow, which seemed to never grow, exposed the long, jagged scar etched across his cheek. His presence always demanding respect, forcing others to listen to his words during the rare times he spoke. A natural fear arose in the hearts of others, but along with it came a distinguished line of respect, leaving a curiousness as to why he exuded such attention? Why the dead eyes? The truth behind the scar? That's when at twelve years old, my mother informed me about how his once gentle smile, now rarely seen torturing his face, was stripped away after an explosion from a nearby car bomb captured the life of his wife bulging with a son yet to take his first breath of the earth's tainted air. When time finally healed his lacerated body, there was something missing, missing from the very depths of his soul. When you looked at him, no one was looking back, but a pair of glossy black marbles.

This is when he completely devoted himself to my mother. Even though he lacked an education of anything other than Islam, he had obtained a vast degree of knowledge from the various businesses and members of the royal family he had established relationships with over the years. I could never figure him out exactly, but one time through the impenetrable shield that protected him, I recognized a weakness in it. It happened when a car was far surpassing the speed limit, when it suddenly swerved onto the walkway. My mother unaware of the impending danger and only seconds from smashing into us, Kamal dove, tackling us into the wall of a business, crashing to the ground, barely missing the sure death of the car by inches. As I popped my head up, seeking an answer for what just happened, I watched the car plow over shopping bags people frantically dropped when dashing out of the way before colliding into the back of a black Toyota Tacoma as it tried making its way back into the street.

In that split second, I looked back to my mother laying on the ground next to me, then up at Kamal propped up on one hand staring down at us. In that moment, I saw a small glimpse of love, of life, breaking through those dead eyes. Since that day, I think deep down, when he looks at us, we faintly reflect his lost wife and son.

I'm still undecided on what to do, but I owe it to him to wait until the final decision is made.

"I hope it's soon," I say, softly.

"Don't allow anyone to discourage you. People will always try to convince you you're not talented enough. Don't listen to such nonsense. You have a gift to play; never give up on it; never let it slip through your fingers."

There is no denying the joy I have out there, squishing the fresh blades of grass underfoot, as Kamal is commanding me through intense workouts, devoting his time, knowledge and encouragement to me year after year, allowing our minds the freedom they've been asking for in the quietness of this stretch of land.

After a healthy rest, we head to our cars. He tells me he'll visit me soon. We both pull out going opposite directions. When I reach the main streets of the city, darkness touches everywhere. Shops, retailers, coffee shops are closed or with only one worker able to be seen from the street. Something serious is happening. Then as I see the delayed traffic ahead, funneling to be stopped by a group of officers grabbing papers through windows, it hits me. A roundup. The ring comes from between the consul. Tariq.

"Hello."

"Where are you?" he asks, anxiously.

"I'm on Dammam, why?"

"The police are enforcing document checkpoints on all main roads. It's about time they do something, making good on their promises."

"I'm coming upon one of the checkpoints now. I'll call you back when I get home."

"All right, yallabye."

I set my phone down, finally coming to a halt behind a short line of cars at the checkpoint. Then, catching me by surprise, the white reverse lights become engaged on the car in front of me. Suddenly it begins to roll toward me. Only a few feet remain before smashing my front end. I quickly check the rear view for room to maneuver, not an inch. The truck's bumper is nearly touching mine. I punch the horn hoping to alert the officers ahead. One of them turns and begins walking in our direction to assess the commotion. However, the call for help is too late; the impact jolts me a little, anger instantly filling my body. The doors come swinging open; two African men spring from the gray Honda, breaking in opposite directions. The alerted officer instinctively pursues the one heading north. Shifting my attention toward the other getting away, I quickly pop the door taking chase myself, the adrenaline-laced anger dictating my every move.

He is about forty yards ahead of me making his way down the long-crowded walkway, leading to a hard left. The first corner I take at full speed, noticing I've gained some ground on him. He whips his head around, checking for a tail and for the first time unexpectedly finds me. Fear shocks his face for a split second, causing him to exert more energy. He quickly hits a short right. I'm right on him, relying on the agility, the endurance I've gained from soccer to close the distance. With another peek behind him, realizing I'm uncomfortably close, he begins weaving in and out of men, women and children, hoping to trip me up, to cause one false move. But he's finding out real quick, his footwork is no match for mine. Within six feet he still refuses to surrender, suddenly dashing recklessly into the oncoming traffic. Barely evading the first car, he makes it across two more lanes, when a green SUV breaks, locks up, but doesn't stop soon enough. The rubber screeches until flesh and chrome grill meet. His extended arms take some of the impact, the rest connects at his torso, mercilessly launching him to the pavement lying motionless.

He may be dead. I feel satisfaction inside at the thought, concerned with only making it safely to his side. Maneuvering through the first two lanes, waiting for this last truck to pass by and as soon as it does, I'm stunned at the sight. He is back on his feet, our eyes meeting, aware of what's next, determined by who makes the first move. Then he's off again with me in pursuit. However, the injuries are affecting him, slowing his pace some. In about fifty yards I catch him, shoving him from behind. The relentless concrete is unforgiving, shaving off a few layers deep of raw flesh beginning from his hands stretching down the length of his entire right side, all blending in with the injuries sustained moments ago.

I stand over him, watching the blood leak from the pervading wounds, contemplating on what to do. Wait for the police? Walk him all the way back? Or leave him? He's afraid. Fearful. Not knowing what my plans are. I can see it radiating off his dark, anguished face. In an authoritative voice, I demand an answer. An answer I already know.

"Why are you running?"

He doesn't say anything, continues to stare up at me as if he doesn't understand.

"Where's your documents? Your visa?"

His blank face tells me all I need to know.

"Do you speak English?" I ask, his final warning.

Still nothing, Cautiously I bend down to check his pockets, but before I make contact his mouth moves.

"No, no, I'm illegal. I have no papers. Please don't hurt me! This is the only work I find here, in your country, to feed my family. I have no other way. Without this, my children will starve to death."

I find no sympathy for him, but am reminded of specific verses in the Qur'an about infidels. Infidels in our land. I continue assessing him, allowing his nervousness to escalate. I propose one final question, one carrying clout to the utmost degree.

"Are you a Christian?"

Without much delay he responds, "Yes."

My mother's bound body flashes before me - she died a Christian. This man is deceived like all the other men and women like him. Repulsion, disgust, is rapidly growing while analyzing his feeble condition. The blood drains from my face, leaving behind a clenched jaw and tight fists. I can't withstand it any longer, the first one grazes off his cheek, as he tucks his chin. The next one connects solidly into the right forearm being used as a shield. Left, right, left, connecting flush on his nose, releasing a cracking noise, splattering blood into my face and body. I continue unabated until I feel a firm grip latch sturdily around my right arm and body, simultaneously pulling me up from the ground. Off balance, surprised by the raw strength, I struggle to see the identity. The hold is too powerful to escape. After carrying me a few meters away, he let's go. A massive man awaits our introduction, six feet three, two sixty, daring me to provoke him. The smooth wooden club clutched in his left hand finally registers, police. I take a few calculated steps to my right, clearing away from both of them, inviting his next move - arrest me or the African. He looks behind himself, back to me, then walks over to the man on the ground, forcing him to roll over on his stomach, securing his hands with handcuffs, waiting for the approaching cars.

"Why were you beating this man?" he asks, in a calm, prying manner.

"He's an illegal, who ran from the checkpoint after hitting my car, but most of all, he's a Christian."

The interest in his eyes remains on me until the opening of the car doors breaks his concentration, shifting away from me. A skinny man approaches with a long beard falling off a gritty smugness. They exchange words, pick up the foreigner with an undisturbed trail of blood leaking from his nose, escorting him to the backseat where they throw him in, then drive away as if nothing happened.

My hands are still shaking uncontrollably, the adrenaline taking its time to dwindle from my body. A sense of relief has draped over me though, release from some of the rage that's been manifesting inside. I don't know the extent of damage he endured, but at least one of them has suffered. However, still unworthy to taste what was left when they took my mother from me. The small pool of blood covering the street invites the robe of honor to cover me, satisfaction in the air I breathe.

Remembering my car at the checkpoint, abandoned, door wide open, incites urgency in me to return. I begin transitioning into a light jog, retracing the blurred path. Back at the checkpoint, the car's the same as I left it except for the officer standing beside it, the same one who began the pursuit. He must have received help if he is already back here. A smile parts his lips when he sees me approaching.

"There you are. I was minutes from moving your car to a safer location, as we need to resume our procedures."

"He was fast. Running with resilience, purpose, aware of the repercussions if caught. Deportation, no job, no money, no means to provide for his wife and children."

He nods in agreement. "Why did you chase him down?"

"I'm tired of them coming into our country taking all of our jobs," I say, as if I really care.

"We all are. Hopefully this is permanent. We wouldn't have caught that one if it wasn't for you," he says, thankfully as he departs.

He walks ahead to the line of cars signaling for one to pull forward. As I pass through, I catch a couple of officers rummaging through the vehicle the men abandoned.

At home, I put forth a defeated effort to calm down, the tenseness still alive. Those eyes bulging with fear still crying out to me in help-lessness, for mercy. I can feel something new within - not remorse, not regret, but a releasing of pleasure, of something healthy. This must be my calling.

In the stale afternoon air, I sit, reflecting on Noor's words to me in the car, the commands of the Qur'an, the deceiving infidels, my life. A noise from outside attracts my attention. I go to the window to find Tariq coming in. I meet him at the door with a loving kiss and em-brace.

"Marhaba akhi."

"Masaa al-khayr (Good evening). How long have you been home?"

"For about thirty minutes."

"You never called me back, so I decided to stop by," he says, frustra-tion in his voice.

"Something came up unexpectedly," I say, as he follows me back to the sitting room where we both are seated.

I keep my eyes focused on the small bowl of dates centered on the table sparing me some extra time to decide on what to reveal to him. His dream as a young boy, kicking the ball around the dirty streets, was to play professionally one day. Should I be the one to lead him down another path? To rip it from his wishful hands?

"Umar, there's blood all over your hands!"

Turning directly to him, catching an intense curiosity traced with worry, then down to my hands spreading out now, I see the splattered, dry blood across swollen knuckles. I picture the stream running over those black lips finding an exit at the bottom of his chin, then soaking into a faded blue t-shirt. I feel Tariq's desire to know the truth. So, I don't keep it from him, I disclose the situation at the checkpoint, but more importantly about the specific question triggering an unleashing of rage upon the foreigners' face and how the overweight policeman left me there alone. He is listening intently until the end, then says something, taking me by surprise.

"The infidel deserved everything he got. They've been pouring into our country illegally stealing opportunities away from us, bringing with them their religion, values, culture, even if they aren't allowed to display them publicly or privately, it is still known to all Saudis."

I ponder his comments, whether I should share the new chapter in life I'm beginning, to follow true Islam according to what the Qur'an teaches and Muhammad lived, instead of the following of what seems convenient in life at the time. Carefully I choose to tell him. It is my responsibility to make him choose, to obey Allah and the Qur'an or to disobey and remain an infidel. My body welcomes the comfort of the chair when I lean back. Before I tell him, I rotate my hands back and forth studying them, the dried blood, the swollenness, how I used them to inflict pain on another man so effortlessly.

Without looking up, I unfold my plans. "I'm leaving the country soon."

I wait expectantly for the question.

"For what?"

"For training," I tilt my head up until our eyes meet, "then joining my brothers in jihad."

Astonishment strikes his expression. "What about soccer?"

"I've been waiting on it for too long. I can't say I believe anymore my purpose in life is to play soccer."

"How can you say that? You've been given a gift - you're just going to throw it all away?" he asks justifiably, with a hint of disappointment.

"Tariq, I can no longer live my life hovering along absent of any true meaning, without a clear purpose, choosing to live as an infidel by not adhering to what the Qur'an commands, but following a corrupted version because it makes life comfortable. Suppressing the truth to meet our wants will not reward us with Jannah (heaven). Only hell will be awaiting such a lifestyle. Look at our society, the corruption, the greed, the working with and pleasing other Western nations. What's next? To become like them? I will gladly die a martyr's death given the assurance of paradise before such treachery." I briefly pause, giving him time to contemplate the insight. "I've made my decision."

Now, I present him with a life altering ultimatum: "What's your decision going to be?"

He's silenced, at a loss for words, recognizing the ramifications of his answer, the life changing consequences of this pivotal moment. I don't expect him to answer right now, just as Noor didn't from me, only to make him ponder the future of his life.

"I don't know," he eventually says.

Thinking of Noor, I look to the table spotting the folded piece of paper settled below the bowl of dates right where I left it. Scooping it up, I hold it out to Tariq, hesitating briefly before taking it from my hand.

"It's Noor's number. If you decide to join me, give him a call. Tell him I gave you the number. He'll inform you on everything you need to know."

"Noor? He's in Riyadh?"

"He recently returned, not staying for long though."

Our father never liked Noor, his extreme views of Islam, telling us to count all his words as misunderstandings of what Islam truly is. I'm sure Tariq heard much more about it than I, being much closer. I know father must be in his thoughts, what he will say, what Tariq will do if he decides to leave. This is his predicament though, not mine, for our father possesses no influence over my choices in life. He never really has. I look at his young, bare face, trying to envision him with a weapon in his hands, taking another life. Growing up he was always weak mentally, lacking that leadership quality, the kind that can attract anyone to follow you, to give their life for you. This is why I don't see him coming with me, giving up all he has, defying our father's demands. Neither of us says another word. We welcome the quiet room, the fading sunburst rays creeping out of sight, the emptiness of the house. Then comes the call, the muezzin's call to 'asr. Tariq rises, looks to me for his next move.

"Go ahead without me, I'll be right behind you," I insist.

After watching him close the steel door, I make my way into the shower, washing the stranger's blood from my hands, watching the little red streams travel the shower floor. The hot water pours down my neck and back, as a therapy, forcing the tension to flow with it down the chrome exit. Unaware of the stress my body's been enduring, my mind moving nonstop. I can't afford to slow down, to worry about life's subtleties. When I step out to grab a towel, I'm disappointed in finding only an old one. I'm reminded of my mother's tender care in always providing in the most convenient ways: clean towels, folded clothing, rich aromas invading each room.

In resentment, I rip the towel off the rack, dab at my face and body, then throw it to the ground. Realizing the quickened onslaught of drowsiness taking hold, there's no way I'm making it to the mosque, so I gather up a rug, unravel it in the courtyard facing Mecca and bend in prostration. The air is beginning to cool, offering some relief for my overheating flesh. After 'asr, I crawl into bed, remembering lastly the dark, quiet room around me.

The following evening a video from a sheikh on how Muslims should treat infidel Christians and Jews feeds my thinking. I continue to listen, watch the small, wiry man in his loose shemagh and long gray beard intensely giving his message, feeling the truth emanating from his screen. I begin to wonder how I have been living astray for so long? Living as an infidel against all that Allah has required of me. Have I been so blind? Are Saudis, Muslims that blind? This explains the absence of meaning in my life. The inner emptiness I've always felt, aware of its existence, but suppressing it, conditioning myself to ignore it. It's said that one can only restrain the hungers of the heart for so long before it devours itself. This must be Allah leading me to my destiny, revealing my lack of obedience and pointing me toward what's important because I have lived a life of offense.

I check the time, 6:58 PM. Tariq will be here any moment. I click out of the video, shutting the computer off, then head out front to wait. The day has drifted by faster than expected, much of it while exploring the various sheikhs, imams and religious leaders across the internet all claiming to speak the truth, establishing fatwas on everything imaginable. Some are clearly recognized as being given for some greater purpose of the government, while defying the traditions of Muhammad, others faithful words from the Qur'an.

Standing along the street, I anxiously wait for the unexpected plans he has this evening. The fiery waves of heat busy with scorching the day are finally disappearing into the colorful mosaic of reds, yellows and oranges painting the sky above, inviting the cooler night to replace it. Such moments have always been my favorite. This is the best time to play soccer, when traffic slows to merely a trickle, leaving a lifeless maze of walls in every direction, allowing for the sounds living in the silence to awaken to a low growl. Even the slightest rumbling of an engine can be heard, echoing many kilometers away. This is a time where the streets can be listened to privately, where the motionless rule, except for the occasional disturbance of bright lights shooting through almost unseen. I cherish such unappreciated freedom and privacy. However, the burning desire of Saudis is to find some flaw, some mistake, some action that they can use to defame the reputations of others, while exalting themselves.

The blue BMW encroaching reminds me of why I'm here, but I don't pay it much attention, until it pulls up beside me. The passenger seat window begins rolling down. Tariq's face is on the other side, along with Noor driving. It surprises me he called, especially so soon. I carefully slide into the backseat behind Tariq. There's a peculiar seriousness present. What has Noor told him? Given him? Promised him? We greet each other before my question.

"What are your plans tonight?"

Eyes fixed on the street ahead, as we pull away Noor answers, "I'll tell you when we get there."

I relax into my seat, betting this has to involve some kind of preparation before we leave the country, before our training begins. We pass through familiar streets I traveled when growing up, close to where we live. After a few miles, the car comes to a halt alongside a wide street where traffic is scarce. I know this area, know it well.

"Let's go," Tariq says, stepping out.

I tug on the metal handle, climbing out. Tariq walks out into the street where kids are playing soccer, forced to use the streets because of the shortage of public fields to play on, especially for the poor. We approach the edge of their imaginary boundaries to watch the young kids sprinting back and forth, fierce, determined faces willing to sacrifice their bodies for victory. However, through all of this, you can recognize the joy, the freedom, the escape from their lives, from the trials and suffering faced daily. We study them intently. My eyes find a taller, quicker kid who reminds me of myself, with a similar style of play. He can get by anyone at will, but forgets he's on a team, that he can't do it all himself. I glance over at Tariq, finding a smile tearing through his boyish face. Noor's absence was predetermined, probably Tariq's doing. He brought me here for a reason, either to convince me from going or to say one last farewell to the very game we've lived for all our lives. A high pitch shout grabs my attention, noticing the goalie chasing after the loose ball behind the goal.

"A little more to the right," says Tariq, studying the kid with hands on top of his head in disbelief that he missed. The open street here makes it ideal for playing. The makeshift goals are almost identical to the ones we used to make.

"Remember when we were searching everywhere for a place to play, too young to be on the fields and we stumbled upon the kids running up and down this street?" He takes in a deep breath. "I always had to be on your team for some reason. Never wanted to play against you. I guess I viewed us as a team. What a great team we were too!" He turns back to the game. "Do you remember me sprinting to retrieve that pass from you, when suddenly, he came out of nowhere crashing into me, sending me onto the unforgiving concrete below, where I rocked on the ground with clenched fists because of the pain? You ran over and helped me up off the ground, encouraging me to continue. Can you recall what I told you?"

"You told me to win for you," I say, re-envisioning the request, the redemption in his eyes.

"And you should have seen the expression your face molded into, a look of pure determination, one that struck me deep, leaving an ever-lasting impression on me as to what standard we should play at. When I watched you score the goal to win the game, right then, with all the gratification, satisfaction pulsing through me, I forgot what happened to my ankle. I attempted to stand, as you were running over in celebration, but I quickly collapsed with searing pain shooting through my foot."

His eyes remain steady on mine. "You helped carry me all the way home hobbling on one leg. I will never forget that."

"Those were fun times," I say, reminiscing, as the ball whizzes by the net, blocked by the goalie.

"Do you remember when we were little kids running around on that small, dirt field, the edges littered with random pieces of garbage, playing there for the first time? I can remember how much fun we had, but most distinctly, as we were leaving, we looked at each other and without words communicated the same burning desire that had just filled our hearts. This is what we wanted to do for the rest of our lives together. The excitement felt thinking about it, the happiness doing it, I will never forget those dreams of ours, the escape from the rest of the world when kicking that ball into the net.

He lowers his head, trying to suppress the emotions coming on. After a brief period, when turning to meet me, a new hardness is present, as if he just severed the last thread holding onto anything meaningful in life.

"Deep down I knew I was never talented enough to make it, but held on for you, to be with you when you did. To make sure you knew I would never leave our dream to play together. A part of me still knows you're destined to make it. And the only thing I ask of you is when you do, you will quit whatever you're doing to go play, to play for both of us. Promise me this, Umar."

The intensity of his request is something I have never experienced from him before. The feeling of a man's last request before the darkness of death overtakes his soul. My curiosity perks as to why he is asking me this right now? Regardless, I won't be able to gather enough courage to tell him no, to refuse him the peace of knowing one of us will fulfill our dream.

"I promise you," I say, seeing the comfort relieve the heaviness weighing on him.

"I should probably tell you now. I brought you here to tell you I'm no longer pursuing soccer...have decided to join you in leaving the country to fight. We have always been a team and I'm not going to be the one to abandon it. I can never let you go alone, you know that," he says, smirking. "Noor has been helpful, offering me five thousand riyals and bought the plane ticket today scheduled to leave tomorrow morning."

Tomorrow! What about the unfinished business in finding the person responsible for giving my mother those papers? I can't leave without reconciling this issue first. Wasn't this the very thing striking within me the anger - driven determination for revenge?

"I can't leave tomorrow." I tell him. "There's something important I must do first; I promised it to myself. It shouldn't take long, a week or two at most. Just enough time for you to get comfortable, so when I arrive you can inform me on everything I need to know."

He doesn't have to speak the words for me to know the impact of my response.

There is fear, anxiety, anger, of having to go all alone now. After a minute or so of looking at me in a disappointed, but needy way, he finds the kids again as an escape.

"I'll be waiting for you when you come. Do your best to hurry," he softly whispers, making his way back to the car.

The children finish the game as twilight warns of its imminent presence, parting them to go their separate ways. The street is naked now. I'm still staring at it as if continuing to be entertained by the game, not wanting it to end, not wanting to enter back into the reality I'm now living in. How all it took is one significant event, one choice, to change life's course in a matter of moments, is mystifying when properly examined.

The shadow emerges upon me, dispersing the thoughts, the questions, the uncertainties of what lies ahead. I stand for a moment before getting in, leaving behind a part of my childhood I will never again revisit, severing what used to be my life.

Chapter Seven

The images of both their faces are seared into my memory. It's been thirty minutes, waiting, AC regulating the sweat filling my palms, especially the one grasping my plan. Recalling how my mother would get off around six in the evening, emerge from these doors accompanied by other women, I make sure I'm here early to pick the ideal parking spot, providing a clear view of the entrance. Every time those broad glass doors fling open my eyes are peeled, searching the faces to identify her, but this place expands over a vast area, making it difficult to follow every figure moving in and out, the parking being situated about fifty meters from the walkway to the entrance, offering directions on where to enter and exit. Fake date palms scatter the perimeter of the tan, three-story building, decorated with numerous, deep, rectangular windows lining the soaring walls. The benefit of this being a women's facility is many men like me are waiting to pick up their wife or female relative, making my presence inconspicuous.

Traffic is pouring in as the top of the hour draws near. The passing of every truck obstructing the view for some seconds in front of me contributes to my worry of missing my opportunity. Every time it occurs, my heart speeds up. I watch a Saudi woman cross in front of me traveling toward the entryway. The moment she reaches the stone overhang, the doors swing open, exposing a group of five Saudi women and two foreigners. My finger hovering over the green call button, ready to push it at the first recognition. Ten meters closer...it's not them, they all have dark skin. I relax, waiting for the next group. The doors open again; this time two Saudi women emerge followed by two more foreign women. I quickly realize a problem, and the closer they come the more panic arises in me. I can't get a clean look, because the two Saudis in front are walking too close, blocking my vision! My right hand straddles the door handle. If I have to get out for a new vantage point, I'm prepared to do so in a split second. As they keep heading to my left the two foreigners finally break away, turning right in my direction and as they do, my heart skips a beat. It's them, neither wearing full niqab - the same two in the photo. My finger drops on the screen, connecting the call. I study both of them closely, waiting for the treasure to open for me. Nothing. Still nothing.

"Come on, reach for it," I say, mumbling to myself.

Suddenly, the taller, light-skinned one reaches into her pocket retrieving her phone, then studies the screen. Found her! Praise be to Allah!

What a confused expression she has, looking up from the screen staring afar off, a contemplative investigation, sliding it back into her pocket then continuing to move as if now distracted by something. Before disappearing from my sight behind me, I slowly start my car and back out, monitoring the vehicle they enter, an old, brown Toyota pickup. Accelerating into a crawl, disregarding the cars backing up behind me, they finally pull-out merging with traffic. I follow at a safe distance, never removing my eyes from the black male driver. We navigate about fifteen minutes outside Riyadh when they pull into a compound. Decreasing my speed, I cruise by, scanning the interior as they enter. I will be back tonight, sneak in, find her place. This compound is in shambles compared to the rest of them: a bunch of little tenements hugging one another on all sides, dirty and packed with foreigners. I've seen and heard that most Westerners live in these compounds or gated communities making life easier and more comfortable, but I've never been inside of one. I return home and wait in the silence of my place for darkness to fully encompass the sky determining the means by which to take her life, possibly their lives if that's what it must come down to. I've never killed anyone before, but don't anticipate it being too complicated, especially the one who deceived and lied to my mother causing her death. This is the least I can do, to seal up loose ends. The more all of this stirs inside of me, the more intense the rage becomes, the hate for anyone who dares to speak to a Muslim of any religion other than Islam, any God other than Allah.

I pick up the Qur'an always resting atop the small side table, turn to one of the passages Noor spoke to me during the ride home last night.

"Fight them, (unbelievers) and Allah will punish them by your hands and disgrace them."

When I heard him say it, a sense of duty, of permission, radiated within my conscience, a duty to live by Allah's final authority. And now, the existing feeling is confirmed. The table accepts the Qur'an back, as I kneel to ask Allah to give me strength through this war I'm entering. When finished, I lift my head, peering through the bay window, heeding the mature night in its blackness. It's time.

Chapter Eight

One truck has entered within the last ten minutes. I can't be here much longer without drawing unneeded attention to myself; I'm already suspicious enough lurking around this compound for foreigners. Finally, my window of opportunity has arrived. I leave my car parked nearby in case I'm forced to make a quick getaway. In a brisk walk, I move along the unlit street toward the entrance of the compound when I feel it, feel it manifesting in the bottom of my gut, fighting to free itself, a newness that reaches far beyond the parameters of what is felt before a game because of its powerful grip on me, on my heart, squeezing it to its maximum potential. However, regardless of this intrusion, my mind remains sharp, clear, on the mission at hand, rather inviting the new sensation, excited to discover all that it offers.

The tall, thick concrete walls stop at the entrance, offering enough room for the two lanes to fit. Little lights are stationed at the front of each group of tenements offering essential light for me to find the brown Toyota. I stealthily maneuver inside the walls, shifting my eyes between the lines of parked vehicles resting barely beyond the front doors of each residence. The further I go; nervousness establishes a stronger presence. After making it halfway into the compound, I spot the brown rear-end protruding slightly past a white Honda. I check behind me, confirming it's clear, before taking a sudden sharp right.

The thought of this possibly being someone else's door brings another level of uncertainty, of anticipation upon me. I stop, standing before it, undecided on the next move to make: knock or open the door and walk-in? What if there are several people inside? The un-limited scenarios cause pause in me, the cool air offering some relief from the sweat beginning to seep from beneath my thobe and keffiyeh, but I'm helpless against fear's steel blade pressing against my stomach. I know I need to make a decision quickly, to ignore the sickness of fear whispering ever so slightly to turn around and leave and follow through with what I came here for, for Islam, for Muslims, for my mother. Then, as if for the first time I notice the brightness shining down from the scattered balls of bright light above, somehow infatuat-ed by them at the moment, my awareness delayed to the ever-growing threat getting closer, getting brighter, I whip my head toward the light, seeing the car inside the compound heading in my direction. Are the police carrying out a raid or routine walkthrough? They will punish me severely for being here, the shame being the most consequential to me and my family. Hastily, I hit the door three solid times.

Looking back at the encroaching headlights, then back to the door, the car, the door, my pulse pounding against my chest waiting anx-iously for someone to answer. My inner voice finally advising me to turn the knob and walk-in. A final command: if there's no answer in a few seconds, I'm entering. The moment the thought ends, I hear the metal bolt grinding, the door opening a meter or so. On the other side stands the same woman in the photo, the one I followed, the one I'm here to kill, suspicion leaking through her calm expression as she uses the door to guard against my intrusion.

"Can I come in and ask you a few questions?" I request, taking one glance over my shoulder in urgency.

Her eyes are studying me if I'm a potential threat or not, but I can't afford the time. I give her one last chance.

"If this is the police heading our direction you know what will hap-pen to both of us," I tell her quickly, in the most honest way possible.

Without a word, she steps aside, pulling the door open wide enough for me to fit through, granting permission to enter. I act immediately, needing only a few steps before I'm safely inside. The clicking of the shut door behind me registers, then she glides past me a short distance taking a right into a small bare room with two black, worn-down couches facing a faded square wood table centering the room. The light illuminating the room is coming from a lone lamp posted in the corner below the only window covered with a tan curtain. I watch her settle down upon the furthest couch, laptop open, papers disheveled all over.

"Take a seat if you like."

After lowering myself down on the soft, cotton cushion opposite her, she gives me her full attention.

"I'm sorry, I didn't get your name and why you have come here at such risk to ask me some questions," she says, with a tinge of hostility.

"I'm Um...Moddi!" I blurt out, barely catching myself.

"Well, Moddi, I don't have much time, so if you can ask your questions and be on your way it will be helpful," she says, in a dry, assertive tone.

For the first time, I capture her natural beauty up close: long, wavy, auburn hair curling over her slender shoulders with the deepest penetrating green eyes you only find in a remote, undisturbed lagoon. Her body is covered by a thin, black, short-sleeved shirt with gray sweats. This is new to me, being so close and intimate with a white woman, especially one this attractive. I remind myself of the purpose of my visit, to find the truth.

"I didn't intend to come to your residence in this kind of blunt manner, but was left with few options."

She doesn't flinch. I move straight to the point.

"Did you work with a Saudi woman named Aisha Abdullah Al-Sindi?"

Her eyes fall to the floor, a connection occurring, memories surfacing, before recovering. "Yes, I've worked with her for two years at King Faisal Specialist Hospital and Research Center."

"Did you spend a lot of time together, talking, sharing thoughts unrelated to work?" I question, studying her body language as she responds.

"We were required to spend much time together, as was demanded by our line of work. When you're around someone closely for a substantial amount of time, of course, personal questions about life are going to arise."

"Did you ever discuss religion with her?" I ask, methodically building on the previous questions, laying the groundwork.

Her gaze doesn't break from mine, as she shifts forward understanding the questions' implications. I can sense a new carefulness.

"Yes, we have discussed religion," she says, with stern confidence. I think of the text I sent that morning. Did she go? Was she there when my mother was executed? Again, my mother's face appears, haunting, drowning in a puddle of blood.

"Do you know what happened to her?" I ask, hinting of accusation.

She looks away, dealing with her attack of emotions, refusing to display them in front of a complete stranger.

"She was murdered," she says in a bitter kind of disgust.

"No," I immediately snap back. "She was executed. And do you know why? Because she apostatized. She rejected Islam, became an infidel."

All I can feel is anger burning its way through all my body suppressing the grief, the pain, existing somewhere inside.

"Are you a Christian?" I ask, finished playing games.

Without the slightest wavering, she stares directly into my eyes saying, "Yes, I'm a Christian and my time with you has come to an end."

"I have one last question before I leave," I say, not asking.

She doesn't respond, only glaring at me, expecting it.

"Did you give her any Christian material?" Recruiting all of my focus, senses, I examine her every movement, expression, anything that may reveal the truth.

The moment her lips begin to move, we both hear it: the clicking of the front door. Instantly, she explodes from the couch, startling me as she grabs the crevice of my arm, yanking me up toward the direction of the bedroom.

"Go out the window," she commands at the bedroom door, her face revealing a surprising calm composure.

Someone must have seen me on her doorstep, called in. A raid. I push through the half-open door, quickly closing it to a sliver, then move around the narrow mattress situated on the floor by the window, when my heart suddenly stops my body. "Wait. See who it is." I try to refute the demand, but find myself already peeking through the crack in the door into the room.

He appears from the corner, determination crunching his brow tightly together, then another one...five total entering the room swiftly swarming her petite frame. She lifts her head from prostration to study their faces one by one. All of them are advanced in years, carrying beards of differing lengths, except for one bare-faced youngster. I can see the agenda on their faces, to inflict pain, punishment and possibly death if need be. Maybe no one did see me; this is just a routine walk-through.

The first man who enters the room, clearly possessing authority, fearlessly steps inches from her face. A scowl is permanently creased into his broad jawline with a scraggly beard failing in its attempt to hide the sagging skin beneath. He finally opens his skinny, parched lips, releasing a deep raspy voice.

"Who are you praying to?"

"To God," she says, in the fearless tone I've been recently introduced to.

A part of me is urging me to leave, knowing what's coming next, to put some distance between us while they're busy in here. She deserves the punishment that's about to be unleashed upon her, doesn't she? She's a Christian. If they didn't show up her blood would be on my hands. I ponder how I so easily forget the mercy she showed me, directing me to this room to escape, to prevent a great shame and criminal charges. Then freely falling to her knees obliging to the consequences assured to come. She never answered the most important question though.

Should I wait it out, risk getting caught and arrested? Is it worth it? Before I can dissect the thousand thoughts ravaging my mind, the man asks a critical question.

"Are you praying to Allah?"

"No," she answers, remaining steadfast in her resolve.

Without a second to spare, a left hook smashes into her delicate cheek, knocking her to the floor, a grunt of pain sent through the tenement. The five other officers come closer, smelling the weakness, halfway encircling her. She only sits, propped up on one elbow, aware of the beating she must endure. It comes down in flurries. Fists flying wild, kicks connecting flush into her rib cage, stomps mostly being deflected by her elbows and knees now tightly tucked into her chest. Every kick that lands forces out a deep exasperation of pain. Now it comes, the scarlet splattering everywhere, down her arms, into her hair, puddling up below her head. Are they going to kill her?

I begin to feel that familiar presence manifesting inside me calling me to help, to pull open the door and save her from potential death. So many times I've found myself in this position, watching, listening to the moaning, the cries, the pleas, but never possessing enough courage to interfere after that first time. Fear's authority holding me in the darkness, out of harm's way.

The older man takes a step back, chest expanding with each quickened inhale in desperate need of oxygen and gives the command. The others finish with final kicks to the abdomen. She's not moving. I keep my eyes fixed on the officers, waiting for their next move. They haven't searched the place, but after the beating, the likely death of her, their pleasures should be satisfied for the night. Their hungry eyes stare down at the limp, motionless body, pride stretching over their faces. They exchange a few words, following glances at her body, then all turn, following one another around the corner out of sight. Are they trying to lure me out? I listen for the door, for any sounds, not like they can't be deceiving me though. Lacking the courage to find out, I stay put, keeping my ears alert, my eyes switching from hallway to bloody body. She's dead, must be. Hasn't moved in minutes. Then something down below captures my attention. Movement. Fingers moving. She's alive! Instantly I tug at the doorknob, only to stop myself in the process, realizing what trap could potentially be waiting for me. Suddenly, a still small voice, coming from someplace within, overpowers every other voice, compelling me to go to her, to help her. And for some strange reason, I comply. In less than a second, the door swings open and I kneel at her side. The sight sucks the air from my lungs. Almost every inch of white flesh is stained in blood, her hair gobbed together sticking to her face and neck, blood still freely flowing from the long gash above her right eye, from the split in the middle of her bottom lip and from both nostrils.

I reach out pressing my two fingers against the nape of her neck. The rhythmic beating brings confusing relief, thankfulness in a way. Without delaying any longer, I rip the keffiyeh from my head, collect the hair sticking to her face with my free hand, gently pulling it aside so I can clearly examine the extent of damage. However, I am taken aback by the swollen knots bulging from her forehead and left cheek. This is not the same woman I was conversing with twenty minutes ago. Rana flashes through my mind, spread out across the floor along with my inability to help her or rather my decision not to. Now, I'm at this Western woman's side, able to help her, willing to for some odd reason I can't figure out. I don't have to. Pressing the keffiyeh onto the biggest gash above her eye, I hope to stop the leaking. I swivel my head around the room searching for anything that can be used to place against the other wounds. Nothing. The blood is beginning to slowly crawl over my fingers. I use my other hand to hold her head straight, needing her to wake.

After analyzing her condition, the damage, she needs a hospital. My instincts are to call an ambulance, but I'm not willing to take the risk. No matter the means, I'm breaking the law.

"Please, wake up," I whisper to her lifeless body while checking her pulse again. "Come on, open your eyes."

I think of her sacrifice for me. Willing to sacrifice her life for my safety. Why? I would never do the same, especially after coming here accusing her in her own home of committing the utmost offense. I intended to harm her in just the same way. A taste of disgust makes its presence felt inside. Then, one thought spurs the motivation, the perseverance in me to keep her alive: if she dies, I will never know the truth about my mother.

I pull the keffiyeh from her forehead, ring it out, try wiping up what's left, moving to her lip and begin dabbing at it. The moment I apply pressure, her head moves, releasing an agonizing moan. Staring intensely at the back of her eyelids, pleading for her to open them, needing her to live, another deep moan leaks out; the struggle is apparent, but little by little her eyes begin flickering open.

"You're going to be okay. I will get you to the hospital, all right?"

She's locked onto my face. I can't tell whether or not she's coherent or waiting for her mind to recover.

"I need...my phone," she suddenly mumbles, clearly on the brink of death.

Instantly I scramble through my thobe until retrieving my phone. I hold it out to her. She takes it and begins tapping at the numbers leaving fresh bloody fingerprints. During the ringing, she never averts her eyes from mine. The guilt crushing my heart, as I wait what seems like forever. I don't know what to say. Nothing can be said to relieve what she's feeling. I know this. So, I decide to keep my mouth shut.

"I need your help...I'm at home - hurry please!" She pleads, with a kind of hope in her voice.

I accept the phone back from her extending arm.

"You better go."

"I can help carry you to the car," I insist, feeling obligated to offer, owing her at least that.

"No, please go," she requests, the words breaking in weakness.

How worthless I feel. How rejected. I've failed at such times all too often in my life, especially recently, but there still must be some need for my help. I don't care if her friend sees me. But am I ready to confront the police if they're waiting outside?

"Why did you help me?" I ask, desiring to know her reason before I go, probably never seeing her again.

She holds my gaze with those soft emerald eyes, "Because I love you just as Christ loves you. Please, you must go now."

Recognizing the urgency in her voice, I rise to my feet, moving toward the front door. When I approach the hallway, a couple of words chew their way out of my mouth, stopping me. Turning my body slightly, enough to catch her bloodied body resting on the floor, "Thank you," I whisper.

"Umar," I instinctively respond by returning my attention to her, "you resemble her even more in person."

In the moment her words surprise me, leaving me momentarily stunned in silence taking in the significance of her observation, before leaving her behind.

The cool night air covering the empty street inside the compound provides relief. I set my pace faster than usual, to avoid being seen. No police so far. Suddenly, they're right on me, shining brighter and brighter until eventually zooming by. I tuck my chin while turning away, preventing the driver from a clear view of my face. This is when I realize there is no keffiyeh for me to hide behind, blood smeared across the front of my thobe from wiping my hands off on it and there's no doubt they saw it. I glance back checking the destination of the car. It aggressively pulls up in front of her place. Two figures quickly emerge, sprinting to the door. In a split second, they are illuminated in the headlights. I faintly make out long, black hair flowing from a slender frame. The other I'm unable to tell. I have an image of them running through the front door, taking a right, then instant panic, fear, as they race to help. The guilt reminds me it never left, only hidden behind the stress of escaping myself. Are they capable of carrying her to the car without hurting her? I could have picked her up myself. Too late now; I must keep pushing ahead, watch my own back. I transition to a jog, exit the compound, down the darkened street finally reaching my car. Just as I'm opening the door, I look up, seeing the white Honda come speeding down the street. Will she make it? Life or death can be decided at any given moment. Whether one freely gives it or has it taken away from them, life ultimately holds value. Her willingness to give hers to protect mine means something. I'm entangled in my thoughts for the entire drive home.

Many hours into the night, I'm wide awake, unable to chase away those penetrating green eyes, the battered, bloody face, the grace and love shown me and an unfamiliar feeling, one that I have never felt towards a woman before. After failing over and over again at suppressing them, I now invite them in, one by one, providing me with the opportunity to examine the contents of each one. I think of her departing words of the love she has for me along with Christ. I think of the unanswered question only she alone holds. What if the answer is yes? Do I still implement the same punishment as before? The fatigue eventually wins out, forcing my eyes into the darkness.

Chapter Nine

The sun is at its zenith, casting down the relentless heat of a typical day in Riyadh. The streets are busy, the buildings alive with life, yet it all feels like a dream, following a predestined path, dead to the world I'm living in right now. Is this numbness, this exiled state, what true Islam offers? I no longer even taste the fresh acidic sweetness of the orange citrus I sip on. This lack of closure is continuing to suppress my concentration on the mission, to the next flight meeting Tariq. And each successive hour that dwindles by reminds me of her, keeping me guessing of her survival.

I watch the compact, familiar Filipino man waiting on the list of new customers who enter. He's always respectful, never late, prompt in his serving, running to and fro for a minimal earning. My eyes follow him until an idea registers. A solution. It doesn't take long before I'm calling Rana on the phone.

"I don't know what kind of condition she's in or if she's even alive, but I know she's here. You will have to find her. Remember the questions, especially the one about giving mother anything?" I say, emphasizing the main reason why we have come to the hospital.

Rana nods before rising from the passenger seat, carefully passing in front of an impatient driver, then tailing two other women through the entrance of King Faisal Specialist Hospital and Research Center. I find a parking space close enough to see the human traffic going in and out. Three women emerge, two younger and one older, faces glistening in the sun's rays. The distance at which I'm able to notice it is what holds my attention. As they draw nearer, the tears continue to stream down their puffy little cheeks. I can only think this woman isn't their mother, a relative comforting the raw emotions of a tragedy to a loved one.

As they fade from my sight, from my mind, I ponder Rana's venture inside without a name. She only has a description of the woman's battered body and the date and time of arrival. The only thing she has in her favor is the fact that she's looking for a foreign white woman. Odds are the only one. This is only the first obstacle; additional difficulties pile on after this, but I have faith in her that she will navigate through all the required procedures to accomplish the task requested of her. She understands the importance of it, that my future plans hinge on the answers received and delivered to me.

Cold air blows against my chest, climbing up my neck into my face, preventing the determined beads of sweat from forming. I begin feeling anxious, wondering what is going on, what is taking so long. Something is calling me to go in, to see her myself, to experience that distinct aura of hers, exuding a confidence in life despite the unexpected when it comes, something quite similar to what I felt, sensed, when around my mother toward the conclusion of her fate, now that I think about it. I have a strong feeling she's survived the beating, is alive and well, ready to go back to her daily regimen unaffected by the merciless trappings that catch most men, fear.

I check the screen. The hospital's closing in one hour - still no sign of her. I begin playing with possible scenarios in my head, estimating the approximate time it would take. None of them suffice unless, for some reason, she's sharing the complete history of their relationship. My finger habitually taps the side of the phone; I contemplate calling. Minute after minute passing turning into hours of looking at the glass doors, to the phone, back to the entrance. There she is! A surge of energy bursts through me, anxious to find out what happened. Instead of pulling out to meet her, I stay put in case there is something further that must be done. For a split second, doubt enters about whether it's her or not, but as she approaches the car my instincts are confirmed. Her thicker stature, height and most of all her unmistakable shuffle.

I don't deviate from her eyes as she reaches the door, patiently waiting for the update. Yet, the moment we share the confined quarters once again, I notice a peculiar change in her.

"Is she alive?" I ask, invasively.

She faces away from me toward the hospital organizing her thoughts, the events, how they played out.

"She's alive."

My heart experiences a relief, yet an attachment I find disgust with.

"I asked the woman at the desk if she could help me find a patient I knew little about. Once she agreed, I informed her of the few details you told me about a white foreign woman badly beaten. As soon as I finished speaking, a spark ignited her memory prompting her to type away at the keyboard, finally delivering me the room number. When I reached her room, the door was open, but I stopped immediately before to gather my composure, my thoughts. When ready, I stepped inside the doorway and peered inside. There was a slim, Indian woman, hunched over in a chair, adjacent to the raised bed where a bandaged figure lay fast asleep. Instead of intruding, possibly startling them, I lightly tapped against the open door. At the sound of the first knock, the Indian woman whipped her head right at me. The absence of recognition caused her to hesitate, arming her defenses for potential harm, then wearily greeting me where I stood.

When she asked if she could help me, I asked the name of the patient. She told me, Lydia. I explained to her how she knew my mother and I only wanted to check on her condition and if possible ask her some questions. She told me it wasn't a good time because of the surgeries and medication she's on from the many sustained injuries. That it was a miracle she survived. I was at a loss for words. I stood there for a second thinking of what to do next, but before I had a chance to decide, she told me to hold on. I watched her go to the bedside and gently touch Lydia's leg. She stirred awake rather quickly, listening to the woman's whispers, then Lydia turned her head toward me, covered in gauze except for the small opening of her swollen stitched-up lips. All she did was stare at me for about a minute, until I began feeling uncomfortable, averting my eyes to the long hallway. I must have missed her granting permission because suddenly the Indian woman was in front of me explaining Lydia agreed to speak with me. I thanked her on the way by.

Once I made it to the edge of the bed is when I could feel the entirety of her condition. There loomed a hint of recognition, but her wrapped face denied my memory the details. After introducing myself and offering my sympathy for her tragedy, I wasted no time in presenting the first question to her, whether or not she was staying in Riyadh or leaving. Her expression transformed, hardened, I had no doubt she knew I was sent to ask this, that I was informed of what had happened and was here to find out her intentions. The answer reaffirmed my assessment when she said she was undecided and had to pray about it. Unwilling to be there any longer than I had to staring at her ravaged body, I asked the only question that mattered: Did Aisha Abdullah Al-Sindi ever give her any Christian material? Without flinching, she gave me a stern no. I thanked her for her time, then walked through the thickness of the room."

Something inside me is suspicious of this account, refusing to believe these two short questions took more than an hour, especially remembering the bold but gentle way she spoke to me in what seemed to be leading up to a definite yes that night, before the intrusion and beating when those soft, ocean-green eyes demanded my full attention. Does this mean I'm denying Rana's word? Accusing her of lying to me? The mere thought of it is suffocated by the memories of her within our pact.

I concede for the moment that Lydia is not important to me, however, for some unknown reason, somewhere deep inside my soul, I don't want this to be the end; I need to see her again. Confused on what to do next, knowing I can't enter the hospital, I gaze out the driver's side window at the complex. Acceptance eventually settles in or defeat. Encouraging my hands back to the wheel, I watch the hospital fade away through the rear-view: goodbye Lydia.

It's a rare, silent drive back to Rana's. The lingering possibility of her not telling me everything discussed in that room I refuse to let go. Maybe because I don't want it to be all. Maybe I want an excuse to see her again. No matter how hard I try in convincing myself the end has come, the rage still resides deep inside me, begging for a release and for some unknown reason, she's the only one possessing the power to do it. I don't say anything though. Before opening the door, I thank her for the help. She refuses to look away from my apathetic expression, asking, "Akhi, have you ever asked yourself why you believe in Islam? I know this is prohibited, but why Islam and not one of the other religions?"

Her loving, innocent face is truly curious. I know she's asking me because of the unique trust we share between us, the openness that exists, a critical piece of our relationship. However, I won't allow her to be deceived. I've already made that mistake too fresh in my past.

"I don't ever want to hear you ask this question again. Do you understand?" I say, angrily. "Now, go repent, pray and read the Qur'an."

This is the last answer she expected to hear, proved by her disappointed countenance, by her stepping out of the car speechless. She will understand one day this was out of love. This kind of love doesn't always make you feel warm inside, but a greater purpose lies behind it, realized only later on in life. And truth with love triumphs over love by itself. This is what our mother would tell us growing up when we disagreed with the response she would give. Anyone else who dared ask such a question would be charged with blasphemy. I'm thankful she still feels comfortable enough with me to ask such risky questions; however, at the same time, I'm worried about the direction of her thoughts. Watching her black-cloaked frame enter through the door, closing it behind her, I allow the only softness of my heart to gradually harden over, for there can be no harboring weaknesses moving forward or they will be exposed, used against me when under the pressures to come.

The azure sky is dimming, inviting new light from the million bright little balls of whiteness. I decide to take the rest of the night off and rest some. I'm going to need it. When I arrive home, there's still no sight of my father. His absence is leaving me wondering, mainly because of Tariq's departure. This is something I must check on with Noor, about Tariq's status and my joining him. The place is silent, scentless, something I'm unaccustomed to. I would have to learn to adapt to it if I were not leaving. I go to my room to relax, think, read some surahs, anything to make the last two days vanish from my memory. The black Qur'an stationed beside the bedside is chosen.

Undecided on what surah to read, an invading thought comes: Why do you believe in Islam? Rana's question surfacing. It must be the way she presented it. I've always questioned why others believe in other gods, but never have I asked myself why I believe in Islam in any kind of objective manner.

My eyes find surah 4:74 temporarily ignoring the reflection for now.

"Let those (believers) who sell the life of this world for the Hereafter fight in the Cause of Allah and whoso fights in the Cause of Allah and is killed or gets victory, We shall bestow on him a great reward."

Before I can fully absorb the affirmation from the verse, the vibration of my phone shakes my leg unexpectedly. I argue with myself about whether or not I should answer it. After the fourth pulse, mixed with curiosity, I check the caller. Noor. Just who I need to speak with.

"Hello."

"Umar, assalaam alaikum."

"Wa alaikum assalaam."

"It's going to be a week before you leave. Many things are happening right now. There's one more reason why I called...I had a conversation with your father today." Suddenly my father appears in the doorway startling me, I wasn't alerted by the faintest sound of his presence entering the house. A cold chill radiates from him, shooting his look of death into me. Immediately the words of Noor make sense - my father knows about Tariq leaving, why he left. The brief pause from Noor coincides almost perfectly with my father's steps toward me ending.

"Tariq's in paradise."

I don't respond, keeping my eyes fixed on my father, who's showing no sign of stopping. Without breaking eye contact, I remove the phone from my ear, hang up and routinely slide it into my thobe.

"You knew he joined, didn't you?" he accuses. And you didn't do anything to stop him? You let him go? It's difficult to imagine him leaving without you. That he would give up soccer if you didn't agree as well." He stops within a foot of me, peering down with his welling up smoky eyes. Stunned by the words of Tariq's death, I'm still attempting to fight against it, against the unexpected hollowness taking up residence in the pit of my gut. Guilt that has latched itself on to my conscience. I never anticipated death so fast. I figured it might come only after the training when in the midst of warfare. The pain of loss is no surprise, as the numbness from my mother's death still lingers. Questions of how it happened arise though, to quench the thirst for closure.

Positioned at the foot of the bed, survival instincts offer a warning of an immediate threat: the slight shaking of my father's hands against the hem of his thobe's sleeves, muscles bulging in his cheeks from a clenched jaw, grief deepening the crevices in his face, all needing a release and that release is me. Certain of the wrath to come, I still tell him the truth; not for him, for Tariq.

"Yes, I knew about him joining; we joined together. I had to stay behind to take care of some business first."

I receive no blink, no word, no movement at my response. So, I give him the one thing that brings me some kind of hope with Tariq's death.

"He's in paradise now."

It comes whizzing at me expectantly. I lean back, dodging the out-of-control right hook. He quickly steps closer, throwing a flurry of blows at my head knocking me to the bed. Very few penetrate my arms and knees tucked securely against my chest, to cause any damage. The power behind the punches begins to weaken, as the fatigue and frustration sets in. When I don't feel any more punches coming down, I peek between my elbows catching him grab the small wood table near the bed, dumping the books onto the floor, aggressively returning back to me. A deep fear surfaces, recognizing the potential danger it can cause me. I can't allow it to happen. I must put an end to this. No longer will I sit and take it. I wait for him to come a little closer and as he does, raising the table overhead to smash me with it, I strategically aim my foot at his midsection, then with everything I have, release. It connects directly into his sternum, launching him back into the wall, dropping the table in mid-air. Instantly, I spring up off the bed, rushing toward him before he has a chance to recover, quickly deciding between two options: try to flee past him or inflict enough damage preventing his pursuit. Right as I come within a couple of feet from the doorway, he places his hand on the floor leaning partly into my path attempting to press himself back to his feet. I can see the strength, the awareness, surging back into his face and through his body. He's not letting me escape, leaving me with only the latter option. I dig deep, from the hips, mustering up all my power and when I unleash my fist, his eyebrow catches it solidly, smashing him back against the wall, stunned, bleeding. The left hand follows suit connecting square on his chin, this one leaving his head limp, slumping off to the side, unconscious.

Relief washes over me, like a relentless ten-foot wave crashing down on me, stripping away a suppression I've always felt, but could never quite shed. Captivated by his bleeding face, I never imagined seeing him in this condition: vulnerable, helpless, especially by my hands, finally experiencing what my mother and I did all of these years. Defeat. However, when he wakes the pride and anger will fuel his revenge. So, I take one last glance at him, knowing this may very well be the last. And as I do, I search my heart for any piece of it that will miss him, that will hope to see him again, yet find none.

Before leaving, I hurry to the head of the mattress, pulling it away from the wall, reaching underneath forcing my hand through the thin slit along the seam, grabbing the ten thousand riyals and my mother's phone. After safely tucking them away, I sprint from the room to the car, then hastily depart. Once a reasonable distance from the house, I dial Noor, confident he will provide a discreet place for me to stay until my departure.

"Hello."

"Hey, something has come up forcing me to leave the city," I explain in a calm, but serious tone.

"Don't worry, I'll take care of it. I'm at an istirahat on Abi Said Al Khadri Street. Meet me here. I'll send you the address and be waiting out front."

"I'll be there in fifteen minutes," I say, tension easing some.

The drive drags on longer than expected from the inescapable events fresh on my mind. Noor's confession of Tariq, of telling my father, my father's appearance and uncontrollable rage, then the pivotal decision on my part to cross that boundary set when I was a young boy, changing our lives forever. Is he not at the brunt of loss in all of this? In all this, he's lost a son to paradise and now lost the son he refused to ever love from birth. This severance, as expected, is bringing me closure. It's still too early, too obscure, to fully understand the implications of it.

All the city's lights are coming alive, illuminating the hungry streets, as the dull, powder-blue sky transitions to its nightly reveling. The traffic is heavy right now, workers rushing to make it home for the night. After passing the last green light, the place is now in view. The closer I come, the more cars I discover packing the parking lot, making me question whether there will be a vacant space to park. I feel a little jolt as I pull in, running over the small lip in the pavement, immediately scanning each aisle for an opening. I wonder what's going on inside? Must be something important to attract an audience so numerous. Then I catch the beaming red brake lights of a Toyota pulling out ahead of me, choosing to take its place. Adrenaline still fresh, circulating freely, as I step out and stride to the entrance. The door surprisingly opens a moment before reaching it, revealing two men: the first a bulky man with a rigid stare and the thickness of a forest growing from his face. The second is Noor. He's wearing an expressionless look on his face approaching me with his confident composure, a look I have come accustomed to seeing on him.

"Marhaba akhi, khaif."

"Bakhair," I return, as we embrace.

"Sheikh Khalim Ahili is here tonight speaking on important issues, issues pertaining to all Muslims."

He grabs my hand, leading us to the door, then, right before he clutches the handle, he turns with a hint of compassion in his eyes, saying, "We will have time to discuss things later, but right now let's give our full attention to this message."

I nod in agreement.

We enter the building, cross through the main floor, passing by Saudi's leaving or waiting in the lobby. Through a small line of people gathered at the front desk, an Indian man is greeting and serving customers with rooms, a kind of privacy equally observed and respected by all who attend. After traversing down the hallway, we come to our room. Noor enters first; I'm at arm's length behind. The room is crowded with devout Saudis'. Sheikh Khalim Ahili is already at the front of the large square room delivering his message. We are required to navigate toward the back until we lower ourselves into two seats next to many other men. Bouncing off the many faces, I catch a glimpse of an overbearing man sitting on Noor's right. Something registers of familiarity, yet I can't recall from where. Then it hits me - the policeman who yanked me from beating that foreigner. Why is he here? With Noor's face intently focused on Khalim, I decide to do the same, dismissing the man for the time being.

Khalim's a stout man with a solid white beard settling on a wrinkly, sagging face unappealing to the eye, yet containing power. His white thobe rides high above his ankles. By the introductory phase in his speech along with a few more men still sauntering in, he must have begun speaking shortly before I arrived. I clear all distractions from my mind, focus on this intense man, welcoming his words with open arms.

"Are you Muslims by name only, falling under the title of Islam while compromising to live by the true ways of Muhammad? Are you the defeated ones who sit by powerless in overturning any people, government or country to Islam? Did Allah desire for us to live under subjection to infidels and heathens? The ways of men today are an insult to Allah and his lordship over this world. Muslims are not only living the same way as heathens, but adopting their thinking, their values, their culture and even their tolerant laws. Look how far we have strayed from true Islam. Islam is a way of life; the way of devoted life Muslims have been failing to live by. We are a special people unlike any other, for we have been chosen by Allah to conquer the world. This is our responsibility, to bring about global submission to Islam with the truth in our mouths and a sword in our hand. Any man-made government must be destroyed..."

At this point I wander into my own violent images against infidels, bringing honor upon myself, partaking of more good deeds. I float in and out of deep contemplation for the duration of the message. When Khalim finishes, everyone stands, many greeting one another and conversing, while others exit the room. Some men surround Noor, waiting patiently to pay their respects, as I take a few steps back, opening up a wider path for people to pass by. A pair of eyes meet mine, exchanging recognition, the officer again. Almost immediately he turns to greet Noor. It's more than a greeting. They engage in long conversation blinded by a certain closeness. This intimacy causes suspicion on my part. How long have they known each other? Does he know me? Is this why he let me go that day? I wait for Noor to finish. He motions for me to lead the way, placing one arm against my lower back, the other outstretched in front of him. Outside the building in the parking lot, alone with Noor, he gives me the first instructions.

"We're taking my car."

The warmth of the leather seats helps me relax, to know that I don't have to worry about where to go or what to do. A feeling of purpose has never before been so dominant in my life like tonight. I ride along watching the traces of white and colored lights streak by through the window, waiting patiently for the questions. And they eventually come.

"You can't return can you," he asks, "to your father's house?"

"No, I can never see him again without one of us losing our life," I answer, "making it difficult for me to fly out of the country without having to run into him at some point."

"There is no need to worry about these things; they are minor distractions in our agenda," he says, immersed in confidence. "Now, tell me, what you learned from Sheikh Khamil Ahili?"

Unprepared for the question, I say what first comes to mind.

"He enlightened me on some controversial surahs and the different interpretations surrounding them, while reinforcing the inclinations I've been feeling lately, even acting upon, regarding our living according to true Islam. However, there are several new questions that have formed as a result. Unanswered questions."

With his eyes still locked onto the road ahead, he says, "Well, there will be plenty of time for answers to prepare you in the coming days."

The remainder of the lengthy drive is felt through the muffled rumbling of the tires heading deeper into the darkened desert. I'm unacquainted with the area, but satisfied with its remoteness. We pull up to the high concrete walls surrounding a secluded, two-story house just outside Riyadh. Noor jumps out, slides the heavy steel gate to the side, then drives us inside the mini fortress. We step from the car and while Noor walks back to close the gate, I take the chance to survey everything I'm able to make out in the dark with the only light beaming down from the second floor, easily clearing the height of the outer wall, providing clear vision to the streets all around. A one-level guest house is stuffed tightly against the NE corner of the compound adja-

cent to the main section. The area of the courtyard separating the two
is sizable, offering plenty of space for activities.

"Follow me," Noor says, almost disappearing into the blackness. I
come to stop behind him, as he gives the front door several light taps.
I notice little black blotches covering the sides of the door frame and
splattered on the wall above. The door cracks open, diverting my in-
spection. Through a narrow passage, we are observed for recognition
by a small pair of eyes, gleaming from within, out from underneath
a keffiyeh. A second later the door is released from its constriction,
revealing a younger man, about my age, average build, with a clean
smooth face holding those distrustful eyes I've already been acquainted with. But his face instantly softens toward Noor, stepping to greet
him with a warm embrace. Noor turns to me, extending his arm, "This
is our brother, Umar."

"Assalaam alaikum," he says, before embracing.

"This is Basmah," says Noor. "You'll be staying here with him for
some time."

At a loss for words, I remain silent, studying Basmah's face.

"Let's go inside," he says, spinning around entering into the dark
doorway. I follow after Noor, shutting the door behind me.

I'm led through a barely lit room furnished with two brown sofas facing each other, complemented by two wooden tables. There
are small shadows of objects grounded in the corners I'm unable to
make out with the limited light. We enter the next room possessing
the source of white rays that are struggling to reflect their way out. A
laptop is stretched open on a black table with several chairs tucked
encircling it. Basmah closes the laptop, pushes it aside, pulls out three
chairs from the table, insisting we be seated, then disappears through
an adjoining door. Moments later, he appears carrying a tray loaded
with a ceramic teapot, empty cups and plates of fresh bread and dates.
Hunching over, he gently places it on the table, pours the steaming hot
liquid into each of the three long glasses, setting one before each of us
before sitting. I guide the cup to my lips, taking a conscious sip of the
scorching, yet tasteful Moroccan mint tea.

Noor speaks first, looking directly at me, "Let me see your phone."

Confused, suspicious, I take it from my pocket handing it over. He
pops the battery out, sets both pieces on the table then asks, "Do you

need anything off the phone."

"No," I reply, always keeping a backup.

"Good, they'll be tracking you on this one. I'll give you a new one, but remember, to wait at least twenty minutes from the house before inserting the battery. This is very (important.") I nod while telling myself at the first opportunity I must take the battery from the other phone stuffed away in my thobe.

Noor gives Basmah a quick glance, returns to me, then in his re-assuring tone says, "I must go to the city. I'll be back tomorrow. Until then, Basmah will take care of you. If you need anything, ask him."

They both stand, I do as well to give my farewell to Noor, then return to my seat watching them walk from the room. My eyes survey the entire room. There is nothing else to it besides two other doors connecting to it. When I come upon the fresh bowl of dates, I can't resist the temptation no longer. In seconds my teeth are crushing the plump, purple fruit unleashing their distinct sweetness gushing throughout my mouth. My thoughts continue to roam, not landing on any one particular thing, which is quite unusual regarding my life late-ly. Right after flooding my mouth with a drink of tea, Basmah enters the room.

"Are you hungry?" he asks, not expecting an answer.

My mind is saying no against the battling of my stomach's cries. Realizing I have been given no choice in the matter, I willingly surren-der to his hospitality.

"I haven't eaten since this morning. It's been a long day."

Our conversation is directed to Islam and the reality of living it out properly until interrupted by the echoing knocks from the furthest door in the room on my right.

"Time to eat," he says, walking into the other room.

The moment I enter it hits me, a wall of savory aromas emanat-ing from the rich display of Kabsa set below. Smelling the mixture of spices always makes my appetite intensify. I lower myself to the floor opposite Basmah, as he begins du'a (prayer). Once finished, I fill my dish with Kabsa, biting into a chunk of perfectly cooked chicken. It is seared on the outside, while juicy and tender on the inside, making me recognize how truly hungry I am. Through the reflected light bounc-ing off the shiny glass, all that can be seen is blackness outside. This is where my eyes fall while enjoying the meal in silence, a mutually agreeable position.

After finishing, he takes a small sip of coffee then addresses what I've been wishing to know, yet at the same time, fear what comes with it.

"Tariq was a good man, a faithful brother. I know Noor delivered the news to you without the details. He felt it best if I did so."

I steady my focus, my attention entirely on him.

"When he came here it was known he wanted to wait for you before engaging in any training. We respected his request, his loyalty to you. It was evident you two would excel together in ways unimaginable. We supported such a close union between brothers. It was our plan to implement you both as a team, convinced it would bring better results. Nevertheless, things don't always go according to plan.

"A rare opportunity presented itself to us, coming under very difficult conditions and heavy restraints offering us only the tightest window to act. And with the constricted time frame for preparations in assembling the preferable manpower, we were forced to make it a solo operation. Tariq," he pauses, eyes drifting through the room, before returning, as if he was replaying the past over again in his mind, "volunteered. Our target was a prominent sheikh, a renegade infidel, who has been teaching his corrupt view of the Holy Qur'an among our people for many years now. He was scheduled to speak privately at an istirahat in Medina. We knew the only way to get close enough with such tight security, would have to be by vest alone. I'm sure you've heard the rest, a few killed, many injured, but not a scratch on Sheikh Ahmed Rahmani. The full details are still unknown. When I'm informed, I will share them with you most certainly, if you still desire to know. Tariq gave his life for Islam, for Allah - now he's in paradise. That is what's important."

All I can do is listen, confused why he volunteered and what really happened inside the building. Knowing some of the answers will never be discovered, they keep my mind occupied on a solution as opposed to the loss and to the traces of guilt tormenting my conscience. When I finally respond to his words, I can't determine the length of time that has elapsed since chasing thought after thought in a motionless world.

"Let me show you where you'll be staying," he says, sensing the uncontrollable grief mixing in my words, in my bowed head.

We get up as he leads me back through the house, into the courtyard, arriving at the guesthouse. He opens the door without entering, "Everything you need is inside. If you need anything else do not hesitate to ask. My servant will come by occasionally to drop off food and other materials while cleaning. Tomorrow I'll be gone most of the day, but Noor will return sometime in the afternoon. Rest easy my brother."

Chapter Ten

The living quarters are small, furnished with a heavy black couch pressed against the east wall, a round wood table resting at its front, holding a Qur'an. Only one other door exists leading to the lone bedroom. I take a seat on the couch peering at the semi-lit courtyard through the small window in the room. My body slowly melts into the soft cushions beneath me, relieving some of the pressure that's been weighing me down physically for weeks now. Right when my eyelids close, the phone comes to mind, causing me to get up, welcoming the privacy of the bedroom. I find very little room to maneuver outside the mattress lying in the corner. I pull her phone out ready to take the battery out when something inside urges me not to, instead to peruse through it. But when I'm faced with the choices displayed on the screen: her contacts, her messages, photos, email, I pass them all hitting the safari icon gambling it's still connected. I tap it; sure enough, it is. I instantly go to YouTube searching for Islamic sermons. A familiar name stands out to me, a Saudi who is known for speaking on a moderate aspect of Islam, a false way leading Muslims away from the truth; however, out of more curiosity than anything else, I click one of his sermons. After about ten minutes, I'm nodding in and out of consciousness already concluding that this sheikh is taking surahs out of context, trying to spiritualize what is intended to be a physical reality, as is demonstrated in the Hadiths. I strip the battery out, place them back into my thobe, then crawl back into bed, submitting to my body's pleas for rest.

I'm suddenly standing inside an enormous empty stadium. Turning to survey the rest of the place, there it is, a figure at the other end of the field kicking the ball into the net, gathering it out and doing it again and again. Something pushes me forward toward the person who won't show their face, strangely backpedaling when returning to the same spot before striking the ball. As I come closer, my vision clears, helping me notice the flames suffocating the soccer ball between his feet. Why is it not being consumed? Standing motionless a few meters away, wearing one of our team uniforms, I shout at them. No response. I try again. Nothing. I take two steps closer.

"Who are you?" I inquire.

A sudden burst of hot air consumes every inch of my body, as the figure whips around in one quick motion to face me. I shudder at what I see. Fear follows a repulsion so severe the bile can be felt crawling up my throat. The mutilated flesh hanging off his face makes it almost impossible to recognize him at first until I look into his suffering brown eyes, those same ones I grew up with side by side on every field with a goal. Then his lips part.

"This is where I should be, Umar, under these lights, playing in front of the whole world, a star in the Kingdom, scoring the winning goal," he says, resentfully, kicking the ball to me.

I stop it with my foot before fearfully hitting it back in reaction to the hot flames it carries with it. He doesn't stop it; lets it pass between his legs toward the net behind him.

"I didn't want to go! Didn't want to die, to kill those people, but you made me." He slowly begins advancing toward me.

"Why? My own flesh and blood. I would have done anything for you. Why take my life? For what purpose?"

Now within a foot of me, I try to fall back but am unable to. Panic causing shivers to ripple through my every fiber. His face, freshly bloodied, burning pieces of flesh never fully being consumed, a sudden swarm of flames engulfs him.

"Where were you, akhi? I waited and waited, but you never came. I needed you. Needed your help."

His voice grows into an agonizing scream. Unexpectedly reaching out grabbing hold of my thobe.

"Help me, akhi. Please help me," he pleads for a moment, before the anger, the hate resurfaces. "You abandoned me. Left me to die alone."

The horror filling his eyes scare me, the heat causing me to veer away, stumbling backward. Without a wasted second, he lunges forward onto my legs shouting in a piercing tone, begging, "Don't leave me, don't leave me here alone. It's tormenting me day and night; I'm unable to escape it. Please, take me with you."

All I can do is kick him away, my legs burning, the flames now consuming the hem of my thobe, the unbearable pain penetrating deeper than the flesh, an inner pain of the soul, suffocating all of me, but with no escape. The thought of burning alive prevents me from responding, frightening me with fear only survival can tame.

The next moment, the next image my sight focuses on, is a mysterious white wall of clouds before me, then I'm suddenly sitting upright in bed, instantly scooting myself backward, profusely pouring sweat, heart pounding against my chest, frantically swiping at my legs, in hysteria, eventually coming to the realization there's no fire, but finding my gaze darting around the room for Tariq. It seems more than a dream, something so real I can't pull myself out of. Can't release myself from. Every detail vivid, every word of his directly entering into my soul. Why was he on fire if there was no fire where he died? I wipe my brow, allowing the stream of sweat to descend from my fingers to the mattress.

The rusty squeaking of the door hinges awakens me to Noor's figure carrying a pot, two cups and his calloused face. I sit up, sucking in the chilled morning air billowing in through the open door, wondering in this early morning hour what he has planned? Before I push myself up, his deep tone reaches me. "There's no need to get up, I'm only dropping this off. I'll be back later to speak with you."

I continue to lay in comfort until the fresh air is cut off from the closed door. I'm up now, filling one of the spotless ceramic cups full of black coffee. Feeling almost claustrophobic now that my lungs tasted the crisp morning air I'm so used to spending time with. When reopening the door, the courtyard comes into view revealing details disguised in the darkness last night. I allow my eyes to drift into the openness of it, then something disrupts it; a soccer ball rolls by. I lean to my right in hopes of finding the source of where it came from when suddenly, I'm startled by the little body quickly jetting by after it, causing my heart to jump.

The sight reminds me of how much I already miss it, playing, training and even watching it. I step out into the courtyard, studying the boy's skills: ball control, footwork, agility, speed, as he continues practicing giving the occasional glance over at me for approval. Unexpectedly, he passes it to me, testing me, if I possess the skills as well. I carefully stop it, while simultaneously launching it off the ground from foot to foot, to my knees, and up to my head in a continuous cycle of intense ball control without ever allowing it to touch the ground. After a few minutes of this, I shoot it back. His face brightens, as he stops the ball with his foot while walking toward me.

"Can you teach me how to do that?" he asks, in great excitement and hopefulness.

"I don't have the time," I answer.

He's crushed. His downcast expression says it all. I think of Kamal and what he did when I was a boy. The tiniest fraction of guilt changes my mind. Not giving him a chance to react, I steal the ball from between his feet in one quick motion startling him.

"You must always protect the ball, keep it close to your center," I say. "Come over here next to me."

Once he's beside me, I begin showing him the proper technique in the fundamentals to get him started. Afterward, I give him the ball challenging his ability to apply with coordination. He fails, tries again, fails, as this will be a never-ending process.

"It's going to take a while to progress; keep practicing a few hours every day. Hard work and perseverance," I say, hoping to instill in him the required mindset to reach elite status, to distance himself from the average players packed together on the same level.

I spot Noor emerging from the house, crossing the courtyard joining us.

"Abdul, you're being taught by one of the best players in our country. So, listen to every word he's telling you if you want to be the best," he says, staring down into the boy's deep brown eyes glinting with sparkles of hope.

"But for now, go see your father inside."

Abdul stands upright and proud, shifting his attention to me,

"Thank you," he lets out, before sprinting toward the house practicing along the way.

"Let's go inside; we have some things to discuss," says Noor, stepping into the guest house.

The welcoming golden light can be seen climbing over the wall warming the side of the house. That bland smell of desert air is also expected here. These people are still unfamiliar to me, creating an uncomfortable feeling deep down that continues to withstand my attempts at conquering them. I walk inside, keeping aware of this. Noor fills a second cup, leans back on the couch taking a sip, waiting for me to join him. I lower myself down next to him, disturbed by the advice he gave Abdul to listen to me, knowing the boy will never be given the opportunity to play competitively, destined to be a soldier for Islam.

When I was age ten or eleven, there were kids not only playing organized for clubs but in the streets and on those dirt fields scattered throughout Riyadh. What if I wasn't given that freedom to play? What if my uncle never challenged me that day? Where would I be right now? Even though I played, I still ended up here. It makes me think of how my mother supported me in soccer, most of my family did, yet it was the path of infidels to some and up until now, I was blind to all of it. Wasted my childhood devoting it to soccer instead of studying the Qur'an and walking as Mohammad demonstrated for us.

Setting his cup on the table, the words come calmly. "It seems your father has taken your conflict in one of two ways: he will take care of you himself, on his own time or will completely cut you off from the family without physical revenge." He paused momentarily to taste his coffee. "My opinion is he's taken the second path. It's in your hands now Umar. Do as you please. I know this has been on your mind, distracting you in a critical time where your mind must be clear."

"Thank you," I say, aware that he didn't have to tell me.

He must have heard from someone in the family soon after it happened, maybe one of his mysterious connections. Whatever the source, at least my father never went to the authorities. What about Rana? The family? Will I ever see them again? Rana's face flashes in my mind, when we were last together sitting in the car when I dismissed her question. How would Noor answer such a question? I see him pull something from his thobe, setting it on the table.

"This is for you," he says, the black phone resting next to the coffee.

Before I'm able to respond, the words flow out unexpectedly, "Why do you believe in Islam?"

He locks onto my eyes, with a grave expression, studying me intently, my motivation. "Since you already know the answer, there can be only one other reason as to why you're asking," he says, now taking a glance into the courtyard.

In the silence, I ponder his response, its implication, the consequences that may come from it. Therefore, I attempt to express the question differently, one to clarify the meaning, to soften my mistake.

"The reason for the question is rather, why are there so many different views and beliefs among Muslims all claiming to be the truth?"

He turns to me, his tight commander face stern. "You know the surahs that speak about those who will take the Qur'an and twist it to suit their own desires. These infidels will meet their judgment in hell, suffering in great measure. And one of the easiest ways to separate true believers from infidels is whether they are a mirror image of Muhammad. Do they follow in his steps, doing what he did and commanded to do?"

I stay quiet, contemplating, not knowing if I should respond, if he's expecting me to, although feeling reassured about the path I'm on, that this is Allah's will for me.

"One more thing, Umar," he says, closing the distance between us, "don't ever ask me a question like this again, understand?"

I nod, experiencing for the first time a cold, murderous glare on his face, one devoid of any regard for human life, sending a chill through my body.

He takes the last drink of his coffee, rises to his feet, alerting my defenses, strolls to the door then before exiting, tells me, "This evening Basmah and I will run you through some of the basics. Until then repent, pray and recite some surahs."

For a while I don't touch my cup, move for that matter, only ravage my mind with what ifs, with potential danger I may have carelessly brought upon myself, never thinking such a question would bring with it potential consequences. Interrupting my thoughts comes the shout from a minaret close by nudging me from the cushion to the floor in prostration for zuhr. It does nothing to relieve the fear now burrowing deeper into my mind. I pick up the Qur'an hoping it will suffice in abolishing the relentless worry putting me on edge. This also fails as I can't recall anything I've just read. I don't know what else to do, where to go, so I call out to Allah.

"Oh, Allah, I repent for doubting you even in the slightest way. Whatever you want me to do I will do. Lead me and I will follow." Nothing happens, no assurance, no comfort, but enough to remember what I'm reading, as I clutch the Qur'an again.

Chapter Eleven

"Assalaam alaikum," I hear, looking up to find Basmah's athletic frame entering the guest house.

"Wa alaikum assalaam," I return, feeling the pace of my heartbeat quicken. "Has Noor returned?" I ask, but before he has time to answer Noor's dark brown face shows in the doorway.

Did he tell Basmah what was said? An uneasiness falls over me of a potential plot planned. Maybe I'm overreacting. Realizing they're both coming to join me on the couch, I slide over to one side as a precaution. After they're seated, the old fragile Afghani enters carrying two pots, three cups and kebabs. He replaces the old tray then shuffles away disappearing into the evening courtyard.

Basmah takes one of the pots, fills all the cups, rips a piece of charred chicken off the skewer with his teeth, then turns his boyish face to me with eyes possessing the power of an elder.

"Plans have changed. There will be no need for any training today. Something important has come up. An opportunity for us to further Islam."

He pauses, washing down the chicken with a sip of steaming hot mint tea. My natural reaction is to follow suit, but this time the nerves that have already begun churning my stomach prevents my hand from propelling forward. Is this how they approached Tariq? Then it becomes clear, our exchange earlier. Basmah knows. They're looking to use me as quickly as possible. I'm nothing but a perishable life. I patiently wait for what's next. The contents on the table remain an island I can't reach.

"We've received word that Prince Ghazi, who heads the anti-terror strategy, one of the top puppets for the West, is meeting with a prominent Imam at King Khalid Grand Mosque tonight. They're not going to be there long; this is why you've come, to honor Allah with your life, who promises paradise," he says, in a cold, steady voice.

My pulse begins racing uncontrollably listening to every word, understanding this is not an offer. Clawing to find a legitimate way out, a surah rips through my mind, a conviction in my gut.

"It is not fitting for a believer, a man or a woman, when a matter has been decided by Allah and his Messenger, to have any option about their decision." As the pressure grows, death becomes real, causing my life to flash before me. Is this my destiny? What Allah has chosen for me? I swallow hard, stare directly into his eyes. "Why me?" We sit in silence for a few moments. Then Noor says in a deliberately calm, emotionless voice as if expecting the question, preparing for it, "We feel you are the only one who can accomplish it. This will be a great victory for Islam, for all true Muslims not only in our country but all over the world. A strong message will be sent to the noblest of dynasties about serving American interests, to the religious leaders teaching lies through our mosques and their imposing of secularism and to the Muslim world that we are raising the banner of jihad."

I betray no hint of the doubts I'm feeling. I learned early on in my childhood to hide my true feelings beneath an indifferent face, an essential survival tactic. However, a sense of duty, of being obedient to Allah, overcomes me. Can I adjust my beliefs because it's going to cause me pain or even death? This is what I've been called to do. I must accept it, must carry it out.

"What do you require of me?" I ask, steadying my demeanor.

Basmah is grave now. "The meeting is at 9:00 PM. There will be extensive protection, guards inside at the entrance, other positions as well. Their one weakness is where we're striking: the entrance. This will come unexpectedly; however, it will give us the best chance to reach him. This should allow you the opportunity to drive right into the building as they are entering, igniting the explosives.

Noor hesitates only for a moment before adding, "This is if our information is correct, which is another reason we've chosen you. We have confidence in your abilities to maneuver around whatever obstacles they set before you in order to complete the mission, taking you straight to paradise."

Paradise echoes through my ears, resonates within my body. I'll be reunited with Tariq, blessed, rewarded.

"When do I leave?" I ask, noticing the natural light escaping faster from the room.

Noor peeks at his phone, "An hour."

"Until then, we must go prepare some things," Basmah interjects. "If you need anything, go to the house and ask."

"Thank you, I'll be ready when you return."

They stand, disappearing once again from the room. The tension eases with the absence of their presence but fails to erase the fear of death residing on the surface, of losing Rana, Kamal, the entire family. Then her face appears, that soft creamy skin surrounding those wells of sparkling green, how they glow with a unique substance, a peace, from the same source my mother possessed in her last days, that Rana had on the bedroom floor. They all share this same characteristic. Why is this something they share? Why has this infidel woman come to mind anyway? The flow of questions keeps coming in uninterrupted, inviting with them weakness, doubts, which will only end in a dishonorable death followed by scorching fire.

To distract my mind, I decide to get some freshwater from the house, hoping in combination with the fresh air it will help keep me occupied long enough until they return. Outside, the air is still warm, dropping considerably though, as the last portion of grayish, blue sky fades behind the horizon. My slow pace allows me the time to observe the only black SUV sitting inside, the surrounding silence in the courtyard. After a couple of taps on the door, the old man answers, ushers me inside to the sitting room.

"What can I get you?" he asks, indifferently.

"Some cold water," I request, staring into nothingness.

While he's en route to fetch the water, I pull a chair from the table and wait. The instant I do, little Abdul stumbles in from the adjacent door, exhaustion tugging on his fragile frame. But as soon as he lifts his eyes, recognizing me in the room, excitement explodes across his face, reviving those chocolate brown eyes bringing him to my side in no time with a request.

"Can you teach me more tomorrow? How to be as good as you are?"

He's innocent, filled with hope, aspirations, an imagination you only experience as a small child. Am I going to be the one to steal that from him? To crush his little spirit? I see myself in him, standing before Kamal like a fresh sponge soaking up every word, every new skill he shared with me filling me with endless doses of happiness upon every kick. What would I have done if he denied me that first experience with soccer? Only now can I truly realize and appreciate the many benefits it has given me over the years, all for this last summer night in Riyadh. The reality is regardless of what I say or do, Abdul will be granted his wish to be like me one day, whether it be a soccer star or called upon to give his life for Islam.

"Yes, tomorrow I will teach you," I answer, picturing his dark plump face distraught in disappointment when aware of my absence. "Would you like to know the secret on how to be the best?" I whisper.

His eyes widen in anticipation. "Yes," he blurts out in anxiousness.

"Never quit under any circumstances."

He holds his gaze on me for a short time logging my words in memory, contemplating the deeper meaning behind them. The biggest smile stretches across his face, then he trots out of the room. I think of the odds of him becoming a fighter in the not-too-distant future, dying young as a result, a shadow of me.

Not long after leaving, the cold water appears on the table, the man courteously gesturing. The first drink carries a freshness with it, a satisfying effect I thought all but vanished since the Square. The house is quiet, except for the occasional opening and closing of the doors, which invites the restless surge of events to invade my mind nonstop. The chances of failure at any level establishes itself as the most prominent. In the slightest breath, it will all be over. Possible pain from bullet wounds will be felt temporarily. In what feels like a brief moment, I hear movement behind me, turning to find Basmah and Noor entering. It must already be that time. Their expressions are more steely than usual, as they join me. With no time to waste, Noor opens first.

"Everything is ready to go," he says, "you leave in ten minutes."

I take down the last of the water in my cup, look to him, presenting a legitimate possibility that may arise.

"What happens if vehicles are blocking the path to the entrance?"

"There shouldn't be any if they are abiding by the law, but if it is blocked with traffic, you will have to improvise. Yes, it will make things more complicated, this is why we trust in you to make it into that mosque by whatever means necessary as they enter," Noor says, in a confident, relaxed tone.

We sit in silence for the next five minutes, none of us finding anything worthy to be spoken. Only surahs circulating within affirming my final destination in paradise for martyrdom.

"It's time," Noor mutters, in my distraction. We stand together, Basmah stepping in front, leading the way, guiding us out of the house into the courtyard where a rusty, black Toyota is parked behind one of the SUVs. The night has matured making it difficult to see much of anything beyond the reach of the house light. With each breath, the crisp air penetrates my lungs, awakening my body to a new acceptance of what's ahead, of a journey I have no experience in. We stop at the driver's side of the car, Basmah embracing me, then Noor. Keeping one hand resting on my shoulder, he speaks his last words.

"Paradise awaits you where you'll be richly rewarded, my brother. The detonator is on the passenger seat. "He pauses, then clearly emphasizing one last time, "You will succeed in this service to Allah in the obedient furtherance of jihad."

I nod in understanding, open the door, carefully slide onto the driver's seat, while spotting the black three-inch device next to me. Wasting no time, I turn the key, firing life into the engine. Noor steps forward pushing the door shut. Basmah is already at the steel door pulling it open behind us. Feeling Noor's eyes still digging into me, I glance up to meet them, finding the coldest black I've ever known, devoid of any goodness. For a split second, I tremble in fear, before attempting to absorb the apathy for myself.

"This is the same way I sent Tariq off. The only difference is I have a great confidence in you," he says with certainty.

The mentioning of Tariq encourages me, as I tightly grip the steering wheel with one hand. He finally backs away granting me permission to depart. I shift it into reverse, begin moving out of the court-yard. I connect glances with Basmah, at the last moment before the tires touch the road, only to find the same emotionless expression. Our final goodbye. As quickly as it began, it is gone, far in the past.

Why was the urge so strong yesterday to question Noor? Even as a young boy I usually avoided discussing controversial or offensive topics and those I did engage in were with my mother. However, the one time I came to her, confused, asking why some soccer players from other countries didn't pray like us, followed by my petition to live by the same standards. This ended immediately with a rebuking, teaching me that anyone who doesn't follow Allah and Muhammad as his prophet is evil and going to suffer greatly on judgment day. Her words shook me with terror to the point of never wanting to play against anyone other than Muslims. And now, when following true Islam, apart from any other time in my life, I end up peeling back the deepest layers of my faith.

Carefully navigating into the crowded streets of the inner city, ambient light swarms around everything. Headlights, streetlights, endless businesses and buildings gleaming with life. Yet, I'm unable to focus on anything other than my imminent death. Can this be a dream? I take a deep breath, exposing a weakness inside my body somewhere. Doubt urging me to turn around.

The closer I come, a thin, steady flow of adrenaline pumps through my bloodstream shaking my body in nervousness, imagining the scene playing out before it happens: the spraying of bullets ravaging the car's body, spitting debris into my face and torso without remorse. Very likely my flesh will be introduced to that hot burning sensation of lead intruding, before crashing through the entrance, concentrating on maintaining possession of the detonator through it all. Then with the target in sight, the last courageous moment of my life will be taking my life with theirs.

My heart begins pounding rapidly, so fiercely I can hardly take a breath. Without warning it comes rushing into my mind carefree: Tariq screaming for me to help him, his melting flesh dripping from his body. Is this my fate as well? I begin wondering if Tariq had any doubts? If what really happened in the building that night was Tariq backing out at the last minute, his retreat causing the failure or because of insufficient preparation? Was this dream a warning to me? A warning to abandon this mission? I was the one who presented such an opportunity to Tariq. How can I do that to him after giving his life away? I'm responsible for his fate; I pressed him despite his reluctance, prevailing through my perseverance. He never wanted life to end this way. My father reassured me of this. He was simply following my lead, my influencing presence.

Taking a left at the intersection, I'm close. Checking the phone, it reads nine o'clock exactly. The presence of uncertainty grows stronger along with the pain in trying to sort out the mosaic of disturbing emotions tearing through my mind at a million miles per second. I slowly come to a complete stop behind a large black pickup. I can't miss the immense pure white structure settled up ahead on my left. This is it. The moisture seeping from my palms gathering on the steering wheel, gripping it tighter to avoid the uncontrollable shaking of my hands.

In fear, I cry out to Allah, "Oh, have mercy on your servant! I have committed my life to you since childhood. If this is what you desire me to do then give me the strength to press forward. If not then reveal it to me. I have given up everything for you and am willing at this very moment in time to sacrifice my life for you. Guide me through this mission for your glory."

A flash of neon green light triggers the traffic in my lane to move. Stalling, allowing a gap to build between me and the truck in front, I gather enough room to reach the required speed. After the comfortable cushion is reached, I drop my foot onto the pedal, propelling me forward on the straightaway. No longer occupied by fear of any kind, the adrenaline taking charge now. I scan the entire perimeter of the entrance up ahead, processing all the available information. No vehicle is blocking my path, but several men stand guard at the entrance, more on the street near the vehicles, everything I expected. All of a sudden, I hear rubber squealing, offering me a second's time to see the grill of a tan Ford Expedition before smashing into my passenger side.

At the moment of impact my body is viciously whipped to the right, then relentlessly ripped back against the door with a force I'm helpless to oppose, sending my head shattering through the window, throwing chunks of glass everywhere mixed with blood. The air instantly squeezes from my chest, blurring my vision while tunneling it to a pinprick of white light. I struggle with all my might to hang on, to not allow the light to escape from my grip, my head bobbing, wavering from side to side attempting to gain control completely unaware of consciousness trapped in a lingering realm of mystery, until my thoughts slowly begin regathering, enough to notice the stillness surrounding me, the ringing inside my ears. Then it comes back reminding me about the explosives in the trunk, the detonator lost from my grip.

In a hazy search, I scour the seats in urgency, the floorboards, the consul. Nothing. Only glass, metal and debris. A sharp localized pain becomes increasingly intense and frightening to the point of groaning in agony. I try desperately to focus on the source when the entire left side of my face and head feels like it's on fire. Investigating it, I drag my fingers over wet, lacerated flesh embedded with pieces of glass. Crimson covering my hand when I finally pull it away to examine it. Panic arises. I need to get out, escape this wreckage. The police will be here any moment and are bound to discover what's in the trunk. I tug on the handle; surprisingly the door opens with the slightest nudge of my shoulder, glass falling out. My left leg dangles out, comfortably finding the safety of the street below, followed by the right one. With tremendous effort, I'm able to stand on my feet, holding the door for support. In front of me, a few meters away, the side of the street is empty. It's a desirable direction to flee to, especially with the crowd beginning to form. I take the first step - my knees buckle almost sending me to the asphalt, a weakness rippling through my limbs. Voices are rising around me, but I'm unable to decipher the words through the mist. Such little time I have, so with a new vigor, I pathetically stagger my way across the lanes, reaching the sidewalk and safety of a metal post.

Taking one look over my shoulder, a crumpled hunk of metal lies seven meters from the impact. The demolished front end of the Expedition is not far away, the door opened, men aiding the driver safely out. Traffic's halted, sirens can be heard closing in, but most disturbing is the trail of warm fluid running down my neck to my chest and my inability to locate the source. Shock, adrenaline, the tingling sensation from partial numbness is keeping my senses at bay. However, noticing two men in the crowd pointing in my direction, then heading toward me, ends my time of recuperation.

I release the post, feeling a little more stable now that my legs have regained some much-needed strength, quickly look for an escape route and without much effort discover it's on my left on a street heading north away from this threat. Without another glance behind me, affording no time to be lost, the surge of energy comes filling my fragile body, exploding with all my power down the sidewalk.

The first few meters are awkward, wobbly even, until my natural stride settles in, moving me gradually up the street about a block, taking a hard left cutting through traffic to make it. Assured that no one is following, I wave down a taxi, knowing I must get off the street as soon as possible. The moment one pulls aside, I waste no time jumping in, instructing him to the destination, while situating my body deeper into the seat in order to evade a direct path of vision, imagining the horrific condition I must be in. My bloody thobe screaming out to the police to arrest me. I try not to make eye contact with the driver, a short Asian man, as we weave through the streets, keeping my head low, while discreetly dabbing at my face with the sleeve of my thobe in hopes of soaking up some of the oozing bloodiness. Fear won't allow me to calm down, fear of being caught, of the seriousness of my injuries, of the repercussions for failing the mission. Thoughts flicker of what my next move will be. Depending on what happens back there will significantly influence my decision. The safest move is to lay low for a day or two waiting on the news. The descending speed and slight bump alert me to check our location. We've arrived. The istirahat holds a half-filled lot. It doesn't seem right that we're already here; however, I ignore it, instructing the Asian man to the back of the lot. I intentionally have him stop a distance from my car, ensuring a clear view of our surroundings for anything suspicious and to prevent the driver from getting a look at my plates. Convinced that everything is clear, I slide out, leaving the door open, hurriedly making it to the car with key in hand.

In no time the doors open, my hands counting seventy riyals out of my stash under the seat, swiftly returning to his window passing the paper into his palm. I don't look at his reaction, unable to sacrifice any more time. Back in the driver's seat, I crank the ignition. My next glance is at the taxi exiting the lot, prompting me to follow. I turn in the opposite direction when entering traffic away from the lively city toward the safety of the darkened outskirts.

Chapter Twelve

"Was this your answer, preventing me from carrying out the mission or was it by chance?" I cry out to Allah. "What am I supposed to do now? Who am I to turn to?"

Confession continues driving my thoughts. Then Lydia strangely comes to mind, her unique position.

"No, I'm not asking an infidel for help."

I review friends, family, everyone I know, one by one disqualifying all of them for putting me at risk in some way, a chance I'm unwilling to take, except for her. She faces the least risk. Is there no other way? Continuing to cruise along the mostly empty streets, the pain escalates to a new level now that the spike of adrenaline begins fading. Time is my enemy; a decision must be made. Realizing I'm close to her compound, approaching a side street, I jerk the wheel, ripping the tires right at the last moment. Only this once. A quick patch up, then be gone.

In urgency, I pull up behind the rundown apartments, check the area for any movement, drag myself into the compound, up to her door. Frozen. The fear renders me paralyzed. What if she refuses to help? After what happened last time, I wouldn't blame her. I can't ignore the thumping of my heart splitting every wound open on my body, as if with each beat a few more drops of my life are being forced out. The coldness helps though, helps slow the leaking down my forehead.

I take a deep breath, a breath of trust I'm unaccustomed to taking, reach out and tap the door. Out of the paranoia, I briefly examine the compound in both directions making sure history doesn't repeat itself. Darkness's habitation is all that is found. As I bring my hand to investigate a stinging below my left rib cage, I hear a minor commotion behind the door, then a sliver of white light cuts across the cement doorstep, revealing part of Lydia's averse expression, but most memorable are those irreproachable, penetrating green eyes still glowing with life.

A standoff quickly evolves, my pride against her immovable stare. We resume this position until a shred of surrender finally comes through my pain.

"I need your help," I say, exposing the bloody landscape. "One last time, I'll pay you."

At this point, I'm not too concerned if she is offended by my offer. After all, she laid her life down for me in the face of my hostility. She doesn't say anything nor withdraws her gaze from mine. As soon as she appears to be saying something, the light disappears leaving me alone in the darkness once again. Stunned, I remain in my position, long enough to absorb the disbelief, the disappointment in her decision. Prepared to leave, to decide on the next best option, the door opens wider, her gentle frame inviting me in. A part of me hoped she would be back; that her unique heart couldn't reject someone in desperate need.

I carefully pass by her, instantly recognizing the familiar layout of the apartment. She shuts the door, leads me to a chair next to the lamp ordering me to sit while disappearing into the bedroom for a short time before reappearing with her hands full. A spicy aroma in the room draws me away from the pain for a second, to the hunger of not eating all day. She must have finished eating recently, not too long before I showed up. Now standing beside me, she holds a white towel, an assortment of bandages and gauze, stitches and a few steel instruments. A dark blue blouse softly flows from her delicate shoulders to the floor. Slightly tilting my head toward her, I examine her face for the first time since I was last in this room. I run my eyes down the contours of her smooth cheeks to her tight plump lips. Everything is sharp, pleasing to the eyes. The only change I find is a moist, healing wound above her left cheek and a section of hair that's not fully grown back still revealing the stitch marks. Her lip healed up nicely, no sign of the gash. I know her body still aches in pain from that night. Nightmares no doubt a regular occurrence. And here I am, once again, putting her life at risk. Something inside tells me I should get up and leave, go to the hospital or to Rana. But then she looks at me, reminding me of a rare kind of love she possesses, a connection surging in me, the only person to ever cause this. It feels too perfect to leave.

"Look forward, please," she commands, clearly all business.

The next thing I know, one hand grasps the right side of my head firmly holding it in place. Folding my hands in my lap in anticipation of the pain ahead, it comes quick with an unmet ruthlessness, forcing my jaw to clench, without measure. The texture of the cold, wet cloth is felt, as it comes over every tender serrated piece of flesh on my face and head. I close my eyes attempting to lead my mind away from the anguish, but soon realize it refuses to comply. Its refusal to not feel her every touch, gently putting me back together. There is a tugging and tearing sensation as the stitches slide through pieces of tough skin. After what seems to be hours of agonizing treatment, the words of relief finally come.

"That should be it unless there's anything else?" she says.

"My chest and rib cage have been stinging also," I say, as I begin to slide my thobe down exposing my upper torso.

She takes the towel wiping off the blood from my neck working her way down to my stomach. The moment she travels over my left ribs, I grimace in pain pulling away, before slowly settling back into position. Her hand gently surveys the area, trying to find the source, when suddenly she touches it again, except this time I'm prepared, keeping steady long enough for her examination.

"No more cuts, but two broken ribs it feels like," she says, turning away, gathering up all the supplies.

"I'm sorry, but there's nothing else I can do for you."

I pull the thobe back up over my body confused about the strange attraction I feel for her, but being oppressed by the hatred and disgust for who she is and what she stands for. It's her unconditional love for me, her gentleness, her inner joy that can be felt miles away. She possesses everything I don't, yet she's missing the true god. This is why I despise her. She must enjoy witnessing my pain, my wounds. Payback to some degree. Standing, I take the one thousand riyals, extending them out to her to fulfill my promise. Her expression softens in a precarious way.

"I didn't help you for money. I did it because I wanted to."

"Listen, I offered to pay for your services, take it. You can use the help," I say, firmly.

Her eyes remain fixed on mine, but her face changes, divulging a hint of disappointment.

"I won't accept it. My God provides for me everything I need."

I remember that confident demeanor of hers, respect it even. With her mind made up, I tuck away the riyals, turn, giving her one last glance, then walk out.

At my car, I open the trunk, recalling there being a clean thobe stashed away in reserve for times in urgent need. I take the fresh set, toss them into the passenger seat then drive from the apartments, body aching, reminding me of how fragile I am.

Where now? Somewhere quiet, where I can be discreet, until hearing the update on the accident. Al Aziziyah district. I know an area there suitable for me. The window stays down, permitting the cool air to ease the burning of my wounds. Wanting to see the quality of her work, I maneuver the rear-view to where it shows the side of my head. All the gashes are neatly stitched, still swollen and a little bloody though. She really helped me out. Why is she so kind to me? So loving? It must be her cunning methods being a minority and all.

Not five minutes have passed since leaving her place when the familiar tone rings from inside the car. I grab both phones, discovering the phone Noor gave to me glowing in the darkness with an unknown number. Undecided on whether to answer it or not, I let it keep ringing. It's Noor; it has to be him. Eventually, I swipe the green phone icon but hold it to my ear without saying a word. I can feel the presence of the person on the other end, breathing in short sporadic bursts, until a voice shatters the silence.

"Umar?"

Instantly recognizing his voice.

"Noor?" I say, delayed in a vague tone.

"Where are you?"

"I'm still in Riyadh."

"Where at?" he asks calmly, chased with suspicion.

"I'm not far from the istirahat we visited," I answer in partial truth.

"Meet me near the tents in thirty minutes," he instructs.

"All right," I say, concluding he's already been informed about the incident.

I watch the phone go black, questioning his motives in wanting to see me immediately. To prepare the launching of a new mission? To ask me to finish what I started? I'm still confused about the accident, about the flash of Tariq preceding it. It almost feels as if I was stopped for a reason. Therefore, I allow such thoughts free reign for the time being. At the next intersection, I make a right, taking me in the direction where I planned on staying for the night. Conveniently, the mostly sparse streets allow me to arrive earlier than expected.

Tents are in shambles scattered everywhere along the edge of the street. A dense, foul odor hovers above, occasionally sending an invitation to the bile in my throat. Trash litters the area seen only by the beams of light shooting from the front of my car. With no electricity, all is dark except for a rare flicker from a candle here and there. A perfect place to hide, to conduct a meeting, as very seldom do any law enforcement venture out this far for lack of wanting to recognize the despairing poor when walled million-dollar palaces dwell not too far in the distance.

I remember coming to some of these places as a boy to play soccer on dirt patches bordered by troves of garbage. The competition wasn't as high as we hoped it would be, but the kids enjoyed the game more than in any other place, always smiling with the utmost respect during and after the games. Something about the games, with those kids, gave me a unique perspective about soccer, but most importantly about the Kingdom, its blatant disregard for the suffering poor.

The first thing I do is look for Noor, yet find only the emptiness of the limited open space straddling the road. I pull over, positioning myself for a quick getaway if needed, then hit my lights allowing the natural glow of the night to come forth. Dealing with him, anything can happen. Anticipating having to wait another twenty minutes, I spot a pair of headlights creeping their way toward me. The car slows, pulling next to mine, leaving on its orange emergency lights offering enough illumination in the shadows to see one another. I wait for the figure to emerge before I finish pulling all the way back on the handle, while simultaneously scanning inside the car for another body. The moment he steps out the small amount of light glares off his sullen face. In no time, I'm meeting him halfway between our cars, studying his movements, his every expression.

"Good to see you made it out of there alive," he says, leaning in for a soft embrace. "You were always the most resilient."

"What about the car?" I ask, hoping they never found the explosives.

His face sets calmly, the tone returns to the fearless authority I'm used to. "It's taken care of. No one will know you were there."

I can't bring myself to question him, being knowledgeable of his deep influence into all areas of the kingdom. This is all it takes to strip away some of the stress assailing my body.

"Where are you bleeding from?" he asks, unable to see my injuries in the obscure lighting.

"The left side of my head," I answer, turning it slightly. "A few slashes that have been stitched up, nothing serious."

He doesn't need to know the extent of the injuries. He cannot be trusted. Silence follows until the compulsion to tell him is far too strong to contain.

"Noor, he came out of nowhere. There's nothing I could do. It's a miracle I walked out of it alive with only a few minor cuts. I understand that was our opportunity to inflict great loss upon them and I failed."

"It wasn't your fault. You did good by fleeing when you had the chance. It could have turned out a lot worse for you. Don't allow this to worry you; there will be more opportunities for you soon akhi. Fortunately, our mission was not exposed at the crash, drawing unneeded attention to us at a time when we're about to implement a new offensive strategy. I will take you to a different location where you are able to regroup and prepare for what's next," he says, reassuringly.

"More opportunities soon..." his words sink deeply into my soul while keeping my gaze fixed onto the shadow within the shemagh. Do I want to continue on with this? Too many questions are still unanswered leading me in opposition to this path. Something is telling me the crash wasn't merely by chance, that maybe it was intended to happen.

"You need some rest; follow me to a place nearby and in a few days we can revisit it," he says.

With little thought, the courage flows out from within. "I don't know if this is what I'm supposed to be doing. Maybe I should take some time alone to examine all that's happened."

He straightens up in a new, rigid tenseness. The idle engines become a distant humming, the air thickening with division. I wait through the uncomfortable standoff for his reaction.

"This is the second time your words have been in direct confrontation with Allah and the holy Qur'an. Repent and ask him for forgiveness," he commands, laced in fury.

"I just need a little time to think; there is no sin in such a request after what I've been through," I defend.

He slowly takes a step forward within half a meter of me, when his almost black lifeless eyes are now penetrating mine. Instinctively, my body shifts into combat mode expecting an attack. His voice then transforms into a low whisper with a general's fierceness.

"Infidel! Unless you repent, don't ever show your face again to me."

He turns his back in one motion, disappearing back into the darkness, leaving me standing alone, destitute. Why didn't he try to kill me? To hurt me? There couldn't have been a more advantageous time for him than this. I quickly brush aside the questions, aware of the higher priorities that need to be tended to.

Ten minutes of driving pass and I arrive at Nouf Al Yamamah, walk past a skinny, bare-faced Pakistani who greets me at the hotel door before I enter the well-lit lobby, empty besides the two smiling Lebanese men sitting behind the check-in desk as I approach. Both smiles fade to exasperation when I catch their eyes drawn to the stitched gashes.

"What can I do for you?" the shorter overachieving one asks, pressing into the desk.

"I need one room."

He turns his attention to the screen below punching away at the keys. "That will be seventy riyals."

In a few quick swipes, I hand over the riyals, accepting in return the entry card.

"Room seven," he says, giving my face one last glance before I'm gone.

The room is small. One queen-size bed fills the middle of the west wall draped in fresh white linen with a brown, wooden side table nestled up beside it. Wasting no time, I lock the door and head for the bathroom. When I flick the switch illuminating the entire room and look at myself, it's bad, worse than I expected. The gashes stretch from the edge of my left eyebrow vertically up the side of my head. She did a professional job. The hospital couldn't have done better. I gently stroke my fingers along each path of pain. I still can't explain why she did it. Such kindness, selflessness inside of her. Showing me love despite the degrading way I treated her. I turn away for a second catching the shower in my sights; I'm in great need of one.

The steaming hot water loosens up the knotted muscles through-out my body, tight from constant tension and the methodical onset of soreness. There's no other place my body cries out more for than the comfort of the bed. Laying on my back, I reach over to the table, take hold of the Qur'an, but before opening it, retracing the incident, the vivid details rushing to the surface, the very mystery of being prevent-ed from carrying out the mission. If this is what Allah has commanded me to do, then why would he stop it? He wouldn't.

Once again, Lydia's flowing river of love comes, confusing because of my hatred toward her, yet she accepted me into her home, helping me when I needed it the most. And I didn't even thank her; I'm unde-serving of her hospitality. I would have rejected her if our roles were reversed. Where was Noor's love? Threatening my life, classifying me as an infidel, everything short of attempting to take my life. Muslims are said to be loving toward one another; however, experiencing such a love has been lost in my life compared to this foreigner's love. Only my mother and Rana have equaled this kind. But am I not obeying Allah by not loving her, by not offering her friendship?

Maybe her love is a cunning love covered with fear in order to survive being surrounded by Muslims. Just as the Qur'an says, "They were covered with humiliation and misery: they draw on themselves the wrath of Allah." However, I realize how easily this falls apart when I recall the beating she endured for me. Regardless of what kind of question I may propose, I must first answer why my inner being feels so comfortable, so peaceful when this love is being poured upon me, as if this is what belongs inside of me also. Is this what my mother felt? Is this what sparked her search? Maybe I should find out where such kind of love derives from.

Instantly, feelings of fear, of shame, cover me, causing my lips to cry out to Allah asking for forgiveness, to lead me back to him. The pages flip through my fingers until landing on a surah that feels right. My eyes meet the words and begin reading, "Strongest among men in enmity to the believers wilt thou find the Jews and Pagans; and nearest among them in love to believers wilt thou find those who say, 'We are Christians': because amongst these are men devoted to learning and men who have renounced the world and they are not arrogant."

Convinced this wasn't by coincidence that I randomly picked this surah about the love of Christians toward Muslims, I decide to search through the entire Qur'an finding every surah speaking about Christ and Christians, realizing it will be a relentless investigation.

Hours pass by, forcing my eyes open until finally collapsing. Almost every verse sparking a new question, sending me off into another direction, exploring all it has to offer.

The morning brings an intense pounding in my head. I try rolling over into an upright position only to discover a soreness so deep, my bones ache. Instead, I remain still in uncertainty, gathering my composure. The room is peaceful, a refuge from all the chaos making its way into my life lately. I thankfully welcome the tranquility, as it is giving me the time of reflection needed to choose what's next for me. A wide range of questions come flooding back to me from last night's journey, questions that I plan on taking to a well-educated Imam, the only one I can trust with the kind of controversy they will infuse and even with him I still can't be entirely certain, fully transparent.

I slowly make it to my feet, physically uncomfortable, mentally confused and spiritually feeling abandoned. Not wanting to dwell on the pain my body's suffering from, I make it to the bathroom, splashing a couple of cold handfuls of water on my face, over my head, down to the nape of my neck and up to my elbows. It wakes me a bit, refreshes me from the grogginess lingering from the lack of sleep. I check my phone for the time: 7:03 AM - this should give me plenty of time to ask what I need.

The check-out goes smoother than usual, no questions asked, only a thank you and invitation to come back again by the taller reserved Lebanese man, beaming with that permanent ear-to-ear grin. On the drive, I keep the window down inviting the crispiest air a place to reside in my deprived lungs. The blinding rays are already making their presence felt with an endless backdrop of untainted blue. Traffic is congested as expected, every driver testing the limits in every possible way. Thankfully, I'm close enough, allowing me to escape the long delays behind endless lanes of impatient men. Yet, at one of the red lights, I question where my new home will be. I miss my family already, all but my father, especially Rana and Kamal. What has my father convinced them of? That I'm an extremist? A radical? A terrorist that got Tariq killed and plans on carrying out an attack myself? That this is why I attacked him because he tried stopping me? Maybe I should see them, tell them the truth. But how do I explain about Tariq if asked? I set it all aside for now, remembering my decision to settle the current dilemma before moving on to further matters. However, it always takes me a brief period to get past the sickness generated by the thought of Tariq, which is strange knowing he's in paradise right now.

It will never get old admiring the beautifully laid mosaic decorating the underside of the archway of the mosque as I cross beneath it. The bright blues and pastels always captivated me as a child coming here after weekly soccer practices to pray. Over the many years of this daily ritual, the Imam and I became friends. He was always eager to teach me about the history of the Muslim people, so much so that it was almost impossible to slip a word in or leave for that matter, once I gave him my ear. Several times I would disguise myself by hovering in the midst of the crowds until I could reach the exit, all to avoid his long speeches. But today, I have come armed with an array of questions more than willing to listen to every word he shares.

The courtyard is deserted when I enter, in between prayers, the only element of life being the water for ablution. Stepping into the doorway, I spot Sanafi about thirty meters away speaking with a young brother. His eyes shift to me for a split second, recognizing my presence, then back to the man's face. I retreat back into the courtyard. In my peripheral, I notice their conversation ending with an embrace; I greet him as he passes by. I hear in excitement Sanafi coming to meet me with open arms.

"Umar, assalaam alaikum! It's been a long time, I thought you left Riyadh."

"Wa alaikum assalaam, I've been busy lately. You should know I would never leave without first coming to say goodbye," I say, flashing a smile of appreciation.

"Tell me what's brought you here?" he asks, knowing it must be of great importance for me to come at this time.

"I would like to discuss the Qur'an. Last night I was reading when coming upon some verses raising questions I couldn't answer. So, I have come to you for the answer, since I know you're very knowledgeable in the Qur'an and I highly respect your opinion."

The wrinkles droop down along his long serene face partly hidden beneath the scraggly gray beard hanging to his chest. Looking up at me, honor radiating by such a request.

"I'm always willing to share my understanding with you about the Qur'an and Islamic history."

Before beginning, I take a moment to organize my thoughts, to decide on my approach. Then, with an eagerness to know the truth, I present the first one.

"In some surahs it says that Christians are a righteous people who also worship one God, making it permissible to befriend them. Yet, in other surahs, it commands us to force a Christian to convert to Islam, pay a tax or be killed. Why the contradiction? Which is correct?"

"There is no contradiction here," he responds with assurance. "These early verses on making friends with Christians are abrogated by surah 8:39, which is the last revelation on Jews and Christians."

I interject respectfully, "Then we are to force Christians to convert, pay or kill them in jihad?"

"No," he blurts out harshly, but under control, "this is not the definition of jihad. It implies a spiritual war against all of the evil, sickness and sin in the world. Taking another life is not praised or instructed by the Qur'an except under self-defense."

I've heard this answer many times before from every sheikh and Imam in Riyadh until Noor showed me otherwise. He opened my eyes to the undeniable truth that about sixty percent of surahs speak about jihad and Allah commands us to fight in order to fulfill our faith, as we saw Muhammad live out during his life. However, why the contradictions causing such dispute and division?

"If all the contradictions are explained by naskh (abrogation), then why did Allah change his mind so much?" I ask, confused.

He stares at me with an abstracted look on his face for some moments. "Allah is the sovereign one. This is the way he chose to make it be."

This wasn't a satisfying answer for me. I don't allow it to preoccupy me for long before continuing forth in a different direction.

"Sanafi Amu, forgive me if I offend Allah or Muhammad in my questioning. My intentions are coming from a pure heart. I read that Isa (Christ) was sinless. If this is true, then why would He be placed equal to or lower than other prophets who sinned?"

He plunges into deep thought, turning away to the far corner of the room as if to discover a revelation by doing so. He continues for some time without noticing my presence, not wanting to notice it. By now he understands that any answer he gives will be insufficient in satisfying my further curiosity.

"Umar, you have many questions, I know," he replies, now giving me his full attention. "These questions, along with many others I'm sure you have, are questions requiring more time than I have to devote right now in order to properly explain. But there is an Islamic scholar close by, a devout brother and old friend who has devoted his entire life to answering these kinds of questions. I rarely do this kind of thing, but I will give him a call on your behalf, to ask if he would be willing to meet with you for a couple hours. I'm only doing this because I've always felt a special kind of closeness to you. With your intelligence, your fiery passion, you possess all of the gifts needed to become a great leader in Islam, influencing the younger generations in how to be a faithful follower of Allah."

Before finishing, he's already pulling the phone out, tapping away at the screen while vacating to find some privacy. I watch him from afar, unable to make out any of the conversation. Anxiety begins to coarse through me leaving an uneasiness within, that I not only have taken the risk coming to Sanafi with these questions in the beginning but now am to ask an unknown Islamic scholar in hopes he won't attack me for such contentious words. This makes me wonder about Sanafi. What does he really feel? Who is he really speaking to? The onset of paranoia comes full force.

The call ends. He returns to his position before me declaring the verdict.

"Sheikh Faisal has agreed to meet with you. He is scheduled to attend a meeting in three hours, so you should have plenty of time to cover your main questions. He is expecting you soon."

"Thank you for the courtesy and respect you have shown me in speaking with me as well as arranging this meeting with Sheikh Faisal. This is important to me," I say, grateful for his understanding.

"You are always welcome here. Be diligent in your search through the Qur'an. For it is the word of Allah," he says, with a softened demeanor.

He gives me the directions, we embrace and I exit the courtyard already debating whether or not I should show up. If I do, how careful must I be with what questions asked? As I pull away from the curb, I head north toward his house, which is a close ten minutes from the mosque. If Sanafi directed me to this man, then he must be open enough in discussing the kinds of questions I have proposed. Either way, I don't have many other options to choose from right now.

His villa is stationed in one of the wealthy neighborhoods of northern Riyadh. The tan exterior holds a strong black gate at the entrance snuggled between two live green palms. Approaching his home, he opens the door to meet me. We greet each other, briefly embrace, then I follow him inside. He leads me to a large room, a suite by definition, displaying a collection of black leather couches and chairs surrounding an elegant black walnut table adorned with pots of tea, coffee, fresh dates and sweets. He motions for me to sit down across from him, the chair already purposefully set out, while he walks to the opposite side across from me.

He's a smaller man with sharp features and deep socketed eyes seeing through gold-rimmed spectacles. His face is stern, set in rigid lines of command, as I observe him pour a cup of steamy tea, placing it in front of me, with the rich rose fragrance I immediately inhale. I thank him, wait for his words, yet he seems to relax, with no inclination to rush, sipping his tea while welcoming the quiet. When they come, his deep force grabs hold of my attention.

"I'm told you're a respectful young brother, very intelligent with an unquenchable desire for the truths of Islam, a follower of Allah in the strictness of terms. Only by this rapport have I agreed to meet with you at Sanafi's request. His word can always be trusted. You have more than two hours to ask me the questions burdening your mind. Begin when you like."

Where to begin? I battle with either minimizing the gravity of one question to fearing the boldness of the other. Finally, I decide on one of the most reasonable ones prevalent to most Muslims.

"If we believe the Torah, the Zabur and the Gospels were all sent from Allah and that no one can alter or modify his words, then how can we claim these books have been corrupted?"

"Good question," he says, sparking a kind of joy in him knowing he holds the answer. "All you've concluded is true, except you've missed one critical element: the originals were incorrupt, unable to be changed or altered, but we no longer possess the originals. These current versions have been tampered with; the very text itself has been altered and intermingled with other human writings. Therefore, the Qur'an, the last god-given writings to come down, is fully preserved exactly how it was received, abrogating all books preceding it."

This did not satisfy my question because if both are true statements then there can be no corruption to god's words at any point in time. And if no one possesses the originals, then how can someone claim they've been altered? No text exists for comparison. Therefore, what standard is there to base such claims? I move on to the fellowship question, not to debate with him, but to hear his answers.

"Who corrupted the books? When did they do it? Where was it done?" I ask.

"Jews and Christians corrupted the books over the centuries. These are irrelevant after the confirmed forgery," he answers, as if wasting his time with the questions.

Who confirmed it? How was it confirmed? I move on with a tinge of uneasiness.

"What about surah 10:94 where Muhammad is directed to those who have been reading the Book (Bible) to solve any doubts he has? Doesn't this substantiate the truth and veracity of the Bible?"

He leans back, scowls at my insolence, but allows it while the silence lingers, granting him plenty of time to form a response.

"This particular surah has been pondered and debated for centuries. Far more time is needed to discuss such an intricate matter than this brief meeting. It would also be difficult to explain this taking into account your ignorance of the text."

I dismiss the insult, feeling his frustration with my questioning beginning. He can sense another question rising up in me. I choose the problem of predestination. Of Allah claiming to be "the one who leads astray," as well as "the one who guides." Another contradiction.

"What about Allah saying he both guides and leads astray?"

"Surah 7:177-179 declares: 'He whom Allah guides is he who is rightly guided, but whom he leads astray, those are the losers. Indeed, we have assuredly created for Gehenna many of both jinn and men.' (6:39,126; 30:29; 32:13) Also that nothing will happen to us except what Allah has written for us. It seems not only a contradiction but eliminates our free will in life." When reading these surahs, the Hadith ran through my mind about how Muhammad slapped Abu Bakr on the shoulder and said: 'O Abu Bakr, if Allah most high had not willed that there be disobedience, he would not have created the Devil.'"

Faisal's eyes flicker at my words. I wonder how many times throughout his long life he's heard these same controversial questions, tried answering them?

"Every thought, word, deed, all of it, whether they are good or evil, has been foreordained and determined by Allah. Everything that has come into existence falls under his command," he says, shifting forward in his seat. "Every decision we make in life, every word that falls from our mouth, every thought that infiltrates our minds, is by his will. When we see all the evil in this world ravaging humanity, all the unbelief, all the wicked who reject Allah, this is willed by him. His knowledge is far beyond our comprehension; therefore, we are not to question his purposes for why he does what he does," he answers.

I take a few moments analyzing his explanation. There was no dealing with the issue of contradiction. Even more problems have arisen. Human responsibility is non-existent, contradicting surah 18:29. I proceed with a different line of questioning.

"Regarding the prophets in the Qur'an, I find that Isa is distinct from the rest. He was given the ability to create a bird which is intriguing because only Allah can create. Christ is the only prophet who received the ability to perform several of Allah's divine attributes. He healed many sick people including giving sight to the blind man after putting mud on his eyes. He was the only prophet who is coming back as a judge in the Last Day to administer justice against the world. Sinless in all his ways and lastly, we know he possessed the authority to give life and death. We see it when he raised Jairus' daughter from the dead."

"Ah, you have stumbled upon what seems to point to Isa's superiority over Muhammad, but you must remember that Muhammad was the 'Seal of the Prophets,'" he says, sternly, "the greatest miracle ever committed by a prophet, Muhammad. It has challenged the world to produce anything as powerful, as eloquent as the Qur'an, yet none have succeeded. It has transformed the world through the individual, into the family, across entire nations, offering a literary masterpiece with intellectual, moral and spiritual aspects. No other miracle recorded in history has affected humanity more. Who can dispute this truth? It is incontestable at all levels.

There are still those who must understand that Allah administered to each prophet the ability to perform miracles according to what was intellectually superior at the time. This would prove the miracles were beyond human power, coming only from Allah. Therefore, since the art of eloquent speech was advancing at a rapid rate, the Qur'an was given to Muhammad causing a blanket of silence to fall upon the greatest poets of his time."

Mudjiza comes to mind. Does the Qur'an meet these nine characteristics to be considered a miracle? Why would Muhammad admit he was only a man – an apostle, when challenged to perform miracles? He knew God confirmed other prophets before him by miraculous feats of nature; he even recognized Moses' response with miracles when challenged by Pharaoh.

The doubts continue to multiply under scrutiny. With more to come, I monitor Faisal's demeanor as he sips his tea, surety bringing a familiarity to him in this setting. I can feel our time coming to an end, his patience dwindling. One more area to address though, before leaving. Gathering my cup in hand, pouring hot, rosy tea into my mouth, delaying in order to recall all Noor had told me, shown me, opened my eyes to:

"There remains one last subject I would like to get your wisdom on, your counsel," I say, feeling the warmth of the tea race into every limb in my body. "I have always been told that jihad is a spiritual battle with the world until someone more skilled in the text of the Qur'an revealed to me what I have always felt in my heart initially, that it's most certainly not a spiritual battle, but a real physical war. The legal definition of jihad by Islamic law is all it took:

'Jihad is fighting anybody who stands in the way of spreading Islam. Or fighting anyone who refuses to enter into Islam.'

"The first objection I raised was over the one hundred verses on love, peace and forgiveness contradicting this view of merciless killing of innocent people." He turned to progressive revelation. All these verses, one hundred and twenty-four, were canceled out by the newest revealed surah 9:5. He guided me through the numerous surahs and verses that instruct every Muslim to carry out jihad. One of Mawlana Abul Ala Mawdudi's passages has stuck with me:

'The goal of Islam is to rule the entire world and submit all of mankind to the faith of Islam.   Any nation or power in this world that tries to get in the way of that goal, Islam will fight and destroy. In order for Islam to fulfill that goal, Islam can use every power available every way it can be used to bring a worldwide revolution. This is jihad.'

"Since I heard this not long ago, I could no longer deny nor avoid the clear teaching of jihad and killing nonbelievers in the name of Allah. So, I ask you, how are we to ignore the example Muhammad lived out for us in jihad commanded by Allah?"

Repositioning himself, face shedding all warmth to an intense callousness, surprising me, engaging differently now: it's personal.

"One cannot deny the propagation of Islam; it is the duty of every true Muslim, but the spread of Islam by force, killing all unbelievers refusing to convert to Islam, no trace of it can be found in the Qur'an. This was not on the mind of Muhammad when revealing these surahs. We see in the Qur'an from surah 22:39-40 Muslims granted permission to make war with only those who made war against them. This was a matter of saving our religious freedom, a holy war in the truest sense. Mosques, churches, synagogues and any other place of worship would not exist if such offense was not taken. Peace would have been unattainable. Foreign beliefs would be forced upon all the people. Islam would have been swept out of existence. Therefore, war with motives as pure as this, was jihad, a struggle to establish divine unity, to maintain the freedom of conscience. Fighting in self-defense, the noblest, the most just of all the causes one may enter into."

He pauses to clear his throat, making it obvious he's not welcoming any more questions at this time by the strict holding of his hand in the air.

"The Muslims were not waging war to force Islam on these various tribes; they were the ones being attacked to force them to deny their faith in Allah. Now, you may defend with Nasikh regarding these earlier defensive verses, yet if you look closely at the principles, they remain the same. Surah 9:5 you've mentioned, which is proclaimed as 'The Verse of the Sword', has been stripped out of its context by many misguided Muslims. When one reads the opening verses of chapter 9, we recognize that the order to kill unbelievers wherever you find them is clearly identifying only those who have taken up the sword in attacking Muslims first, specific tribes only, not all-inclusive. And once religious persecution ended, aggressive behavior toward them ceased and war was also to end. Why would Muhammad sign peace treaties with non-Muslims? Agreements would never be entered into if the sole mission was to fight the world until all embraced Islam.

Wars will forever exist in our lives, but it revolves around the worthiness of the cause and the times when it becomes our highest calling. Fighting for truth, fighting for freedom, fighting for life itself, are all the noblest of causes to sacrifice one's life for. To wage war or die pursuing one of these occasions will bring honor upon one's name. War can be good and war can be evil; it all depends on the means by which one is waging it for. There is endless evidence to support my words delving deeper into the verses requiring more time than we currently have. I have tried to summarize for you some of the essential elements pertaining to the misconception many Muslims hold onto. Before you depart, I challenge you, young brother, to search over these verses asking yourself why Muhammad fought. The Qur'an's answer on this point is very clear. It was a pleasure speaking with you; however, my demanding schedule requires my presence somewhere else. I hope our conversation cleared up some of your confusion, while at the same time increasing your faith in Islam."

We both stand, he steps over to me, taking my hand in his, then walks me to the door with an emotionless face, probably already preparing for the next venture. At the door we briefly embrace, I thank him for his time. He stares into my face one last time with a departing invitation.

"After some diligent study, if you still find questions you're unable to resolve, see Sanafi again; he knows how to contact me." I nod in appreciation.

Back in the car, the engine hums as portions of the meeting replay over in my mind. I try accepting his explanation to put my soul at ease. Something within is still rejecting everything though, unsatisfied with what was being offered. The thought of Isa and his characteristics instantly makes me picture Lydia. I actually awake from my reverie to a man behind me, waiting for me to get out of his way. One hand clutching the steering wheel, I tap the gas, bringing me back into the comfort of the street. I catch the man's glance, offer him a slight nod, an apology in a sense, for the delay. How long was I sitting there before he decided to head toward me? It's too late to care; the afternoon swarm of traffic has my full attention.

Chapter Thirteen

I awake with a scream – bolt upright – clapping both hands around my throat. The rapid thudding inside my chest, the perspiration gathered on my brow, the dryness of my throat, the images still so vividly captured in my mind recalling every detail: crawling along a desolate sea of sand in need of hydration for mere survival. Lips cracked, bloody, dreading every body induced swallow unable to dislodge the many grains of sand that blew in my gaping mouth from the gusts of hot wind. Each forward thrust of my hand would sink beneath the endless flow of golden mountains. Soaked with sweat, being forced from every pore in my body, by the blistering orange bursts refusing to retreat. At the top of the hill, I see it – too delirious to believe at first sight until standing the test of a mirage. The glistening white sheen atop an ocean of life settling behind the lone date palm. Mustering up all my strength, I push myself to my feet, heavily breathing with each forced step, occasionally stopping to control the coughing, the dry-heaving and to rest. However, before arriving, feeling so close I can feel the drops of water falling upon my tongue, my body crumples to the sand in devastation, surrendering to inevitable death, as the oasis vanishes, never existing. Nothing but the palm here. Hopelessness takes hold. I want to cry out, try to, yet lack the energy.

My eyes drift closed, then, in the silence, the whisper pierces my ears, "Umar, I am...," but it fades, jolting me with an epiphany, all the pieces falling into place, the familiarity of the palm, the voice. I raise my head, eyes wide open, to discover her standing before me glowing in an almost blinding white light, radiating a pureness, a peacefulness I never knew existed. In her hand rests a glass of the clearest water filled to the brim. Opening my mouth, the hoarse words battle their way out.

"Mother, please...the water."

A cough begins, won't subside, causing my hands to grab at my throat to calm it. Her beautiful golden eyes are bigger, softer, holding a love so rich I can feel it encapsulating me. The words come with an unexpected power mixed in gentleness.

"Son, this water you seek will neither quench your thirst nor bring you life, for it is dead."

She tilts her hand, emptying the glass into the fiery sand. I throw my arms out screaming, "No, no, mother...no."

The water disintegrates the moment it touches down, leaving behind a small hole in the unblemished grains; I'm too dehydrated to shed a tear from the anguish.

I try shaking the dream off, hoping a shower will help. To my disappointment, her words refuse to leave. Too real. What did she mean anyway? It won't quench my thirst? It won't bring me life? It is dead? Grief, sorrow, has overtaken its territory in my heart from the feeling that she was alive, with me like before. There's no denying how much I truly do miss her. To divert my attention, I focus on my plans for today. Since meeting with Sheikh Faisal last week, I've been mentally weighed down with fatigue, trying to maneuver through the Qur'an for the truth, needing to know who God really is. All the contradictions, the new knowledge, is causing me problems. I feel lost, a stranger to Him. I miss my family, miss playing soccer, miss being home. There's no alternative though; I must figure this out before moving on in life.

There's only one place left for me to examine. Over these last days, I'm reaching a new position, one that's ripping my foundation right from under me, making me an orphan to faith, to the only god I've ever known. After gathering the Qur'an along with the stack of other insightful books on the history of Arabs and Islam, biographies of Muhammad, encyclopedias, Islamic apologetics, one from the black market, I take them all to the hotel room, studying non-stop: After hours of endless study, there remain

After hours of endless study, there remain two main points I can't ignore any more preventing me from ever believing like I have my entire life: the many contradictions in the Qur'an and the godly attributes of Isa, which are strictly reserved for Allah himself. Therefore, the logical questions stand. If there can be no change in the words of God, then how can abrogation be applied? How can a divine revelation be improved upon in any way? It should be perfect when it is received. What about the verses that aren't redacted by abrogation, but contradict each other? Lastly, there can be no denying jihad as a reality. It fills more than half the Qur'an with "The Verse of the Sword" annulling all previous verses on peace, mercy and forgiveness, accepted as the last revelation concerning jihad. Endless wars and bloodshed are all I find in Islam's history. Where's the goodness, the mercy, the love from God to his creation or from Muhammad to the people? These traits no longer exist.

I'm living without a god right now. No prayer. No direction in life. A gaping hole has been left inside my soul. Where do I turn to for help now? Who do I seek instruction from? Guidance? What's life worth living for if I don't know my creator? These thoughts continue relentlessly. Questions about Isa refuse to surrender as well. The loneliness settles in. Speaking these words to anyone will surely be the death of me, except one person. She possesses the knowledge to answer some of what I need. Will she talk with me after how dishonorably I treated her last time? I have no other options. No one else to turn to, a position I'm becoming way too familiar with.

Exiting the hotel for the first time in over almost twenty-four hours, the bright Sunday morning sunlight blinds me. It takes a second to adjust, to remind myself how much I missed it, how much the warmth penetrating my skin refreshes my body. I desperately need something considering my physical and spiritual state. In no kind of hurry, I relax, take ten slow, concentrated deep breaths from the deepest part of my lungs, to calm my mind, to regain some composure in dealing with what lies ahead. There's no doubt in my mind though, that truth will reveal itself. It always holds that promise when one diligently pursues it with an unbiased motive, at least that's what I've been told.

I feel more connected after my hands are clutching the wheel again heading north into the city. Regardless of how much I want things to go back to how they used to be, such a thing cannot be. I think back to the crash, to why I was spared a most certain death, while Tariq wasn't. Was it the calling out to god? Deep inside a feeling convinces me the crash was no coincidence. However, with relentless anguish tormenting my soul from leaving behind everything I've ever known, I wish the driver would have missed me, for I have nothing now.

It doesn't take long to arrive at the restaurant. Through the glass front, I see my lonely table. Inside, the place is more crowded than usual. I seat myself in my favorite spot, against the window staring into Riyadh. Not long afterward, the waiter approaches, the same one who's always working. I can tell by his raised eyebrows he's surprised to see me.

"Good to see you, sir. I thought you moved away. The same as usual?"

"Yes, the same as always," I answer, my voice tapering off as my attention becomes distracted by a woman walking past outside accompanied by a young girl on one side, a boy on the other, with the man slightly out in front. I don't realize when he walks away from the table, for some reason my eyes are fascinated by this family until disappearing behind the wall as the glass ends. This was me, my mother, Rana and Kamal. We were so young, innocent and open to anything; believing in everything told to me. Inheriting, without choice, Islam, to speak the Arabic language and to be a Saudi. I also inherited the pride that has been instilled within us regarding us as the chosen people of the world, the smartest, the only ones possessing the truth. Ingrained in us to hate Jews and Christians, all without ever examining any of it, not even considering the possibility that we may be wrong. I refused to question what was taught to me, especially about the Qur'an, as it's forbidden to do so. Maybe this is exactly why they teach that, to prevent this turmoil I'm currently facing, this confusion. Slowly these thoughts fade into the evolving city life outside.

The Asian man delivers my beverage before quickly shuffling his way to a pair of older men three tables down. I study the tall glass of citrus, calculating how long it's been, raise it to my dry lips, then let its fresh, smoothness flow down my throat. It's everything I remember it being: sweet, tart, refreshing, except something's missing this time. When I set the glass back down, I discover what it is. There's no desire for it. It means nothing to me.

For a while, I don't move, don't blink, only wonder where I went wrong. Maybe if I would have known the Qur'an better, had been more faithful to Islam, this falling away would never have come about. My mother, Tariq, would still be alive and I would be playing professional soccer. This is it, isn't it? My punishment, for not following Allah in all the ways instructed from childhood? My pursuit of soccer instead of Islam? My overwhelming love for my mother compared to Allah? The pressure of the tear pulling itself from my eye comes with the thoughts of her absence, with the regrets of how I handled such precious information given to me, the fear, the cowardice, that has held me at a distance when in the presence of my father after he showed up. If anyone possesses the power to convince her to return to Islam, it was me. I want forgiveness, yet I know there exists none for this kind of sin.

The motion of a figure passing close by awakens me to the time escaping me. I must be going. I pay the bill, leaving behind the glass half empty, empty of beyond only the juice, but a lifetime of memories, of meaning, forever being a grief to revisit. As I depart, a piece of me says goodbye, sensing I won't be back.

Chapter Fourteen

After a while, my impatience overtakes me, searching for the phone. At any moment now it can happen. My pulse quickens, anxiety rises in anticipation of rejection, all I can do is command my eyes to remain fixed on the two glass doors. This time is different. I must approach them.

I watch the doors swing open; women file out in one small group. I turn the key, firing the engine up. There will be no time to waste. As they get closer, I'm able to scan many of the faces. Found her! She's walking alongside the same darker complected woman as last time. Must be the one sitting alongside her bed in the hospital. Estimating the distance from the walkway to the parking lot, I creep along the road, waiting on her to reach the crosswalk. Without delay, I pump the gas, launching me forward blocking their path. The sudden braking startles them, causing them to immediately stop, eyes peeled for danger. Anxiety, fear, uncertainty, resonates all over their faces. The passenger window already down, I lean over finding a better view. Lydia's eyes betray her instant recognition of me, but she stands motionless, curious of my intentions to come visit her publicly at her work like this.

This was carefully orchestrated, with the least amount of risk involved. I could never chance going to her place again. She almost lost her life that way, something I'm beginning to feel more guilty for. To such a degree I've bound the memories in one of the darkest rooms in my heart, however, every time I see her, a flame is ignited, forcing me to answer the knocking. Coming here in this fashion grants me the cover of being a driver.

Looking boldly into her eyes, I say almost desperately, "Can we talk?"

She's silent for a long moment, searching my face, finally turning to her friend on her side. "I'll meet you in the truck."

The woman nods with concern, then rounds the front of the car heading into the parking lot, glancing back twice on the way. Lydia takes a few steps forward, bends down until eye level with me, waiting expectantly.

With the much-needed courage in hand I ask, "I don't know how to ask you this," I briefly pause, searching for the right words, "will you come with me to Bahrain, where we can discuss some private matters?"

"Discuss what?" she asks, suspiciously.

I look everywhere, but in her eyes. Stalling. Embarrassed to be asking.

"The Bible and...Jesus," I whisper, shame casting down my demeanor. In the silence, I can feel her gaze burning into me. She has no reason to believe me, to trust my words after our past encounters together. I return my attention to her, forcing every ounce of genuineness, of struggle through my face. For a second I forget about everything, only her beauty, her seducing emerald eyes.

"Let me go tell them I have arranged some other plans," she says, then navigates around the car along the same path as her friend.

The sudden noise is startling, making me jump in my seat. Instantly, I check the rear-view mirror: a line of cars is stacked up behind me. Irritated by their impatience, something is telling me to make them wait until she returns. But, I remember what I'm doing, trying to be discreet, not attract my unwanted attention, so I pull forward, take a left down the aisle she traveled, catch her heading my way after stepping away from a truck, as it pulls away. When I pull up beside her, she opens the door, gracefully sliding into the back seat.

"Thank you for agreeing to come with me," I say, exiting the hospital parking lot.

"I always have time to speak about my faith with anyone who is genuinely seeking for answers, but if arguing is their intention, I have no interest in engaging in conversation."

I understand her position, respect it. Answers are what I need. We maneuver through Riyadh onto King Fahd Causeway, heading straight to Bahrain. I can't help but watch her admire the blue waves off in the distance. So content. Peaceful. Suddenly glancing up, probably unconsciously aware of eyes upon her, she catches me. I look away as if I wasn't, but on the inside embarrassed for getting caught. What does she think of me I wonder? I don't dare take the risk of returning, such a thing may make her feel uncomfortable and want to leave. I cannot chance that. The rest of the drive is quiet. I pay less attention to traffic and more to the overbearing thoughts and feelings I'm experiencing. Arriving in Manama, Bahrain, we take a right off King Faisal Highway, searching for a certain private restaurant, discreet in the truest sense of the word, near Bab Al Bahrain, something suiting our needs perfectly. About half a kilometer up the street, I spot the name resting high above the entrance. I pull in, finding an open space in the back. Lydia opens the door, waiting for her to join me before asking.

"Have you ever been here before?"

"No, this is my first time in Bahrain," she replies, now walking next to me.

"Mine as well," I say, turning toward her. "Hopefully, this place lives up to its reputation."

Being the middle of the afternoon, I don't expect the place to be too busy, even though the city is swarming with life. Men, women and children fill the sidewalks, carrying shopping bags, walking in and out of every open business. I jerk on the tan door. It is everything that was described to me: thin black carpeting covering sections of the floor, the tables enclosed on three sides by a high, black cushioned partition to offer the privacy so many desire aligning several rows. Windowless walls decorated by colorful, abstract paintings coming alive in the midst of all the black.

From our position, I cannot see a single person except for the two hosts stationed before us at the black podium. Both young Asian men, clean-shaven, wearing long-sleeved, black button-ups with black slacks falling over shiny black oxfords and square white teeth as the first one greets us. His face is softer, not as chiseled, due to the extra weight he's carrying.

"For two?" he asks, directed at me.

"Yes," I respond.

"Follow me, please," says the taller slimmer man, wearing a courteous, but professional expression.

He leads us down the third aisle to our table. For the first time, I'm given a glimpse of the private tables. Foreign women are mixing with Arabs, Arab women are mixing with Arab men amidst half-empty bottles of champagne; no doubt some of these women are prostitutes. Three of them are laughing with the only two Saudis I've come across. Now understanding why growing numbers of Saudis come here to indulge in such forbidden acts, it's relaxed, private and legal in the sheikdom. They can travel here, do whatever they wish without consequences, then return to the Kingdom continuing to promote good and forbid evil like nothing ever happened. A double life. The good thing is, I feel comfortable here because of this, even if they see Lydia as a prostitute I'm paying for. Nobody cares. Hopefully, she will feel comfortable also, enough to open up in my questions for her.

After we're seated, the man retreats back down the aisle. As soon as he's out of sight, her voice penetrates my ears.

"You never told me you were taking me to dinner," she says, hinting she may have denied my request if it was known.

"This is the only place I know of offering the freedom needed to discuss specific things with you, otherwise forbidden to do inside the Kingdom," I say, in defense, expressing my lack of desire in having to bring her here in the first place.

I see her demeanor soften, feeling once again the warm welcome touching me through her endless reservoir of love. Does she show this to everyone? She picks up the menu from the table, begins analyzing it. Her streaky blondish brown hair is flowing over one slender shoulder and down her back, exposing more of her unblemished creamy skin, drawing attention to her appealing beauty, to those deepening green eyes. The table resting between us is draped with white linen feeling the weight from the empty white china and sparkling silver spread before us. Soft black cushioning pulls us into comfort, an invitation to stay all night.

He appears out of nowhere, his black cropped hair hugging tightly against his scalp, brown skin with features from southeast Asia, all wrapped on a short, skinny frame.

"Would you like anything to drink?" he asks, in perfect English.

Lydia speaks up first. "I'll have water, please."

He turns his attention to me.

"Water also," I say, not really thirsty or hungry for that matter.

Alone again, thinking of where to begin, but before I have a chance to decide, she beats me to it.

"So, what have you driven me all the way to Bahrain to speak with me about?"

I settle in, opening my mind to freely investigate all areas in an objective manner. Earnestly seeking the truth, even if that means it rests with the Christians and Jews, no matter how repulsed I am by the mere thought of it.

"Your faith," I reply. "I have many questions, but would like to begin with you explaining what you believe and why."

Confusion falls over her face as expected. Why would I ask such a thing? After studying me for some time, processing all that encompasses this request, the potential consequences, her gentle innocence begins breaking out of its shell, trusting me just enough.

"I am a follower of Jesus Christ. My faith and trust are in Him alone. I understand you were raised to hate us because we are unbelievers, infidels. That we are polytheists who worship three gods, believe god took Mary as his wife who bore Jesus as his son, that Mary is worshiped, even prayed to. There has developed a major misconception regarding these things."

"How?" I ask, intensely.

The waiter returns with our drinks, carefully placing them on the table before us. "Are you ready to order?"

"Yes," I answer, handing him the menu, "I'll have the Chicken Tikka."

He turns his attention to Lydia.

"I'll have the same thing," she says, as he retrieves her menu then scurries away.

She shifts her gaze back to me, continuing where she left off.

"There is no verse in the Bible that says to worship Mary, to pray to her, that God took Mary as His wife or three different gods exist. But we do find and believe Jesus is the Son of God and is God Himself. We worship only one God. We pray to only one God. Mary is the mother of Jesus who conceived supernaturally by the Holy Spirit as a virgin. This is also in the Qur'an.

The belief held claiming we worship three gods derives from a misunderstanding of the Trinity. Throughout the Bible, there are numerous references to this belief, too difficult for me to explain entirely without the Scriptures in front of me. However, it is not the belief that God is three separate gods, rather one essence containing three distinct persons. So, God is a plurality of persons in a unity of essence. One of these illustrations may help you understand. A triangle has three equal and inseparable distinct sides, yet remains one shape. Or we can take one times one times one equals one. Three distinct numbers, yet equal one altogether. However, the most applicable example I feel pertaining to our lives is that of love. God is love according to 1 John 4:16 and in order for love to fully exist there must be a lover, the beloved and the spirit of love between the lover and the loved. The Father being the lover, Jesus being the One loved and the Holy Spirit the spirit of love. These three must be united together as one or love will cease to exist. Every human being experiences love and therefore possesses the ability to relate to this illustration. However, you must keep in mind there will always be a certain mystery about this aspect of God. We should not expect to fully comprehend everything about God anyway. Much can be discussed about this subject, more than we have time for."

I've never seen this side of her, the passion ignited within delivering such knowledge and understanding through her words. She stops, stares at me expecting a rebuttal, a question of some sort. Not right now; I'm content to listen, to learn.

She continues, changing directions now. "Let me ask you a question," she says, pausing, "are you forgiven for your sins?"

I take a second to respond, asking myself this question since I was a boy. "Allah is most merciful."

"Do you have assurance your sins are forgiven?" she asks again, seeking a desired answer.

"No," I answer, giving her what she wants, one aspect of life I tend to prevent myself from thinking about.

"What's going to happen to you when you die?" she asks, wasting no time.

Before answering, I ponder these questions, the reason why she's asking them. Her motivation.

"Only Allah knows," I reply, calmly, all the memories of bad deeds come crashing to the forefront.

Silence fills the air. For the first time, those captivating green eyes disappear behind two walls, her chin now touching her chest. Is something wrong? Then it registers. What courage, boldness, to pray right here, right now. Her face is so peaceful, innocent. Keeping my eyes on her, all that remains of my diminished compassion reminding me of the peace I've felt around her since the first day we met. The kind of peace stirring up foreign feelings, feelings I've always combated with anger or with the hidden grief wreaking havoc deep within. I'm unable to deny the power of love she impresses upon me when in her presence, her beautiful, delicate body sitting there like a lone spring in the desert.

Her head rises, eyes part with a new vitality about them. I remain quiet, no urge to speak right now. She accepts it, receives it.

"I can sit here across from you touching on all the scholastic debates about the origins of the Qur'an, its teaching that Jesus was only a prophet, wasn't crucified, wasn't resurrected, the corruption of the present-day Bible and other notable things, but what will this accomplish? I refuse to engage in this. All I'm willing to share with you is how I came to believe in Isa as my Lord and Savior along with the transformation experienced by doing so."

"Whatever you're open to sharing with me I appreciate," I say, understandingly. "This is my purpose for bringing you here, to listen rather than speak."

She accepts the invitation. Sips her water. Begins. "Right after my eighteenth birthday, I was excited for my new future in the medical field, studying to become a doctor in Russia. I've always had a heart for the sick, the weak, the poor. My parents saved up my entire childhood for this day. In addition to a scholarship I received, we arranged for all my expenses to be covered, only to be surprised one day by some unexpected costs. I thought no big deal, I'll get a part-time job on the side for a while to take care of it. Stumbling upon an ad requesting a house cleaner offering high pay seven days a week for six months, was perfect for me. I reached a man by the contact info, who after a short conversation answering some general questions, told me I got the job. He even said he would arrange for all my travel documents and purchase the plane ticket.

"I was so happy, happy that everything was falling into place, all of my hard work and perseverance was paying off. My dreams were finally coming true. Once I received my passport, visa for job training and confirmation number, I was in flight to Israel. My plan was to work for the full six months saving everything except for minor expenses, then be back in time to enroll in the spring.

"He picked me up at the airport, was polite, charismatic, telling me about the job as we traveled through Israel. We arrived at some old apartments while he described the area where I'll be staying. Once inside, he closed the door, locked it, then he retrieved a black pistol from under his armpit, pointed it into my face, ripped my bag out of my hand, taking all my documents, as another man appeared from out of a room. He told me I was in his debt, that I couldn't leave until it was paid in full through sex. And if I tried to escape at any time, he would kill me then kill my family. At that moment hopelessness fell over me. A fear of death I've never experienced before. Then there was the dread of the unknown: dark, wicked, perverse thoughts entered my mind of how I was soon to be violated in the deepest sense and I could do nothing to prevent it. The despair of never seeing my parents again along with terror gripped me in the realest way. Unimaginable horror shredded my soul in two.

"I was led back to a room and ordered to undress, when I refused, he gave me one more chance to do it or he would do it for me. I was defiant. I was in no way willing to surrender my nakedness. The beating was fierce, relentless until I was unconscious. Awaking to my stripped body aching, spread across the floor, I began hyperventilating. The tears flowed non-stop. After what seemed to be hours, I gained control of myself, deciding to obey his orders until I'm released or the first opportunity to escape arises. When he returned, he asked me if I was a virgin. Confused about why he would ask such a question, I remained silent. However, the moment he threatened me again

I answered yes out of fear of another beating. My stomach turned in sickness as his face brightened in delight. At this point, he gave me my instructions: work six days a week, twelve-hour shifts, sexually serving up to fifteen clients per day. There would be no refusing a client for any request or physical punishment will be administered.

"I was moved to a room a short distance down the hall, which was always locked behind me. It was small, dirty, a lone paper-thin mattress crumpled on the floor was shoved in the corner. The toilet sat on the other side of a yellow cloth curtain inside a one by two meter area. The sink worked just enough when turning its old rusty knobs to taste a flow of metal fill your mouth. Windowless walls left me claustrophobic in such a tight space causing panic attacks on a daily basis. Early the next morning, I was awakened by three women being ushered into the room with me. All of them were deceived just as I was. The only difference between us was they had been here for years having become content, defeated. Their eyes were conquered, lifeless, lost inside their own minds, doing everything possible to take themselves away from the horror of reality. This was the prison they were trapped in. I promised myself I would never be like them.

"We all worked the same shift, therefore forced to share the same bed. However, it turned out to be a blessing as our body heat circulating between us helped manage the cold nights without a heater and the disgrace of one old raggedy sliver of a blanket given for all four of us. After they were asleep for hours that first night, while I layed there staring into the darkness unable to accept the nightmare, two men entered, waking the girls and corralling us into the back of a silver van. They drove us about three kilometers to their business. One brute of a man stood at the bottom of the stairwell patting down clients before releasing them to scale the two flights of stairs, passing by a few run-down apartments along the way. The lounge area consisted of perpendicular corridors stretching down either side of a hallway as a young, very attractive woman sat behind the open reception desk twirling a pen between her fingers like it was just another day in the office. Two red sofas rested against one wall reserved for clients offering them privacy before approaching her.

"One of the men guided me down the left corridor into one of the many rooms, as a younger man followed close behind. The room was small, big enough to fit a single mattress lit by a dim red light. My heart suffocating inside my chest the moment I entered, wanting to resist, to fight back, to be home with my parents as if this was a bad nightmare. His rough grip upon my arm shattered such a hope. He asked me if there were going to be any problems, threatening physical harm if so. I shook my head no.

"The young man wearing a black suit and red tie shut the door behind him as he entered my room. His forward motion toward me caused me to instantly retreat, stumbling onto the bed. He quickly undressed, never taking his predator eyes off me. He lowered himself down over me, grabbed hold of both of my knees forcefully pulling me toward him. Out of reaction, I unleashed a powerful kick square in his chest launching him back onto the floor. Anger covered his face in disbelief of what just happened. In no time he was back on his feet throwing the back of his knuckles mercilessly into my left cheek, making my body go limp, almost knocking me unconscious. At that moment, I surrendered against all my instincts telling me to fight back. I decided to take my mind to another world, completely separating it from my physical body, reminding myself of the hope that one day my opportunity would come.

"Two weeks later is when it happened. My hope almost diminished of ever making it out of that hell alive, of being mentally capable from the endless torture endured. I began even seeing myself defeated as the others, but that particular day, when the client entered the room, I felt different. A stirring inside my soul overpowered my whole being with rebellion, something I could sense wasn't entirely by my doing. I told the man to leave. He refused. I ordered him the next time. He refused again, this time engaging me. With all my strength I kicked him straight in the groin, dropping him to his knees; as I tried running by him, he latched onto my ankle tripping me to the floor beside him. The next thing I felt was all the oxygen getting sucked from my lungs with a vicious pain in my back, then being dragged onto the bed where he struck me repeatedly until blackness poured over my eyes.

"When I woke, I instinctively crawled to the corner of the room, placing my back against the wall, searching for his face, yet only finding my blood splattered all over the floor and walls. Every part of my body ached and was burning with pain. I could still feel the warm flow of liquid leaking from my body. Reaching up to the back of my head, my palm returned covered in red. My vision blurred going in and out, thinking this was it, the end had finally come. Blackness pulled me under once again.

"I awoke the second time to a different man sitting beside me, gently holding a soaked, bloody stained towel. He was dressed in a cream, long-sleeved button-up shirt with black slacks. A middle-aged man, clean-shaven and staring at me through amber eyes. In a heavy Hebrew accent, he immediately raised both hands in a surrendering pose. The towel was tightly bundled up in his fist as he said in a calm, soothing tone, 'I help you, nothing more.' I studied him intently, wondering who he was, where he came from, how he got into this room, where the other man went, then I got a gut feeling to trust him. I was left with limited options anyway if I wanted to live, not knowing the extent of the damage done, only feeling the havoc wreaked on my entire body.

"Without saying anything, he slowly lowered his hands toward my face. One hand carefully turned my head sideways, the other dabbing away at a gash stinging at every touch.

"'You need hospital,' he told me, drawing back his hands. Then he stared at me for a while, pulled a small book out of his pocket and began reading.

"'Jesus said to her, 'I am the resurrection and the life, He who believes in Me, though he may die, he shall live. And whoever lives and believes in Me shall never die.'

"Those words hit me with a power I've never known before. I heard Jesus' name growing up, but nothing more. My parents were atheists; therefore, so was I. God and Jesus were always exaggerated figures who humanity made up in order to cope with life's struggles.

"For the first time, I was able to force out some words, telling him that I didn't want to necessarily believe, but wanted to know how to believe in this Jesus.

"He said, 'You must surrender your life to Him, putting faith and trust in Him alone, that He died for your sins, was buried, then resurrected on the third day.' Then he asked me if I wanted to be set free from darkness, from bondage, if so to join him in a prayer. I felt the urging within the depths of my soul to go forth with it, to surrender to

Jesus. I mumbled yes through hesitancy. He then invited me to repeat after him.

"'Lord, I come broken at your feet, so lost and in need of a Savior. I surrender my life to You. I believe You sacrificed Your only begotten Son, Jesus Christ, on the cross for my sins, that I may receive forgiveness. Come into my life right now, lead me on your narrow path according to Your will that I may serve You with all of my heart, soul, mind and strength. In Christ's precious name I pray, Amen.'

"Tears were pouring from my eyes, as I allowed all of the locked doors of my heart to be opened, letting go of everything I was hiding from, fearful of and clinging onto in life, committing all of myself in faith to this Jesus. When I finished, the man was smiling, joy filling his face.

"He told me I was now a daughter of God, as he gently dabbed away at my wounds. I felt something unique inside me, a release, a freedom, a peace like I've never experienced before. All I wanted to do was cry to God in thankfulness for His grace and mercy toward me. Then he suddenly told me it was his time to leave, but first, he intensely asked me since I was now free in Christ spiritually, would I like to be free physically from this place.

"An immediate surge of anticipation woke me to a new hope, numbing all the pain. I quickly told him yes, confused about how he was going to manage this though. He studied my eyes for a long moment, looking for something, then finally spoke, telling me I would be going to the hospital not long after he left. That when I was taken outside and I reached halfway between the car and stairs, to quickly sprint down the sidewalk to the right, then enter the third business on the right. I would see a soldier at the entrance who would help me. He told me this is all he could do for me. He then blessed me.

"The next moment he was disappearing into the corridor. His words kept replaying through my mind. I wondered; how did he know all of this? Regardless of the doubts, I trusted this man, felt an unusual closeness to him when he sat next to me. It was difficult to sit up, a stream of crimson ran into the wall of my eyebrows, until finally breaking through. As soon as I stood up, the door opened again. This time the stout hairy man who would drive me back and forth from the apartment to the house of horror, walked straight up to me, violently grabbed hold of my arm ripping me down the empty corridor, passing two of the girls I lived with, their docile faces white in shock from seeing my brutal condition, then led me down the stairs. Every step I descended the more I doubted my ability to flee from his tight grip, outrunning not only one, but two men. When we reached ground level, I looked down the street to the distance I had to cover, about fifty meters to the corner. After that, I didn't know. I began talking to God, telling Him how much I needed His help, pleading that if He would free me from this place, I would serve Him the rest of my life.

"With each stride edging me slightly closer to the car, I heard a subtle voice telling me, 'Run now!' Without hesitation, a courage was given to me which I never possessed before, I ripped my arm free from a tightly held grip, sprinting as fast as I could down the sidewalk with all my might. When I made it to the corner I didn't look back, scared to, staying focused on the third business I had to reach. I hoped what the man said was true; if not, I was dead. In two more strides, a soldier came into sight. Heart racing, adrenaline outweighing the pain, the words came bursting out. I screamed for help, from the man trying to kill me. At this point I glanced behind me, relief filling my heart. The soldier was making him stop. I waited to see if the soldier was going to help me or throw me back to the streets. I pleaded for him to help me over and over again, sobbing uncontrollably. He finally pulled a phone from his pocket, touched the screen, then held it to his ear. I positioned myself beside him, as he spoke a few words of Hebrew into the phone. When he hung up, he stared at the heartless man in pursuit of me, gasping for oxygen, still standing about ten meters from us. The soldier yelled something at the man, a language I'm unfamiliar with, causing him to stand there speechless, anger flushing his face wanting so badly to recapture me. That's the last thing I remember before collapsing.

"I awoke in a hospital room, an IV protruding from my arm, body paralyzed, head pounding. Fear instantly gripped me, fear of those men coming there to kill me or kidnap me again, beat me again, rape me again. I tried to get up, thinking I would be safer outside of the hospital, but my body refused to move. Right then a nurse entered the room and seeing me awake, came to my side. The first words from my mouth were whether or not there was a guard watching over my room.

Thankfully, she told me an officer had been routinely checking on my status, waiting for me to wake.

"I asked her when I was free to go; she told me soon on her way out of the room. Those hours of laying in the hospital bed left me much to reflect upon, mainly the Jewish man who mysteriously appeared in my particular room, at the precise time, with intentions of helping me beyond just my physical injuries, leaving me with no logical explanation besides being orchestrated by God himself. I wondered if I would ever see him again. Later that evening, two policemen showed up at my room with a surprising agenda. They questioned me about the incident. I told them everything, yet when it came to the request for my identification, I couldn't provide any documents. As a result, they escorted me from the hospital to an immigration center where I sat for two months, before finally being deported back to Russia. Thankfully I was given the opportunity to use the phone there to call my parents. I couldn't explain to them everything that happened over the phone, their confusion all the more prevalent after telling them their lives were in danger and they would have to move. I was convinced this would only delay the inevitable threat. It's relatively easy to find someone in Russia if you are well-connected. If anything, the move would buy me some time, enough to return with a new plan on how to evade these perpetrators. I wasn't sure how connected they were but wasn't willing to take that risk with my parents' lives on the line.

"Through all of this, I possessed a new peace within, a hunger to get my hands on the Bible, to find out more about this free gift I was given, a new found freedom, the forgiveness received, all through Jesus Christ. When I bought one, I was unable to put it down. The wisdom, the truth, was what I unconsciously sought my entire life. It took me having to face death, subjected to laying in a bloody helplessness before I accepted my need for a Savior, one who could free me from the bondage of the world, to forgive me for all my sins and grant me eternal life. This package can only be found in no other than Jesus Christ."

I sat listening to her words, the power in them, the fire I feel burning with great passion. To see her slender, meek form affected in such a way is moving, intriguing in many aspects I'm unable to fully appreciate. However, it is not without the painful prick on my heart from the torment, the injustice she endured. The presence of the waiter setting our plates before us interrupts us momentarily. This brief break allows me some time to ponder on all she's shared so far.

With the food releasing a desirous aroma, usually causing my hands to begin satisfying my appetite, I choose differently today. The desire to hear the rest of her journey is more important. My spiritual life is a war zone in need of a victor to restore order. Yet the victor remains unknown to me at this time. Her side just received major reinforcements, pressing me to look closely at what Islam is still fighting for, by what is it still holding on? I watch to see her next move, eat, finish or a combination of the two? She looks to me for feedback, for comments or questions of any sort. Noticing my interest in hearing the events by ignoring my plate, she picks up where she left off.

"As my relationship with God grew, a door was opened to me - a unique calling. I fervently prayed on where I was to go, what exactly I was to do. I wanted to help other women who were deceived and kidnapped like I was, who were raped, beaten with no escape or hope in life. God brought me here to Saudi Arabia. Two months after my escape, an old friend I stayed in contact with after school, called me. She was studying medicine in the Kingdom, doing really well for herself, learning a lot. After ten minutes of explaining exactly what she was busy working on, she dropped the question, offering me a job working with her personally. I knew right away this was an answer to my prayers, even though it wasn't what I necessarily wanted. Three more days of prayer with all factors leading me in that direction, I accepted it. Reflecting on these last two years here, I'm able to see the purpose of my coming here. Many opportunities have been given to me, to learn about this country, to help many women here and to be faithful to God. I have no regrets."

Helping women, being faithful to God - my mother comes to mind. They worked together, became friends, shared the same faith. I can see why. She had to have been the one who introduced Christ to her, who influenced her day in and day out. The grief begins surfacing; the wounds still fresh, tender, but this time, instead of conquering it with a justified anger for the betrayal, I suppress it just enough to look myself in the mirror, to look at where my current stance is with Islam, with God. She no doubt experienced this same place of struggle in her search for truth. How did she get through it? What was the determining factor? Do I need a Savior as she did?

She relaxes a bit, expecting an inquiry into her life, yet only the sound is of muffled chatter coming from around us. She recognizes my deep contemplation, decides to try the chicken, respectfully giving me time to reflect. I follow her lead in tasting the meat while it's still hot. It's moist, packed with the soft flavor of lingering herbs, yet not good enough to distract me from the provocative assertions she's made. Still, I keep quiet, continue eating, thinking, catching her boldly staring at me for long periods between bites. She's always captivated me with her beauty, her eyes, her loving presence in general, so much so that I attack it, attack the feelings with hatred. A hatred that I only now am able to recognize, to control.

"What was your motivation for asking me about my faith?" she inquires.

"I've been studying the Qur'an objectively for the first time, causing many questions to arise. Some of them pertain to Jesus, to the Bible, to the beliefs of Christians. I needed a Christian perspective, something different from the same rhetoric heard all my life. You're the only Christian I know, the only foreigner for that matter. It must be somewhat uncomfortable for you, knowing all the risk involved in coming with me, yet you still agreed to. Perhaps in some minor way you're perplexed by my defiance of Islam to go through with it. It is necessary for my purpose in reaching the end," I answer, shamelessly.

"Well, I hope what I've already shared with you has helped clear up some of what you are looking for. If there's anything else I can help you with feel free to ask."

I take the last bites of food off my plate, washing it down with the water. "What is this relationship with God you're referring to?" I ask, sincerely.

"When you surrender your life to God, His Spirit comes to dwell within you, transforming you from the inside out. His love is experienced for the first time, a feeling that is unmatched. There no longer stands any barriers between God and us; you can talk with Him any time about anything, assured that He hears and answers. It's a personal relationship. He leads us and calls us to serve Him in particular ways, always providing us with all our needs. You can feel His presence. There are no words to fully describe all of who He is and all of what He does," she replies, her face radiant.

"How am I to believe any of this when almost every aspect of it contradicts Islam?"

She sighs, looks down the walkway, then back to me. "I can sit here all-night speaking about all the reasons why you should believe, but it will fall on deaf ears if you're here for the wrong reasons. If you've come with the intentions of reinforcing your already held ideology, then this conversation was sabotaged from the start. If you have come tonight with the mind of a child, honestly seeking the truth wherever it may lie, then God will reveal it to you in His time. It always comes down to what you really want." She pauses for a moment.

"It becomes difficult for those of us who have been born and raised into a belief system that encompasses every aspect of our lives to change, to analyze our own views in an objective way when all of our country, culture and people follow the same way; it is almost impossible. We tend to believe we're always right and everyone else is wrong and that's the end of discussion. Why do we never investigate our own set of beliefs? The foundation of our compass? If we can make it past the pride, then comes the fear: fear of the costs if we are wrong, the consequences if we discover what we have grown up believing is false. I understand for you it would be a great sacrifice. It would mean losing your family, your country, even your own life if revealed. This is no easy decision. When your very life depends on the choice you make, the implications contain a sobering reality. This is why many people reject the pursuit of any other view contrary to their own, the fear of facing such a position. I would present to you only one question: are you willing to face the repercussions for even thinking about leaving Islam?"

Anger fills me, tightens every muscle in my body. What insolence on her part to suggest such a notion. Suddenly, I'm reminded of my own uncertainty. And the longer I gaze upon her innocent face, the calmer I become. She has simply asked what I've been avoiding all along, too scared of confronting it myself. A rare feeling of closeness introduces itself toward her now. From her understanding of how difficult it is for me even discussing such a matter to how much I have to lose if I ever forsake my religion.

"This is not an option for me," I answer, with a determined tone.

"There lies an underlying purpose for this meeting besides for gaining a deeper insight into your beliefs, one I do not wish to share with you. I harbor no intentions of leaving Islam, of forsaking the truth in Allah; however, would you be willing to give up everything for another god if our roles were reversed?"

Without any hesitation, she immediately fires back. "Yes, I would. Already have. I surrendered my life to Jesus in order to find it."

What does she mean by this? I take note of it before moving on.

"It must be very difficult to live in the Kingdom, where you can't speak to anyone about your religion and can't possess your own materials," I mention, shifting away from hypothetical apostasy.

"Yes, it's hard, but God opens doors for me to share His saving grace with others. By seeking His will first in my life, staying obedient to the calling He has given me, there comes great blessings."

If I had to guess, she has found a way to read the Bible. She's too intelligent not to. This reminds me of the papers my mother gave to Rana and how she got them.

Setting the glass down after taking a sip, she asks, "Does Allah provide you with everything you need? Can you feel his closeness?"

Already knowing the answers, I take some time to ponder them more thoroughly. "Allah provides me with what he wills me to have; I'm not to question it. When it comes to feeling close to him, I am as close as he desires me to be."

There has never been a time where I've felt close to him. I've always been distant. I remember all of my failed attempts. Going to Mecca for hajj, I was confident after the five-day ritual I would be closer to Allah, yet was disappointed when nothing changed spiritually. I have a feeling she already knew the answer. The question wasn't for her. She has given me a broad range of things to examine. I want to continue in conversation with her, remain in her presence; however, in a different way. Her emanating aura is irresistible, offering me a comfort I forgot existed, a safety I miss. But how long can I keep her here? Maybe she can see through my hardened facade into the lost little boy inside, confused, vulnerable, grasping at vapors for help.

Eight PM. I conceal the phone, surprised how fast the hours have drifted by. Not wanting to present the impression that I no longer desire her company, I take a thoughtful approach. "It's getting late, but before we go, I want to thank you. You've been more than generous agreeing to come here with me, answering all of my questions in a respectful manner, offering me more than I expected."

"Thank you for the opportunity to share," she says, thankfully.

We both rise from our seats. I lead the way past the many private tables with food and intersex mingling, still, an unusual sight to see. When we approach the young, charismatic host, I pay the bill, then exit the restaurant, not entirely composed. My mind is preoccupied with more important matters.

Eyes fresh on the city, a change has occurred, a transformation from when we entered hours ago. The nightlife has emerged alive, active, similar to Riyadh, except on a greater scale, playing with various elements otherwise considered illegal.

I navigate through the congested streets soaking up the different life lived here, the vibe, the new scenery hovering over me, an escape from the confines of the Kingdom, discovering a new found freedom. All of this before me, yet when I glance into the back seat, I'm awakened to the fact that there sits something more precious, more special than any of it. This rejected feeling, pitted at my core, disturbs me. I shake it from my head as fast as possible, turning my attention back to entering onto King Fahd causeway, back home.

Returning to the Kingdom, I can't stop thinking about our conversation over dinner, about the two times I caught her staring at me through the rear-view mirror. What was she thinking about? Maybe she wanted to break the tension residing between us. I pull up to the apartments across the street from the compound, refusing to take any risk where she could be at the brunt of it.

I twist in my seat to face her. "Thank you again for your time tonight, for sharing your personal life with me. You've definitely presented to me some things to consider. If I can make one request of you, it is to keep this night between us, for both of our safety."

"I've always kept our conversations confidential," she says, authentically.

I trust her, more so now than ever before. I have no reason not to. Who else can I turn to right now with complete honesty of where I'm at spiritually? Kamal? Sanafi? Nayef? Rana in some ways, but not without placing pressure on her to follow. Lydia stands alone in this.

I watch her pull on the handle, step out, begin her trek toward her place, when suddenly I remember. The dream. I pop the door, jump up, call out to her just loud enough for her to hear. Whipping her head around, I go to meet her a few meters beyond the car.

"I forgot to tell you about something," I explain, now standing in front of her as dim yellowish light etches across her face through the darkness. "I didn't know who else to ask...I was hoping you might be able to help me."

"Help you with what?"

"Last night I experienced a vivid dream, one that left me waking up remembering every little detail, thinking it really happened. It was different, unique to say the least. I was crawling on the desert in need of hydration for mere survival in unbearable pain, as the relentless sun drained all life from my soul. When I made it to the top of a hill, I saw it, life beaming from a nearby palm. I utilized all of my remaining strength to make it there; however, the moment I arrived, the water vanished. Hopelessness consumed me and brought me to my knees. I closed my eyes accepting death. That's when a sudden whisper pierced my ears saying, 'Umar, I am...,' but it faded away, reminding me of something, the past coming to fruition. When I opened my eyes, she was before me blinding me with the purest white light. She was holding a full glass of sparkling water. Barely able to move my lips, I pleaded to her for a sip. Then suddenly a coughing attacks me and I'm unable to control it. I panic staring into the softest set of loving eyes taking hold of me. Then she told me a profound statement, that the water I was seeking would never quench my thirst nor bring me life because it was dead. Then she dumped the water into the sand, as I cried out in an attempt to stop her. This is when I awoke. What do you think it means? Or do you think It's nothing?"

A blank stare is all I'm given.

"Never mind, don't worry about it; I shouldn't have said anything," I say, embarrassed, upset that I mentioned it.

"No, no, wait, I was trying to recall something to share with you. God reveals Himself to us in many different ways. Throughout the Scriptures Jesus tells people He will quench their thirst. One particular time comes to mind when you were talking is when Jesus was traveling through Samaria, which Jews refused to set foot in, when fatigue brought Him to rest near a well. A Samaritan woman came to draw water from the well. He asked her for a drink. She questioned why He, being a Jew, would ask her, a Samaritan woman, for a drink because Jews had no dealings with Samaritans. Jesus told her that if she knew the gift of God and who it was asking for a drink, she would have asked Him and He would have given her living water. She told Him He had nothing to draw water from the deep well, so where would He get the living water? She asked Him if He was greater than Jacob who they inherited this well from, the very well he and his family drank from? Jesus said to her, 'Whoever drinks of this water will thirst again, but whoever drinks of the water that I shall give him will never thirst. But the water that I shall give him will become in him a fountain of water springing up into everlasting life.'

"One more passage I can recall is on the last day of the feast when Jesus cried out to all the people, 'If anyone thirsts, let him come to Me and drink. He who believes in Me, as the Scripture has said, out of his heart will flow rivers of living water.'"

Stunned. Unable to believe the implications of her words, I can't deny this direct answer to my dream. Conflicting thoughts begin confronting one another, loosening a family of entrenched emotions.

"This is all I can think of. I hope it's helpful," she says, sincerely.

"Yes, it has helped; thank you," is all I can let out.

We hold gazes for a few timeless seconds before she departs from me again. I don't realize I'm still standing undisturbed until she disappears under the night sky. In the car, my mind plays back what she shared. Is this what my mother was referring to? The water I need is not from a well, not from this earth, but only found in Jesus? This is no coincidence; the pieces have fallen where they belong. To believe this means to forsake Muhammad, Allah. The mere thought jolts me with a tremble from a deep-rooted fear. I instantly repent, crying out, "Allah forgive me. There is no God but Allah and Muhammad is his messenger; cast these evil thoughts away from me, please!" What have I been doing? What great deception in bringing me away from the truth of Islam! This must be from my lack of prayer, my ignorance of the Qur'an, turning my back on Noor. I flick the headlights on, pull out into the empty dark streets, foot heavy on the gas.

Chapter Fifteen

Back in the hotel room, Qur'an safely resting on my lap, I comb over the time spent with Noor recently, his heightened zeal for Islam, the talk with Sanafi, the meeting with the Sheikh Faisal and his teachings on the Qur'an and Islam. Comparing it to what I've studied, my understanding of it, all leaves me with three different views. In frustration, I flip the book open and begin reading in hopes of reconciling the differing positions.

Hours of study drift by. Instead of coming to any agreement, I only become more convinced of my doubts, that this book may not be inspired. The conclusions remain unwavering. Then, a voice of warning whispers inside.

"Are you rejecting the prophet, Muhammad? Islam? This means rejecting Allah. Wrath will swiftly come upon you for such blasphemy."

My fear grows. Bones tremble. I quickly pray, "O forgive me these thoughts. Have mercy on your servant. If I have gone astray, bring me back to the truth. What have I done to deserve this? I've loved you from my childhood, attempted to give my own life for your sake the way Muhammad taught all of us by living it out himself, but was it not you who prevented it from being completed? What am I to do?

All I've ever wanted is to please you. Where have I gone wrong? Was it not you who led me to Lydia? Was all the love, all the gentleness she showed me fake? What of the feelings I experience when with her unlike with anyone else? O, Allah, help me! I'll stay here as long as you desire, patiently waiting to hear from you. Please answer your servant." Curled up on the floor, I cry myself to sleep.

When I wake it's still dark outside. My mind wastes no time in picking up where it left off last night. Suddenly a noise coming from behind me by the bathroom interrupts. My body begins grieving in fear that Allah's punishment has finally come for me. I have no chance of escaping or defeating what comes upon me if it's his wrath against me. My attention remains fixed on the small beam of light penetrating through the open window onto the edge of the golden knob, refusing the subtlest blink in fear of missing the initial attack.

After what seems to be about twenty minutes, I crawl up onto the bed, convinced the noise most likely came from next door. Fatigued physically, mentally, unable to sleep, I sit feeling broken, wanting to give up on life. As tears roll off my cheeks, I call out to Allah.

"You know I love you. I've loved you my entire life. I need your help. I need you to show me where you are. In my confusion, if I've strayed from you it has not been intentional. Forgive me."

I take a second to ask myself why I needed to inquire from an Imam, a sheikh, a scholar for answers when I could have found them myself through diligent study and research? Am I really seeking the truth or for answers to reinforce my beliefs in Islam and hatred toward Jews and Christians? Suddenly the dream flashes before me, along with Lydia's statements. I have an unmistakable urge to go to the place only my mother and I shared in order to escape the pressures of life, the one place I've avoided since her death. Maybe this is exactly what I need, to visit our place, to think of her, grieve for her if possible anymore, to look at everything from a fresh perspective.

In no time, I'm on the bare streets expecting anything, lights tracing through the windows faster and faster. I'm not paying attention to any of it, only the destination. As I pull onto the sandy road northeast of Riyadh, it leads me straight ahead one kilometer, before recognizing the shadows in the distance signaling my arrival. I kill the engine welcoming the blackness that swarms me until my eyes adjust to the starlight.

Being here again begins stirring my heart, my emotions, emerging a peculiar memory. About two years ago on the morning of my critical playoff game, she brought me here to watch the sunrise, to talk. The words of advice she spoke to me I can still recite to this day. She took my hand in hers, looked straight into my eyes, then said, "Son, don't ever deny yourself the truth. And when someone gives you advice or counsel, listen carefully, question, investigate, but don't accept it as being the truth or definitive. Search out the matter for the evidence using logic and reason. "Remember, the only way truth can hide is if you're rejecting it." At the time, I didn't regard her words as being relevant to me, never thought much about it, my focus strictly on the coming game. What underlying meaning was she conveying to me?

I step out, feet grinding against the sand below, peering off into the distance, catching the draping branches of a special lone date palm, not far from the others. I slowly make my way toward it, sand sinking beneath my feet with each new step. Halfway there, the separation between the branches is now visible. The deep crevices aligning the trunk are becoming darker, as the light reflects off each little hump above. It sits surrounded by waves of sandy fields, sand of the purest gold harboring not even the slightest trace of camel tracks.

Finally reaching it, I remain still for a moment, taking it all in, sifting through my past memories like a picture book. Then, without preparation, collapse to my knees as a flood of emotions hit me. Everything that's happened rushes to the surface, drowning me in a sea of questions I have found unanswerable. Restlessness leaving me in a fatigued state. Then come the doubts: what if I've been deceived my whole life? That the truth lies with the Christian, with my mother, with Lydia? What will I do?

I try my hardest to ignore them, but they have grown too strong. I can't live like this anymore. The daily torment, the sufferings, the unbearable nakedness and uncertainty, this must end once and for all.

As panic strikes in me, fear of facing Allah's punishment for such thoughts, I cry out to god with all my might, "No, I will not cower this time until I know the truth. There is no more hiding, running in fear of losing everything, of dying. I have lost my precious mother and Tariq. I've lost my passion in life for playing soccer. My relationship with my father and other family members has diminished. Rana, whom I love so dearly, I have been treating with great disrespect lately, along with Kamal because of my dedication to following Islam.

I've found there are no answers outside of you, only a land of shadowed questions. I'm seeking you now God. Whichever side you're on, whether it be the Christians, Jews, Hindus, Buddhists or Muslims, I will follow you. Please show me the way. Reveal yourself to me."

Unchallenged streams begin flowing down my face. I feel the despair, like being lost in the endless ravaging of blue ocean waters, floating in an orange safety raft, helpless, bloodied lips from dehydration, convincing myself it will be better to fall into the water with the sharks than to survive through this. Then, an inner voice tells me, "The truth lies in your hands. But do you really want it? Are you willing to surrender your soul for it? Be honest with yourself."

"Oh, God, do not leave me like this. Do not forsake your servant. Please, have mercy on me. I am now willing to follow you wherever you lead me," I let out in desperation, thrusting my forearms into the sand over and over again, fists clenched like hammers, my eyes squeezing as tight as possible. I lay in a prostrated position for some time, waiting for an answer. Completely submitted, I sit upright, halfway opening my eyes, noticing the stars vanishing, being replaced by a soft shade of blue filling the sky. This is the precise time we would show up, admiring the transformation of the yellow sphere emerging on the horizon. I look to the oasis, to the lush palm before me, then lower my gaze.

What is it? How long has it been here? Where did it come from? The questions rapidly fire at me. I reach down, grabbing hold of the black piece of cotton poking through the sand. Giving it a little tug fails to budge it. Something is anchoring it, something I don't wish to lose. I begin digging around it exposing blacker the deeper I go. The shape of the object is slowly revealed, a book of some kind. I carefully lift it out, unwrap the cloth securely holding it, protecting it from the sand's eroding effects. The gold words gleam against the black background: Holy Bible. I freeze as a stone pillar. A shiver shoots down my spine. There's no doubt in my mind this is an answer to all of what I have been searching for. This has to be hers, but how would she...I know. Just as he used to do, Kamal would wait inside the car while my mother and I visited with each other.

I settle back against the trunk of the palm under the dawn's watchful eye, opening the book. I flip through the pages, briefly reading random verses not knowing where to begin or what to read until I discover a small piece of paper, folded, tucked away in the book named John. I feel an urge to begin here, begin where she last left off.

Through the first three chapters, I'm amazed by the words of Jesus, by the power I feel in what is written, different than anything I've ever read before. Continuing into the next chapter, I immediately recognize the story, the same one Lydia told me last night. Reading it myself moves me, guides me in reflecting back on the dream in excitement: she was pointing me to Jesus, the only One who is able to quench this thirst in my soul! I spend an unknown amount of time pondering the implications, then something strong is drawing me back to the words. Chapter after chapter, I discover a rhetoric unmatched by the Qur'an, an elegance girded with an undeniable cohesiveness. Soon, I reach the second passage Lydia recited to me, this time stopping in astonishment. What are the odds of both of the examples she shared with me being from the same book I'm reading? Can I honestly deny such a divine appointment? "If anyone thirsts, let him come to me and drink. He who believes in Me, as the Scripture has said, out of his heart will flow rivers of living water."

A terrible fear, a feeling of panic grips me tightly, more so than ever before. If I'm considering this book to be true, then all others must be false. "No...I can't do this. What am I thinking?" The book slams shut in my hands. Then, I hear her subtle whisper in my ear, "Don't deny yourself the truth, Son. Open it. Quit running away scared; you've done this for far too long already. With truth always comes sacrifice. You must stand up and face it now."

Recruiting all my strength, taking hold of the little courage I possess, the book opens, I press on. It begins captivating me, entrenched by its depth, time having no importance, unaware of my surroundings. It comes quick – unexpectedly – piercing my heart with one decisive thrust. There's no reading on, no need to. Everything merges here, now, on this very verse: "I am the way, the truth and the life. No one comes to the Father except through Me."

I can feel a new hope infiltrating my soul. The combination of all the experiences over the last week was culminating, leading me to this precise moment in time. Yet, there's the fear of losing everything holding me back. I will have nothing, will be killed or have to flee for my life. The tears come again, pouring from my cheeks in my pleading to God. "Is this from you? Why must it be the way of the Christians? Is there any other way without such great sacrifice? O, God, have mercy on your servant. What do you want from me?"

Out of nowhere, a still small voice consumes all my senses, "Let yourself go; completely surrender to Him."

The powerful force that has bound me for so long suddenly releases me: "O, God, I surrender to you, I choose to follow you no matter the sacrifice, no matter the consequences. I believe that Jesus died on the cross for my sins, was buried and resurrected on the third day. I give my life to you entirely. I surrender to you Lord, I surrender...to you."

Eyes closed, head raised toward the heavens, I sit back pressed up against the trunk, trails of tears traveling down my neck absorbing into my thobe. It comes upon me like a strong gust of wind - the evil I have held in my innermost soul is gone. That emptiness being occupied by hate and anger is now replaced with peace, a peace I never knew existed. "Thank you, Lord, thank you so much," I mumble through brokenness, more grateful than I have ever been.

My thoughts switch to my mother. In this new comfort, a sense of guilt is present in how I treated her those last days of her life. I could have done more. "Forgive me, God. I loved her so much, more than I'm able to express with words."

However, a joy awakens to the realization that she's in heaven right now where we will one day be reunited because of the abundant grace, love and mercy we have been shown by our God. This makes me think of Lydia, all she's done for me, her soft, loving heart that has played a major part in me coming to put my faith and trust in Christ as my Lord and Savior. My disrespect, hardened expressions toward her, ungrateful ways and not once did she waver in the midst of it all but kept her integrity, her loving ways. Oh, how blind I've been.

I have the desire to call her. To tell her what's happened, thank her, ask for forgiveness. I have the urge to tell everyone, Rana, Kamal, the entire family. I know this can't be done though, unless I don't want to live to see tomorrow. The Book calls me to read more. I continue until morning, a blossoming young flower, for the first time tasting the sweetness of the truth. I am coming face to face with the Almighty God. The air is warm now, infiltrating my thobe without remorse, the yellow ball of light hanging in the distance. The day no longer feels dead, but alive, injected with a new purpose. Closing the Bible, I wonder what's next? What am I supposed to do now? Then reality hits me. The sacrifices I must endure: fleeing from my homeland, leaving my family behind and everything I've ever held dear to my heart. I knew this was a prerequisite to becoming a follower of Christ; it just hurts, hurts more now that it's coming to fruition.

"O, God, in your grace you called me to Jesus fully knowledgeable of what trials it would bring me. I trust you in leading me through difficult times by revealing to me what I should do. Please guide me according to what you desire of me, offering me a way out of this death sentence," I call out, eyes in the clouds above.

Time advances. Still no answer. I decide to return to the hotel to eat, shower and rest if my mind allows me. Beginning to wrap the black cloth around the Bible, a thought prevents me. This was my mother's. One of her only belongings I possess. Shouldn't I keep it? My keffiyeh will make a suitable trade. Wrapping it tightly around the book, I place it neatly back inside the hole, then watch it fade under each push of sand. I hate to leave it behind, but the risk is too great taking it with me. The stretch from standing relieves the stiffness accumulated during the long sit. From this position, I have a clear view of the city, teeming with life – with everything I've thrived on, identified with, loved. A few minutes are taken to look at it through the eyes of a new creation, with a new perspective.

Back in my room, I can't do anything but think of Lydia. I know she's working, but maybe if I try to call right now, I will catch her on break, if she even takes one. My phone is already in hand; impatience building, I press the green call button. Ring after ring echoes into my ear. At the brink of giving up, she finally picks up. "Hello," I hear, in a curious, hesitant tone. The excitement of hearing her soft serenading voice causes me to dismiss the warning.

"Hey, I apologize for calling while you're working...I couldn't wait any longer without telling you."

"Telling me what?" she asks, with a trace of caution.

"As dawn broke, I made the most important decision of my life...I placed my faith and trust in Christ as my Lord and Savior," I reply, joyfully.

Silence ensues.

"Did you hear me?"

"Yes, I heard you," she responds, in words broken by the invasion of tears. "I'm so happy for you. Praise God! Glory be to Him."

My heart softens, aches for her, to console her in some unknown way.

"Well, I don't want to keep you too long, can I see you again sometime soon? I have many questions I would like to discuss with you."

"How about tomorrow night at eight o'clock?"

"Where? The same place I dropped you off at?"

"Yes."

"Thank you. I owe you so much," I say, feeling indebted to her. "I'll see you tomorrow. God be with you."

"See you soon. Remember to pray about those questions. He will answer you in ways I never can, directing you to the path He's set before you."

"I will."

"Oh, God, thank you for her." I don't know what I would do without her. Comfort fills me. Always has when hearing her voice. The only difference now is I accept the fiery attraction I've always felt for her, welcome it rather. The love I feel for her has been freed from bondage, just as my very own soul has been. What to do with it is the challenge needing to be confronted.

Tired, noticing it now when reclining back on the bed, I get up in hopes of thwarting it with a cold shower. Pulling off my thobe, the contact from something hard makes me freeze in disbelief. How did I not realize it when I called? I retrieve the phone; the one Noor gave me. This explains her sad behavior I brushed off as nothing. She knows I'm the one who texted her the time of the beheading in Deera Square, who called her...hanging up when she answered in order to follow her home. How did I miss this? Embarrassed, disappointed in myself for such an obvious mistake, I wonder what's going through her mind. The more I ponder it, the more content I am with the situation. Eventually, it would have come up. This way, she has time to process her feelings toward me, about seeing me again.

The ice-cold water splashes against my back, swelling my chest with short gasps of air followed by longer labored ones to maintain the steady flow of oxygen to my lungs. After a minute of this, I jump out keenly awake, rejuvenated with a new vigor. Towel wrapped around me, soaking up every last drop, my post-game ritual comes to mind of spending thirty minutes in an ice bath.

I'm convinced Kamal has spoken with my father about what happened, where I've been all along. He's always treated me as his favorite nephew, loving me like his own, yet always maintaining a respectful distance. This has allowed him the comfort of never getting too attached, emotionally connected, protecting his heart from being ripped again. Out of nowhere, a strong voice tells me, "Go see him." I can feel this is the right thing to do. No time to waste. I'm dressed, out of the lobby, in the driver seat, on my way in minutes.

The city is different now. I'm offered a whole new realm of beauty to admire, a new vision, a new found love for every person I'm given. A new freshness is in the air, a thankfulness for the warm rays reaching my flesh. I take it all in gliding along the course to Kamal, not far from the hotel. A part of me doesn't want to see him, to see the disappointment forming his face. He's spent almost two decades dedicated to me, training me to be the best player in the Kingdom. He's now convinced I've thrown it all away.

Pulling up to the house, I take a moment to pray before getting out. Not confident in what to expect. I hit the door three times waiting patiently. It cracks open revealing Kamal's scarred, apathetic face. Unexpectedly he seems quite delighted to see me, embracing me with affection. He closes the door behind us, leads me to an open sitting area, where he insists I sit before a meal he's prepared, before disappearing into the kitchen. As fast as he leaves, he reappears with a cup in one hand, a handful of kebabs in the other, adding them to the rest.

"Good timing," he says, offering a rare, but powerful smile.

"I'm glad I chose to come," I respond, returning the smile. "It's been a while since my last meal."

He fills my cup with freshly brewed tea, takes a kebab in his mouth, ripping a chunk of chicken off. He's never been one for many words, but there is something different. I can feel it, sense it in his demeanor, learning to read him over the years. He knows. Waiting on me to be the first to bring it up tonight, isn't he? We continue to eat in silence 'til I finish organizing my thoughts, having to convey what happened and where I'm at right now without sharing the significance of my faith in Christ. I finish chewing the last bite of chicken off the skewer – wash it down with tea – look at Kamal, stare into him, until he meets my gaze.

"A lot has happened lately. I don't see any benefit in revisiting it at this time. Much of it I regret, am saddened by, some I still hold guilt from, but in the end, I found an unspeakable gift, which has led me here this day. What's next? This question remains unanswered: a mystery."

"Your father came to me, his heart bleeding grief because of Tariq. What a great tragedy for the family. Many are praying in hopes of not hearing your name delivered next," he shares, hiding any personal position on the matter. "He also briefly mentioned how you attacked him, not showing the slightest inclination of remorse, but with a hateful rage. I'm not going to sit here and ask you to explain what happened. I'm more concerned about you right now. Whatever is pressuring you into this other way of life, you can always come to me to talk about it. We are family, Umar. Everyone makes mistakes, yet you will have to face Allah for taking the lives of innocent women and children who happen to be in the same place as your target." Does he know of my failure? He must be basing this off the direction of my pursuits. I watch his eyes moisten, his focus solely upon me amidst the intense hollow sound in the room.

"My wife and unborn son were taken from me in this manner." He pauses and as fast as the wetness appears it leaves, depleted of its wanton softness, dried up by the thirsty flame of pain. "I don't want to lose you by being on the other side of it."

I'm forced to bow my head in order to hide the rush of emotions, rapidly blinking away the convergence. He's never talked to me in this way, sharing affection so intimately. "I'm all too familiar with the grief that becomes an infection to the soul, slowly eating its way from the inside out, never leaving day or night. Nowhere to escape. It constantly reminds you of the love that once existed, yet will never be experienced again. And every attempt to distract it only feeds it, allowing it to become more pervasive. She's gone forever, Umar. Don't become like me. Don't get trapped in the dark city of your own soul, refusing to return to reality. It is a great deception, offering a taste of comfort, where guilt vanishes and numbness massages your every thought. No matter how real it seems, how heart ripping it may be, you must leave her behind. You must say goodbye."

Drop after drop continues splashing against the floor below, between my feet. Thoughts of how much I love her, miss her, of the guilt and shame, all unleash from the untouched depths of my heart. Once opened, I can't stop it. Unanswered questions still looming. Body kneeling at the feet of death. Then the light breaks through reminding me of where she's at. That we will be reunited one day. Comfort takes over, a gratefulness to God.

When my eyes quit dripping, discreetly wiping at my cheeks with the sleeve of my thobe, I lift my head, am enlightened by how badly I needed to release the pain I've stuffed for so long. Kamal understands this, more than anyone. He undoubtedly cares about me, probably loves me more than I'm aware of under his calloused facade. However, still fighting against what lies deep within the chambers of his own heart. I don't say anything, just show my face. He repositions himself, followed by the sound of his low, steady words.

"Not long after your disappearance, I tried calling you. No one knew where to find you. Your teammates needed you, needed Tariq; they were lost without you," his voice tightens. "From the time you were little, running around infatuated with the ball, I know you possessed the ability to be one of the best if you would choose to dedicate yourself to the game not only physically, but mentally as well. Taking control of the mind is critical. It is what creates the separation between the good and the elite. You have always displayed this, as I emphasized it over and over again during training, after training, all the time. But this vanished when your mother died. Not only the control, the hunger to be the best player on the field could no longer be found either. This is the most pivotal time in your life." He breaks for a moment, fixed on my receptiveness. "Have all these years devoted to training you been for nothing or do you desire to step back on the field with that same passion as before? You have to decide."

This puts me in a complicated position. For one, I owe it to Kamal after all he's done, yet my heart now yearns for something greater than anything in this world. Unless God wants me to continue down this path to serve Him in some way, I can't say yes. At a loss for clarity, for words, I call out to God in my mind, while lowering my eyes to the floor.

"Oh, God, there are two paths in front of me, one leading to another country, the other playing here again with death possible at any given time. Please reveal to me the way You will for me to travel down. Whatever may come, I will gladly accept as long as I know it's where You want me to be. You know the love I hold for You. Let me know which side to take." Waiting, everything is silent; nothing comes. Time is running out. I feel the pressure from Kamal's expecting presence when a memory out of nowhere replays vaguely in my mind. "You were born to play soccer," my mother told me, watching one of my recorded games with me.

"Thank you, God. Thank you," I say within. This is exactly what I needed. An assurance of who I am and what God has gifted me with. "I'm ready to play again," I genuinely let out.

His expression instantly brightens. "I knew you would come back. I was expecting it." He quickly stands, walks from the room only to return holding a white envelope. "I've been meaning to give you something. First, I had to confirm your allegiance to play. A day after I was asked if I've seen you, I received a call from a man representing a soccer club in Italy. He said he was unsuccessful in reaching you." All my senses peek in curiosity, in anticipation for what's coming next. He stalls by breaking eye contact, dipping his head as if disappointment sets in.

"They want to sign you," he finally reveals, face radiating with delight.

God is the first thing that comes to mind. My answer to prayer, giving me a way out, a path to follow. He is guiding me according to His plans. One wrong decision, one wrong answer along the way would have crumbled it all. The news contributes to the live stream flowing from my face thinking of the abundant grace God is blessing me with: a safe place to live, a career I've always dreamed of, all of the little things I so easily pass over. Why bless me? I don't deserve this. Only early this morning have I come to know You. Then the answer comes in a wave of love falling over me: it's not about anything you've done or haven't done; it's a gift from above.

I throw my arms around Kamal as far as they will reach. Excited, thankful, emotions displayed at the highest possible level from all that has happened. When we release each other, he's holding out the envelope. "What is this?" I ask.

"Open it." I reach out, take the envelope, lift the flap. A passport and a thick stack of Liras slide out. "Remember when I drove you to get your picture taken? I've always known this day would come. Prepared for it. The money is what your mother saved up for you over the years. There is enough for the plane ticket, six months of rent if needed and anything else until you sign your contract. I exchanged it for you yesterday."

"When did she give you this?" I question.

"About seven months before her death," he replies, softly, looking away.

She knew the threat on her life was imminent, didn't she? This means she was following Christ for at least seven months. I tuck this information away, will address it at a later date when alone.

"She always believed in you. Loved you more than you know."

"Thank you for everything."

"Are you going to call him?" he asks, his business acumen seeking the finalization of this opportunity.

"I no longer have a phone. That's why I never answered any calls," I explain, recalling the night it was handed over to Noor.

"His name is Marco," Kamal says, pulling out his phone, tapping at the screen, extending it out to me. I hold it to my ear, the echoing of the ring stirring up nervousness, doubting this can truly happen for me, as I'm forever feeling the grasp of struggle around my neck, stripping me of life each moment I attempt to pull away.

"Hello?"

"Hello, Marco, this is Umar Kalawi. I apologize for the delay in my response to your calls. I lost my phone and have been dealing with all of that lately."

"Don't worry about it, things happen. I see your uncle Kamal relayed the message. It's good to finally speak with you. I represent A.S. Roma in Italy. My purpose for calling is regarding a proposition for you. We've been watching you for some time now and are very impressed. You possess a unique set of skills we think can make you an elite forward in this league for many years to come. We want you to join our club, to come play for A.S. Roma. With the addition of your talent, we will no doubt be playing for the championship this year. What do you say?"

I feel the chains of bondage crumble before me, replaced by a grove of love and peace. I control the excitement, hold my composure long enough to answer. "Yes, I would love to play for you."

"Great. We prefer to fly you out in two days if that's alright with you...if you need more time let me know?"

"No, two days is plenty of time."

"I'll take care of the plane ticket and cover all other expenses involved in the transition. Tomorrow you will receive a call from one of my assistants explaining everything in detail. If you have any questions, she will be able to help you. I'm looking forward to meeting with you, but most of all, seeing you on the field. Oh, before I forget, is there anyone else you would like to accompany you on this trip?"

I think of Rana, Kamal, Lydia. What's Lydia's last name? Not knowing what to do, I press mute, take a few moments, ask Kamal.

"He's offering to fly you out with me, if you're not busy."

"I can't go on such short notice," he says, "I will be out there soon enough."

Marco continues before I'm able to respond. "Take as much time as you need. You can tell my assistant your decision tomorrow."

"Thank you for this opportunity...see you soon."

"My pleasure, Umar. Goodbye."

I take a moment to absorb the impact of what just took place. The dream I've been waiting for all my life has finally come true. His words only now begin to sink in. I notice Kamal staring vividly at me, patiently anticipating the details.

"I'm flying out in two days!" Disbelief paralyzes me temporarily by saying it. Kamal's face transforms into a joy I've never witnessed to this day.

"I've always believed in you; it was only a matter of time."

Seeing him like this is bittersweet, receiving the opportunity of a lifetime, but at the same time having to leave him behind, leaving all I've ever known behind for a foreign country.

"You're not coming with me?" I ask, concerned.

His expression quickly dims, releases a deep sigh. "No. You're on your own now. You don't need me anymore."

"You're my trainer. You've taught me everything I know. What am I going to do without you? Who's going to train me? You have to come," I plead.

"You will have new trainers over there teaching you."

"They don't know me like you do, how to push me beyond the limits I set upon myself."

"Umar, I belong here, in the Kingdom. This was the plan all along. You must understand the satisfaction, the glimpse of happiness you have brought to me this day. Now it's time for you to move forward in life, focus on being the best player in Italy. Your mother would be proud of you. She never stopped believing you would make it. Same with Tariq. Go do what you've been called to do."

My heart's crushed at his name, at his dream to play professionally, at the path to death I led him down. God forgive me. Through his words, I'm not too excited to let her name pass by without wondering his mention of her in this manner. What are his true feelings for her?

"Promise me you'll fly out on more than one occasion to watch me play? I will make sure you're on the sidelines next to me."

"I agree to this," he concedes, concealing a smirk as if already expecting to do just this. "Don't for one second think I'll miss a game. I'll be right here watching each one, calling you afterward to discuss your performance minute by minute."

Hours slip by reminiscing about the past, trying to retain the plethora of knowledge Kamal is sharing with me concerning the transition to Italy: the business and contractual aspect of signing with the team, the management of finances, getting into a house, everything that seems to slip my mind. Throughout this time, in the midst of celebration, a loss settles somewhere inside. Acknowledging his lost soul, his desperate need for healing, Kamal is someone whom I love dearly. I ask God if I should tell him. All that comes to my mind is "Patience." Regardless of how badly I desire to share, I trust God's timing and keep my mouth shut. His reasons are beyond my understanding. A loud ring interrupts; Kamal answers, says a few words and hangs up.

"I have to go," he says, cold-faced once again.

We rise to our feet, walk to the door, he embraces me.

"What time tomorrow night do you want me to stop by...to say goodbye?"

"Any time after four I'll be home," he answers, handing me Marco's number.

I enclose it within my fist. "See you then. Thank you for everything."

Chapter Sixteen

The call to prayer echoes through the streets over the monotone sound of voicemail playing back. I hang up, send a message instead, explaining the urgency in needing to see her as soon as possible. Time's running out. I refuse to step on the plane without telling her about the transformation, without inviting her to join me. I love her too much not to, would never forgive myself if I didn't. Exactly how to go about it, what words to use, is where I'm confused. But I trust God will guide me according to His will providing the words I need. Maybe I should just drop by? Is tonight her night or Nayef's other wife's? The comfort of the bed beneath me begins drawing my eyes closed. After what feels like an hour in battle, I'm defeated. Blackness welcomes me.

My mind awakens, eyes thrust open, feeling the worry control my hands in a scramble to find the phone. One eighteen in the morning. No missed calls, no messages. Accepting the circumstances, I turn off the light, lay back down, expecting a draining, restless day tomorrow.

The muezzin's voice once again wakes me to consciousness. My body is still trained to the ingrained alarm. I'm reminded of the required trek to the nearest mosque in order to recite the daily prayer day after day, yet never feeling anything different inside except the well-acquainted insatiable hunger. I kneel and instead pray to my God from the heart, the God who has filled me with that unexplainable peace. Afterward, I shower, preparing myself for this final day in the

Kingdom, my homeland, confident I will stay alive - not by my own power, but by God's. He will align the pieces so they fall precisely where they belong, sustaining me through this last day.

The riyals stack nicely into one thick bundle next to the phones on the bed. I don't trust leaving them, even though I have one more night here. The black outside the windows is shifting to lighter shades of the softest blue, signaling it's time. I conceal the money and the phones in my thobe on my way out. The lobby is quiet, empty except for the same man behind the desk. He must never leave. I step outside the door, the crisp dawn air rushes against my face, invading my lungs with a welcoming morning. I accept all it offers with joy. A new appreciation is experienced for the countless attributes of nature. Unlike before, I'm keenly aware of the new world introducing itself to me. As if for the first time I'm able to see everything in its beauty. It's liveliness filled with the breath of God. I don't allow the busy streets, mostly men filing out of the mosques as they finish fajr, to disrupt my new wonder of the world around me.

The drive is slow, methodical, far different than the previous time with my mind under constant fire, watching the buildings pass by. I have to come one last time alone, to tie together the loose ends dangling from my heart. I park a distance away from the other cars filling the lot. The door opens. I step out, immune from any doubt, slowing my pace. The first step into the square injects me with a flurry of images covered in blood. I ignore them as best as I know how with each successive step until reaching the memory of her imprinted headless body crumpled on the ground. The stone is dry, living in the shadows for now, as the golden sphere is too low to reach it over the arching structures. Completely deserted, I take some extra time. Time to gather my composure, all of my strength.

Ready now, I close my eyes, ask for the courage to face the fear, to slowly open the gates of death, prepare for the unforgettable memories to be conjured up from that day. The scene destined to haunt me to my grave. Giving it permission to come, just this once, with all it encompasses. There she is, kneeling before me, so vulnerable, innocent, petite, yet invigorated by an unbroken spirit sensed in her posture. I see myself, blindly standing there, prideful, selfish, unwilling to stand up for her, speak to her, plead for her life. I'm the betrayer. I left her when she needed me the most. He was with her though, through it all. Her peace, her strength, all from Him. I was too blind to see it. How much did she wish to speak to me about Christ? Eating her up on the inside for who knows how long. What was she thinking? Her heart feeling? Maybe disappointed with herself she kept silent? Whatever was on her heart those last moments, I only now understand the hope she carried with her to death. The hope of life with Jesus after the blade would reach her neck.

Uncontrollable anguish suddenly cripples me to the stone below. Guilt's presence is all I feel, crying out for forgiveness...why did it have to happen like this? Then I'm touched with the realization that if it didn't happen this way, I wouldn't have reached the point of broken-ness required.

My hand hangs low, dragging against the gritty rock, less intense than the thick stickiness of a seducing crimson lake pulling me under. All I'm able to do is stay prostrated in complete submission to the purpose of me being here. Time fades, the yellow rays nearly touching me now, temperature rising, the words come so gently. "Your grief is temporary, your life eternal where you will one day be reunited."

A peace sweeps through my heart, that one of a kind peace I've only experienced at the date palm. I lift my head to the spotless blue sky above, whispering, "Thank you, God, thank you."

My time here is finished. Rising to my feet, the pairs of eyes following me from the shadows, now inside the square, become apparent. Their curious glances amount to nothing though. This is why I leave them behind where my feet will never touch down again. Both visits will be inscribed on my heart forever, embedded in my soul.

I hold comfort in knowing this is what she desired all along. Maybe not in this exact way, but it has been granted ultimately. Finally releasing the nightmares that were ripping away at my wounds. Tonight's obligations surface at the sight of the grayest airplane gliding on high overhead. What to do until then? Yes, one more time, I need to do it. I take the next right, about ten minutes away. Extra attention is paid to my people driving all around me, walking along the city's streets, so hardened, private, I long for their brokenness, for their eyes to be opened.

My family comes to mind. Rana. Reminding me to check my

phone. One missed message. How didn't I hear it? "Sorry it took so long to get back. I've been dealing with some things. Can't meet tonight; Nayef's over. Early morning before work is best for me if this works for you? Oh, yeah, Lydia's last name is Popova." I tap the little message box.

"See you in the morning. It's an emergency. Love you."

I immediately send the information to Marco's secretary. This doesn't give me much time. Guess I don't need it.

In the distance, the field shows itself. The very field my feet have run thousands of miles on. It's empty this early; only the faded blades of green grass and white goal posts reside, inviting players of all ages to compete. Kamal used to pick me up, bring me here, push me until I collapsed from exhaustion, unable to get up. He would then pull me up by a single outstretched arm. My respect for him continued to increase. I never wanted to quit on him, to see the look of disappointment on his face. I'd looked up to him as a father figure I never had, feeling as though the connection was established from the first kick. I will miss his absence, but I have something greater now. It's my turn to share, to pour into him something more significant than his time with me.

Getting out, each step is contemplated, retracing the endless blood, sweat and sacrifice spilled over the years. Ball cresting in the pit of my arm, having pulled it from the trunk where I've kept one since the day I bought the car, I drop it when reaching midfield, not allowing it to touch the ground. Using my feet, head, knees and chest, it pops up and down with an array of synchronized balancing taps learned from years of training. Concentration engaged, coming so naturally, I begin closing in on the chosen number. One more bounce...the ball launches off my head, setting up a strike on its descend. Looking to the net, back to the ball, boom! The one-thousandth hit, my right foot connects just before touching the ground, sinking it into the middle of the net. I stand, watching it, eventually dropping to one knee. How will I compare against my teammates in Italy? My opponents? I take one last three-hundred-and-sixty-degree turn, extracting all the memories created here until filled. Exhale a deep breath, time to move forward. I will never forget. I leave the ball resting in the back of the net, it belongs here in its rightful home.

When I make it to the driver's seat, I take a moment to flip through all my teammates' faces over the years, the friendships built. The likelihood that I will never play with them again, ever see them, yet how desperate they are to be forgiven for their sins, for salvation, for the truth. Each face begins dismantling into the stagnant air. Saddened, I cruise away, hoping they will one day find the truth.

The drive takes me across the street from my house, the only one I've ever known, grown up in, called home. The faintest glimpse of the wall and I know it's mine, years spent looking at it. Every crack winding along the entrance, its precise height, the strategic way aligning the house. This too is lost forever. The longer I focus on them the more memories are revived to the forefront.

A slow-moving Mercedes catches my attention. Dipped in gunmetal gray, it looks like Noor's, which breaks my concentration, filling me with a jolt of fear. My eyes fix on the windshield in attempt to make out the driver, but fails as the glare from the white street light makes it impossible. I patiently wait for the distance between us to diminish. Only when it pulls up beside me am I given the opportunity to see into the car. All I'm able to catch is a keffiyeh covering a black pair of thin-rimmed shades. My mind races. Is it him? It's too late now. No doubt he has seen me. My time is up. The moment he takes a left I punch it, whipping the wheel with an unforgiving grip back onto the road. For a few blocks, there is no letting up, tires screeching, hugging every corner, engine roaring with a mouth full of fumes.

With an urgency like never felt before, I'm anticipating my leave. A fresh start. A new life in a new land being led by my new Father. Recognizing my location being near Kamal's, I check the time. Five forty-five. He should be home. Will Noor think to check his place? When was the last time he visited Kamal? I can't recall. It doesn't matter either way. I convince myself, turning left onto his street. This is my last night here.

When the door opens, a flurry of serenading aromas swarm me, causing a smile to curl my lips. I should have known he would never let me go without sharing a final meal together, always displaying the highest degree of hospitality. His countenance isn't as cold as I'm used to. A warmer satisfying expression is awakened while grabbing me in a bear hug. I welcome it, find comfort in it. Entering the sitting room, neatly spaced along the floor is the most beautiful presentation of different dishes. Kamal's always loved to eat, especially if he's given a legitimate reason for such an occasion. I lower myself to the hard surface holding the savory scents at bay.

"I surprise myself in how well I know you," he says, leaving the room.

What does he mean by that? The curious preoccupation with it vanishes when my future meeting with Lydia reemerges, having never really departed. So many questions to ask her, yet not possessing the boldness, the courage, to actually utter them. Kamal returns, sits opposite me, eyes fixed on mine.

"What did you anticipate I would do?" His amused stare hangs for a while. "The only things you've ever been on time for are soccer events or requests from your mother or Rana. This is why I said four o'clock, really expecting your arrival at around six. Thankfully, you proved me right, allowing us to enjoy one last hot meal together. I finished only moments ago." All I'm able to do is laugh. The truth is undeniable. They have always been my priority, meaning the most to me. When he continues staring at me without any inclination of speaking, I inquire, "What is it?"

"I'm proud of you, Umar. Proud that you never gave up on your dreams," he says, in an unfamiliar tone, where the words carry the tenderness of the heart.

I think about how God never gave up on me. A love beyond my understanding.

"You have much to eat," he says, scanning the feast displayed before us.

Hesitation remains a stranger. I haven't eaten all day, being mentally strapped to fulfilling the urging from the Spirit within. The first bite comes from a tender piece of chicken breast draped in the specific spices of Kabsa. We both enjoy the meal with mutual satisfaction, discussing life in Italy, playing soccer, his visits, the progression up to my current position, everything but the most important aspect of me, my transformation. I patiently wait for the opening, having no intentions of disobeying.

Our time together is needed, however, after finishing the filling of our appetites, I begin thinking of when he's going to ask, offering him an opportunity in the brief silence. It comes as I expected it would, shortly after the thought. "Did you receive the email?"

"Yes, a few hours ago," I reply, tapping to bring it up to my screen. "He says he has a ticket for you, insisting you join me."

"I know, he's a good man. I apologize though; right now I'm unable to schedule the required time to dedicate to this trip. Prior obligations take precedence. Next month I will make sure to set an entire week aside to fly out and visit with you."

There's not a doubt he'll keep his promise. I slide the phone back into my pocket, simultaneously peeking at the time: seven-fifty PM. Anxiety pulses through my body. I can see her standing all alone, waiting, trusting my word. I can't be late. "Kamal, I must go. I have an appointment at eight o'clock."

He nods his head in understanding. I follow his lead to our feet, through the house stopping at the front door.

"Thank you for everything. I will never forget all the sacrifices you've endured for me," I say, from the heart, as he gives me a final loving kiss and embrace. At arm's length, moisture gathering in the crevice of his eyes, he offers the nod of approval, of honor, when a boy has become a man worthy of venturing into the world by himself representing all the values and principles instilled in him by his parents. Searching my mind for something to say, nothing comes, but the slight nod in return.

The darkness has settled as dew on the city, offering to replenish my senses with fresh lungs, with signs sparkling in the heavens above, with a deserted peace the desert is conceiving for itself while preparing me for the mission. All of these wonders, yet my concentration is mainly concerned with Lydia, with organizing my thoughts for her. Each second too essential to waste, the speedometer hits seventy. For this time of the evening, the streets are rather empty, offering a less dangerous route. Every corner I maneuver throws the car sideways, tires screeching, the suffocating rubber smell, all while noticing the blurring of buildings as I pass by. I can't afford to be late, to miss my chance.

Pulling into the apartments, there's no sign of her. I continue searching the dimly lit area for a figure, a shadow hiding. Movement grabs my attention in my peripheral, coming directly at my left side from a black enclave tucked between the walkway of two doorways. I watch the figure closing in on me, waiting for the perfect position when the light will reflect off the face. It never comes. The back door opens and for a split second, I think of Noor, until the overhead light flashes on, revealing a colorful abaya, surrounding that beautiful innocence, instantly calming my nerves. There's something different though. Something I can't quite figure out.

"Thank you for seeing me again," I say, meeting her gaze through the rear-view mirror.

"I couldn't refuse your request after hearing about your experience."

The door shuts, welcoming the blackness. A sweet hint of lemon finds its way through the car, reviving me, luring me toward its source. Our destination is one kilometer east of here, a place we must go to offer her the safety she deserves. In a couple of minutes, we pull inside, the parking lot spanning a great area, colorful signs illuminating the sky. I choose a place way in the back, away from any life. The overhead lights shining just enough through the windows allowing us to see the silhouettes of each other. I step out, walk around to the rear passenger side, getting in beside her. The words come pouring out with ease.

"I desperately needed to share this with somebody. You were the only one who came to mind, the only Christian I know," I explain.

"I'm interested in hearing what you want to share with me," she says, shifting into a more comfortable position. I explain everything from the beginning, with every detail except for the extra ticket, my proposal. Tears of joy stream down her blushed cheeks, short snivels, wipes at the face, the nose. Not surprising though, knowing God's limitless abilities to transform a life when surrendered to Him.

"Glory be to God! Only He can intricately weave all of these unique strands into one grand design. The dreams, struggles, the date palm, the Bible, the verses I recommended that fulfilled the dreams...amazing!" she exclaims, eyes sparkling.

All I can do is think about how blessed I am to know such a godly woman. Loving, kind, giving, selfless, an outpouring of attributes I will never possess like her. Now I'm supposed to invite her to not only come to Italy with me, but to express my feelings for her. I'm not prepared for rejection. I continue filling her in on some personal revelations over the week, buying me time.

"The Lord continues to soften my heart, to mold me into who He wants me to be. When you told me to pray about what to do, I'm still astonished at how he opened the door for me to serve Him in another country so quickly. I know I don't deserve such grace, mercy, for all the evil I've committed. The way I treated you, treated my mother the last days of her life," I say, shaking my head in shame, feeling the shot of pain stabbing through my heart more now than ever before. Even a bit nauseous.

Her expression softens, appearing hurt herself.

"I've asked God to forgive me for my past, but I don't completely feel it yet. Like something is refusing to let go," I admit.

"Maybe because you don't want to let it go? Feel as if you deserve to be punished for your decisions in life. You must fully trust God that His forgiveness is through Christ by His grace, not by anything you have done or will do."

I nod, knowing inside this is exactly why. Only delaying having to face the guilt. Before I'm able to respond, she releases what's on her heart.

"I've been waiting for the right opportunity to tell you this," she stops, takes a few deep breaths before continuing, "I'm...the one who introduced your mother to Jesus."

Surprised by her confession, even though all along the evidence pointed to her. An influx of questions I find instantly flooding my mind, however, standing unwavering in their midst are the soldiers of peace. The anticipated anger remains a stranger to me. Actually, excited for the prospect of having many of those looming questions put to an end. I lean closer, paying greater attention.

"She was a great woman. Loving. Selfless. All of the honorable characteristics to aspire toward. I honestly believe she was rejoicing in heaven during that special moment, watching you at the date palm. This was one of her greatest struggles in life. Not knowing how to present Jesus to you without disappointing you or pushing you farther away."

I bow my head ashamed. Taking a controlled breath, trying to release the chained guilt still imprisoned, thinking of my blindness, the pride constricting me behind a fortress nearly impossible to penetrate, while hostile toward all who opposed my ideology. This is exactly what she was trying to avoid, my attacking her. Would I have done it? Only now am I capable of seeing her unconditional love. Then it comes. Making perfect sense. She didn't want to risk me being the one responsible for sending her to her death or having to live with that internal ravaging of the soul my entire life. I think of our eternal souls, heaven or hell. No doubt this was constantly tugging at her heart.

"How did you first approach her with it?" I ask, interested in the first exchange. My mother's reaction.

"We worked in the same research and development sector, growing closer and closer together during those long hours. Our personal lives slowly became interwoven into our conversations. She knew I was a Christian, but she didn't treat me differently, never mentioning it once. Until one day we experienced an unexpected breakthrough in a particular project we were heavily invested in. Sitting there in a joyous atmosphere, I felt the Holy Spirit urging me to speak to her about my faith. And over the years learning to never quench this inner voice, I obeyed by asking her some questions about the Qur'an, about Isa in the Qur'an, then asking her if she would be interested in hearing what the Bible says about Him. She pondered it for a long moment, then finally hesitantly agreed. I shared with her the personhood of Christ, His life, His performing miracles and eventually His claim to be the Son of God."

"She faced difficulty on the last issue more than any other. Along the way asking questions, reasoning. Every fiber in her body warred against it, never disengaging though, but stayed persistent in finding the truth. This was an admirable quality. Some of her questions stumped me, forcing me to diligently research in order to find the answers. This not only offered her a foundation of evidence to build on but furthered my own knowledge and understanding of the Bible.

"How long ago did all of this begin?"

"In August of last year, about eleven months ago. There was a short period during the beginning where she quit asking me any questions. I could tell it was eating her up from the inside. A spiritual battle. However, as our friendship grew and my relentless challenges, she was pressed to deal with the difficulties raised. When I could see her getting overwhelmed, frustrated in specific ways, I would back off, giving her some space to decompress all of the internal struggles she was facing. Then, one Friday morning, I walked into work, finding her waiting for me, which was unusual. It struck me as strange considering she's never done that before. I sensed a change in her. The curious part of me triumphed over the nervousness in asking her if she needed to ask me anything. Her exact response was, 'I'm ready, I'm ready to give my life to Christ as my Lord and Savior.' Stunned by her directness, by the certainty in her voice, I led her through prayer right then.

It was a powerful moment. When I opened my eyes, her face was shining with tears of joy, with a transformation I could recognize immediately. She reached out, taking me into her arms, squeezing me, as I returned the heartfelt connection. Love coursed through my heart for her, for God in His calling her to Christ. We stayed in the room for a while, intimately talking, until the repeated interruptions of calls forced us to return to work. For the next eleven months, nothing stopped us from spending every working hour together studying, praying, fellowshipping. Our relationship grew stronger, our bond tighter. She took on the new role of a mother to me. I watched her grow in her faith, grow in her thirst for the Word and a fiery passion to live and walk for the truth. We even discussed how difficult it would be to hide from you and her family this new change. Did you observe anything different about her during this time?"

I earnestly search my memory spanning the last eleven months.

"Looking back now, I remember a new vibrant glowing about her, a joy, a certain peace and contentment surpassing my understanding because I was refusing to see it for what it was. I was unconsciously protecting myself from any kind of potential harm that could come to me if she was sinning in some way. Her counsel changed some as well, wiser than I was conditioned to. Physical affection was apparent more often and in a gentler manner, causing momentary suspicion; however, I was satisfied with seeing her happiness, never wanting to disturb it."

"How did you read Scripture together?" I ask, the buried Bible coming to mind.

She folds her delicate hands into her lap. "This brother from Jordan smuggled one to me shortly after I arrived in the country. Your mother and I would read it during our breaks inside a locked room. Sometimes she would borrow it, taking it to a special date palm in the desert to read. It was her way of intimately connecting with God. It was the same one you found and read from. She was supposed to bring it to work some time ago, but never showed up. I knew something went wrong. Felt it in my gut."

She turns away, grief attacking. I patiently remain settled, giving her a moment.

"Did she ever speak about me? Rana? What she desired most in life?"

"Half of what she spoke about revolved around you and Rana. The rest about God, revealing His infinite wisdom and power in our lives. She loved you so much. Showed me pictures, told me all about you. I wanted to meet both of you, but at the time decided it wouldn't have been for the best."

"Why?" I ask, realizing my mistake only afterward, but not wanting to admit it, admit to the pride that would have incited an egregious act on my behalf.

She eyes me with the look I've come accustomed to, grown fond of. "I think you know very well what the outcome would have been."

She took a short pause. "She was extremely proud of you, of your relentless dedication to playing soccer in hopes of achieving your dream one day in turning pro. That's why she and Kamal applied for your passport, saved up money, kept in contact with clubs around the world to sign you. She wanted this to be your way out. She couldn't leave the Kingdom without both of you. I watched her tears splash against the white tile floors many days. I understood this sorrow she carried with her.

You asked about her desires. Outside of you and Rana, she was being called to speak out to Muslims in particular across the world. With her intellect, she could reach a specific group of women that may find it difficult relating to other Christian women. This was her gift. The gift that was cut short according to God's will," she explaines, fighting the tears as they escape her eyes. "I was supposed to help her in Italy, where I own a little villa, preparing the way for us to be used in a great way. We must always remember that tomorrow isn't promised to us."

I sit pondering her words, about how quick this life can end, as hers did. How fast it fades like a vapor. Wanting to cry seeing her cry, my heart hurt knowing she's hurting. However, the glimmer of excitement over the unexpected opportunity to present my proposition to her comes on strong. Before I would contribute this as being a coincidence, but not now. God is undoubtedly the Grand Weaver orchestrating this intricate design of human events. How else on this specific night, with this special woman, about to offer her my whole heart to come with me, just so happens to own a villa there? Lived there. Familiar with the country. I struggle to hold my composure, as His grace and love are clearly seen pouring through this opened door.

"Are you still planning on going back to Italy?"

"I don't know yet," she replies, her mind weighing the option.

The urging won't let up...it's time. Battling against the anxiety, the fear, not letting this moment pass me by, aware of the likelihood it will never come before me again.

"Remember when I last spoke with you on the phone about what to do next?"

"Yeah."

"Well, there's a part I left out. Not long after that, when I was led to my uncle Kamal's house...you could never guess what happened. He tested me regarding my passion for soccer to either continue playing or give up forever. He handed me his phone already ringing. The man who picked up was an Italian recruiter offering me a contract to come play there."

She sucks in a breath, face brightening. "You said yes, right?" she asks, held in suspension.

I hold her gaze for a moment, almost losing it. "Yes, I accepted the offer, filling my heart with the greatest joy."

She leans forward, anticipating a hug coming from her, but at the last second restrains herself. I know I just missed out on something special, slightly disappointed about it. I continue.

"He asked me to think about who I would like to fly out with me."

I can sense her understanding of where this is headed, her body visibly tensing.

"I gave him your information, got your last name from Rana."

I pause to watch her reaction. Nothing. Her expression doesn't change.

"Kamal told me he couldn't come right now because of prior obligations. I've been waiting to ask Rana as well, in the morning."

While studying her face for a clue to a response, I'm thinking of how to break the news about my feelings for her. Eyes shying away, situating herself into a more distant position, all signs pointing to rejection, she finally answers.

"I'm kind of confused as to your asking me to come with you. Perhaps for a day or two, I can come to visit you; however, my work is very demanding here in the Kingdom."

I can't hold off any longer. I quickly ask God for the words, glancing out the window next to me long enough to collect all my heart's feelings into a gift for her to open. When I turn back to her, eyes fresh, courage recruited, once again recognizing why I'm so attracted to her: sharp pleasing features, confident, a gentleness, but most of all one of the most loving heart's I've ever known, pursuing the hope she has in Christ. I don't deserve her, too holy for me, can't hold it in any longer though.

"Remember when you told me you wanted to tell me something, then brought up how you introduced Christianity to my mother?"

"Yes."

"It's my turn to tell you something...from the first time I experienced your presence, I was drawn toward you. During the situations that joined us together by my deceitful ambitions, unwanted feelings began developing deep within for you. Although these feelings were growing unconsciously inside, the hate was also manifesting itself. Lasting up until this week when I surrendered my life to Jesus. The hate has vanished, the feelings, on the other hand, have never left. And the more time we spend together the more I desire to be around you. I don't know how else to tell you this...I want to be with you...in Italy." Her expression doesn't waiver, making me all the more nervous. I finish anyway, with all my heart's agenda. "There's no excuse for how badly I treated you. It was purely selfish, cruel on my part, which causes me grief every time I think about it. You didn't deserve any of it. I affected you in ways I will never fully understand and apologize for the pain, suffering and afflictions I have caused you not only physically, but emotionally. I wish I could go back and trade places with you that night in your place. I hope you can someday find it in your heart to forgive me. For you to still agree to see me after all that happened speaks volumes of the love you possess."

My eyes drift back to the parking lot, catching a rare figure enter a vehicle, leaving us to ourselves. I think of how difficult a position I've placed her in, the guilt I feel for it. "If you don't see me this way or don't want to go to Italy with me, I understand." I look down to the seat, anticipating rejection, relieved it's off my chest though, residing in her hands now.

Her words flow with surety laced in love. "I've already forgiven you. Prayed daily that you would one day see what's behind the veil. My prayers were answered," she says, with a humbling smile of thankfulness. "I'm really happy for you that God answered your prayers by creating a path leading you out of this hostile situation into a place of religious freedom where you will be doing what you've always dreamed of doing." She stops, sighs, then continues.

"About wanting me to come with you...it's shocking. This is the last thing I guessed you were planning on telling me. I must confess this is complicated to answer because it possesses many layers of difficulty."

Turning her head away again, letting out another sigh, then finishing her thought. "I can't give you an answer right now. There's much to consider. Most of all I need to pray about it."

I'm disappointed she didn't say yes, failure invading, even a little anger, attacking all the confidence I'm clinging on to. But, unlike before, that friendly peace makes its presence known telling me everything will work out one way or another if I only trust in Him.

"That's all I can ask for," I say, trying my best to conceal the embarrassment. "I hope eight o'clock in the morning is enough time for you." Her blank expression tells me what I need to know.

"I don't know..." she responds, hesitantly.

I interrupt quickly, "Don't worry about it. It's too much pressure too soon. It would be selfish on my part to expect it. For you to drop everything you're doing to come with me. Many trials have led you on a path to this place for a reason. To come along interfering in this is actually quite inexcusable on my behalf. I apologize...don't know what I'm thinking. This meeting was intended for me to share with you the miracle that happened in my life and to ask you some questions to further explain some things I'm ignorant of. Thank you for what you've already shared with me regarding my mother. It's etched on my heart forever."

"I'm always more than willing to help you in any way that I can."

It comes out of nowhere requesting its disclosure. For some reason, I heed the call. First peering through the windshield, disengaging from the present to travel back to those dark days for a short period.

"When I called you before you might have recognized the number...my mother's. She hid it before he took her. I conveniently happened to be there when it rang. This is what led me to you for the first time. I knew you had to be a friend. Even though I used it with the wrong intentions, I'm glad I kept it. You may wonder why I'm telling you this? You received a text informing you about the time of her death. This should never have happened. Not a memory worthy of holding onto...seeing such horror. You deserved to be notified in an appropriate manner. I hope you can also forgive me of this also."

Speaking of it rekindles the fresh emotions percolating at the surface. Blinking back the water blurring my vision, every movement of her body, every object she's drawn to, I notice.

"I'm grateful you sent it. Figured it was you, showing up at my place soon afterward wearing a murderous look over your face."

Her countenance changes; these words offering me an unexpected soothing. When her head rises, the hurt cannot be mistaken, pouring through her unreachable green eyes in a way that will provoke any man to dive into the raging waters willing to sacrifice his own life to save hers, to comfort her.

"Every time it comes to mind it breaks my heart because she endured what should have been my sentence. I loved her more than I knew. Wish I could have taken her place. I'm the one who is responsible for the materials. I gave them to her. It should have been me kneeling in the Square," she unloads, clearly shaken.

"It's not your fault. How could you know it would play out the way it did? You are not God. What happened is in the past now. There's no changing it except finding peace within this storm. All things are under His authority are they not?"

"I know...it's harder some days more than others. With you here discussing it with me, fulfilling one of her three dreams in life...I just needed to get it out."

I've never seen this side of her, vulnerable, sharing personal feelings, the impenetrable walls being opened for the first time, a glimmering hope almost coming alive at the thought of her possibly revealing any feelings she might have for me. We both stare off in our own separate ways, flipping through the painful memories, emotions, affected by the life of one very special woman who was irreplaceable in every way. These few moments of reflection remind me of my selfish desires with Lydia. God has His own plan for her. Getting in the way of that is something I refuse to do. I will leave it in His hands.

Feeling the need for some time alone, I urgently ask what's left on my mind. "I have one last question to ask, some advice, before I drive you home if that's all right?"

"Yeah, what is it?" she answers, regathering her composure.

"It's about Rana. I really want her to come with me as well, but we both know the only way it's possible is if she leaves in secret. The thing is, I feel the desire to share Jesus with her first. How do I do this when given only a few hours in the morning?"

I notice the shock. Silence and a mysterious face frozen in position are all I receive. Aware of her intellect, I begin to ponder what kind of strategy she's developing. Maybe there's more beyond taking a sensitive approach. Secrets I've yet to become acquainted with.

"Take tonight to pray about it. God will give you the opportunity and the words tomorrow. In gentleness and in love, speak to her from your heart. This is all you can do. But you will be amazed at what can transpire, how the hardened layers of her heart can be penetrated just like your mother's was and just like yours. I have confidence in you. All you can do is your part, leave the rest to Him."

For some reason, I was anticipating an easier path. Looking back in life, I've always endured the most difficult ones. I Consent to the soaking up of her advice with a brief nod. I step out of the car just long enough to slide around the back into the driver's seat. Lights, awakening of the engine, the concrete being trodden. My thoughts too scattered to concentrate. Mentally preparing for the sleepless night, the draining encounter with Rana, the anticipation of Lydia's call, the new life in Italy, all bombarding me with a compressed time frame.

I don't say a word on the drive; I've said enough already. The slight bump when entering the lot of ravaged buildings reintroduces reality, the one element in life you can't escape from. I hate having to drop her off here. Yet, it's almost a luxury in comparison to the compound across the street, her home. The last place a Saudi would look for words of wisdom, for guidance to the answers they so desperately need. And here I sit, with one of these precious foreign women, serving me out of the selfless love she possesses.

Door halfway open, leaning forward, she says her goodbye. "Thank you for tonight. My soul has been stirred by the miracles of God in your life. I'm flattered by the invitation to Italy. I will give you a call in the morning with my decision. And if you begin feeling any doubt about revealing your transformation to Rana, remember how much you love her and desire her to obtain the same freedom you have been given."

So much on my heart claws to come out in some kind of orderly fashion, but remains scrambled, suppressed, only one sentence emerges, "Thank you again for coming to spend this time with me. You've given me more than words can express."

"I'll talk to you soon. God be with you."

The dark figure briskly treads across the street, disappearing into the compound. Expecting at this point of the night to have all the answers for tomorrow, yet I'm still trapped in the same uncomfortable realm of the unknown where worry and stress tend to gain victory. Will I ever see her again, this godly woman my heart has fallen for? I never expected my life to be this tightly woven around three women at such a critical time as this. I entertain the random thoughts of past events for a short time in the heavy darkness.

What now? Ten-thirty. I have to pick Rana up at six. Maybe rest is the most beneficial choice. My eyelids feel the heaviness of my mind's constant work. I lock all the doors, recline the seat to parallel, watch the light turn into blackness, the sharpness of my conscious fading and drift off the cliff into nothingness.

Chapter Seventeen

Shooting straight up in my seat, scanning my immediate surroundings, where did it come from? What is it? Panic prompting me to check the time, fearing I may miss my flight. Four forty-seven. Relief settles me. Guess I needed the rest. The noise is of no real concern any longer. Then, out of nowhere, white light explodes through the darkness, exposing the entrance to one of the apartments. The small car crawls out of its place into the streets not too far away from me. It must have been the door slamming shut that woke me. I start the engine. Let it warm up for a few minutes, head west to Rana's. She should be expecting me.

The streets are bare; the city's still asleep, not for long though. Morning prayer draws near. I crack the window, inviting the brisk air to flush through the car, asking it to ignite my mind with the appropriate words for her.

Hands clenching tight around the small silver handle, it inches open with a tug just far enough to reveal what's needed. No sign of Nayef. I enter. After a few knocks, her loving face appears. Instantly my gut sinks. The bruises on her face are too severe to hide. Her arm holds the door open, as I squeeze by. With each step asking God to take the anger from spreading so intensely. Before I lower myself down into the lush black leather sofa stationed along the wall, the words are distinct, instructive, "Take her to the palm." Without hesitation, I turn to face her. "I want to take you somewhere," I say already in motion back toward the door, taking her by the arm.

She doesn't question nor resists my request. Why she trusts me with this kind of confidence after my behavior, my treatment of her lately, I don't know. The sky's slowly shifting from black to lighter shades of blue the closer we get to our destination. I occasionally glance over at her, noting how close we've been all our lives, how badly I want her to accept Jesus as her Lord and Savior. Can I ever not want the best for her now? The only obstacle is whether or not she believes my intentions. I must keep aware of this.

She doesn't ask where we're going but rides next to me with a security, a comfort, she's not used to. Every street, building, person, all of nature receives my careful attention to their every detail. By the time we arrive, the powder blue sky has fully bloomed. Out of my peripheral, I see she's watching, waiting for me to make the first move. I get out, meeting her on the other side. No need for words, we both venture out into the sinking mounds of gold like so many times before. The air is warming by the minute, rigid in its movement.

The lush greenery draping as the sole source of refreshment now hovers above us. I lower myself down, using the trunk of the date palm to prop me upright. Rana follows, her shoulder pressing into mine. "Just like when we were younger," I say, facing her.

A mummy wrapped in black cloth is all that fills my vision. I can't speak to her like this. Reaching over, I take hold of the niqab, unravel it from her head exposing a shining beauty no longer suffocated. No one but her and I out here. She is lovely, a delight to look at besides the swollen lip and puffy cheek she shamefully turns away to avoid my direct line of sight. She knows I know who it's from. She gradually comes back, studying my intentions while I'm thinking of something to make her smile.

"Remember the time I threw the date at you, hitting you right in the eye? I couldn't stop laughing...the expression on your face," I say, my mouth already stretching in the fullest smile.

Picturing that look of disbelief on her face, partly angry, causes me to chuckle. Her serious, demoralized stature begins cracking, lips turning upward until finally expressing that contagious smile I never can deny. For the first time in years, I feel the warmth we used to share.

The special brother-sister relationship severed by the hardening of my heart. What a blessing it is to feel it once again.

"Yes, I remember, you threw it when I wasn't looking," she defends, in an amused halfhearted way, nudging me in the process.

I allow my laugh to slowly regress, transform into the serious, risk-it-all face, yet with a liveliness flourishing like the freshest wadi. A force is evident within, refraining my lips from moving, keeping occupied with the island of date palms off in the distance, providing for the luscious life hovering below them. It doesn't take long for love to overpower the breathtaking scenery, love for the destiny of a human soul.

"I guess you're wondering why I brought you here?" I ask, locked onto those muddy wells of innocence. "Something happened to me. I've been struggling with how to tell you, stressing over your reaction to it."

"You can tell me anything, you know that," she interjects, reassuring me of how close we are, however, unable to hide the trace of disappointment heard in her voice. "I've noticed a difference in you at the house. I brushed it off as being overly sensitive on my part," she says, expecting for me to divulge what's on my chest.

"Anyone can say that until they hear the secret. Then comes the exception to the promise." I take a deep breath. "I guess the best way is to just tell you...I have found God."

"What do you mean? A different God?" she asks, unsure of my meaning.

"Yes, the true God, Jesus Christ."

The air sucks from between us leaving an eeriness, suspended in anticipation. Her face is stuck in shock, immovable, her eyes refusing to waver from mine. Seconds pass by, silence the only presence. Then, suddenly after a blink, they appear, gushing over her plump cheeks to the crease dividing her lips, finally free-falling off the bottom of her narrow chin. The tears only enhancing the mystery of not knowing her feelings, if they're related to sadness, joy or anger?

Uncertainty filling my heart, wondering how I should respond to her silence. Disclosing such a serious matter, I've risked our relationship of never knowing her true feelings on the issue.

Then, unexpectedly, her tight arm jerks free, wrapping it tightly around me, her wet face finding the safety of my neck, opening the floodgates. The sobbing, the releasing of pressure pent up inside, it all flows out. I accept it with open arms, gently rubbing her back for her comfort. What does this mean? What's she thinking? I badly want to help her, not be the cause of this emotional breakdown. No matter if she chooses to hate me and never wants to see me again or accepts me for who I am now, I will forever love her, hold a special place for her. The words battle through the crying, reaching my ears in a gracefulness unprepared for.

"Praise God...I've been praying so long for this day to come." This can only mean one thing: she's a believer. The unending joy overcomes me, opening up the long-awaited rivers of grace pouring out onto her smooth black hair. My arms squeeze her a little tighter.

"Thank you, God. Thank you so much," I whisper.

Something heavy releases from me, a peace instantly replacing it. Given this assurance of her life after death almost eases the guilt burrowed relentlessly in my heart over our mother. We remain in this position for a while, making up for these isolating past years. I gain back not only what we once shared, but far beyond that, we're both going home one day. Will be together forever.

Her face detaches from my neck, blushed, tears glistening as they nestle in her thick lashes. My joy mirroring hers. The questions emerge, one in particular stands at the forefront. However, in order to properly present it, I fill her in on the last two nights, everything except my confession of feelings for Lydia and inviting her to Italy.

"Glory be to God," she whispers, between sobs, all she's able to get out.

I keep silent, waiting for her to relax some, offering an opportunity to vent any feelings held captive for so long. They come as expected.

"I wanted to share with you so badly, even tested you one time to see your reaction in the car. I asked you about believing in another religion, but you scared me with your response. I feared how far you would go if I told you. I know I should have anyway, am a coward for not. Please forgive me?"

Her words cut me immensely. A slap in the face for the merciless monster I was even to my own flesh and blood. My heart has so much to say, yet the words refuse to oblige. Can say only what's on the surface.

"You have nothing to ask forgiveness for. You have been beyond what I could ask for in a sister," I pause, eyes locked. "Will you come with me?"

Her attention wandering to the distant city, showing a deep concentration before returning.

"You know I can't go. Nayef will never allow it."

"He will never know. Our flight leaves in about three hours, we can go pick up your things right now," I say, pointedly. "Trust me on this."

She lets a sigh out of indecisiveness. Traces of fear can also be detected. Fear of Nayef's brutality, of revenge for committing such an abomination in rebellion. I reach out, tilting her head up slightly with thumb and forefinger.

"Let's pray about it. If He wants you to come with me, it will be revealed to you."

"Okay," she says, eased by the suggestion.

We each take a moment taking our own turn calling out to God. The maturity I hear in the way she's speaking surprises me – makes me proud of her. Finished, I look to her earnestly hoping for an answer. My impatience gets the best of me once again. It will happen when it's intended to if it's God's will.

"I'm going to miss this country," I say, eyes exploring the stoic presence of the unique palm giving us the comfort easily dismissed. It's family nearby, the ocean of golden sand surrounding this city of hungry souls.

"The longing of home will attack me, I know this, but I'm ready. Ready to do whatever God is calling me to do. For the life I've been given, it's the least I can do." The softest gust of silence breezes through.

"What do you think mother's doing?" she questions, eyes flickering to defend against the swelling sadness.

"She's rejoicing, praising God on her knees, confident we all are part of the body of Christ and will be reunited."

She hesitates before speaking again. "Do you think she...forgave me?" My heart taking the brunt of the strike. Pain the inevitable consequence. How did I miss this? The guilt, the burden she's been carrying all this time. The same as Lydia. As me.

"There's nothing to forgive you for. You feel as though you betray her, I understand, but she would have forgiven you immediately. You know this better than I do. Remember Peter denied Christ three times after He was arrested and sent to be crucified? Peter was forced to deal with this same feeling of betrayal, but we see how Jesus came to him after His resurrection, forgiving him and calling him to spread His saving grace to all the world. If you hold on to this unforgiveness after asking God for forgiveness, it will kill you from the inside. Mother could never stay angry with you, she loved you too much," I reply, placing my arm around her, pulling her closer.

"You're not responsible for her death. This happened according to God's will. She was worthy enough to die for Christ, to lose her life for Him. What an honor. This is the main reason why I ended up here last night. The way in which it all transpired left me broken in pieces with only God capable of healing me. To build me back anew."

"If I never said anything to Nayef...she would still be here."

"And you probably wouldn't be," I say, envisioning Nayef beating her in uncontrollable fury.

"I would have been content with that. Didn't possess the courage to stand firm though," she says, bowing her head in shame, shaking it back and forth.

Lips quivering, I can see it – something deeper, struggling to come out. Not wanting to scare it away, I keep my arm tight around her shoulder, bringing her body into my chest, relying on her trust in me to feel safe enough to open up.

"What is it?" I softly inquire.

She leans back just enough to look into my eyes. "After I gave up mother's name, when asked if I believed what was on those pages, I said no. I...denied Christ!"

Her head returns to my chest in a condemning sorrow still very fresh. I search for some words of comfort, yet come across a numbing emptiness. Loving her so deeply, I yearn to help ease her suffering. but realize this reconciliation is intended to be between her and the Lord. For a short time, we don't move, speak, only float in the tense air, inciting the closeness of our old connection, an attempt to move beyond that.

She finally pulls away, saying in concern, "We should probably get going. You don't want to be late."

Based on the suppressing answer, I gather she's staying here or at least leaning this way. I firmly plant my palm in the porous sand, rising to my feet, assisting her up with my arm.

Before taking our first step, I scour the date palm, how meaningful this place will forever be to a mother and her two children. How God revealed Himself to me through His word here. It provided us with a place of refuge to search out His ways, without knowing Him, but ultimately calling us to enter into a personal relationship with Him. I retrace the path my eyes took last night, acknowledging the ungratefulness that built upon me for so many years. I've always heard growing up that one doesn't appreciate what they have until it's taken from them, yet if one's life is taken from them there's no life to appreciate. I have found if one is unwilling to give up everything to receive life, they will never know what life truly is altogether. Their freedom to choose has left death as the only other option.

I carefully transition through each one of my senses, nature's interaction with them, the treasures being offered: seeing...smelling... hearing...tasting...touching. However, with time as of the essence, I crouch down, plunging my hand into the gritty sand, instantly colliding with what I'm after. The red and white keffiyeh bursting forth so vividly against the tan terrain.

She intently watches me unravel the cloth exposing the precious book. "You found it!" she exclaims, eyes sparkling.

"You know about it?" I ask, curiosity enlivened.

"I knew it was here, but not exactly where," she explains. "Mother told me about it a couple months ago – was never given the opportunity to read it though."

A thirst is evident in her overflowing delight to at last hold it within her grasp. I hold it out as a gift not intended to be given by me, but destined to reach her at this moment, given by all those before me who risked their lives to smuggle it into the Kingdom. She accepts it, not breaking the finest thread of concentration, as if it's the best gift she's ever received. The teardrops explode in all directions at the moment of impact against the black leather. I take it there may be more history to this book than I'm aware of. I study her opening it, flipping through the pages, coming to a destination, then silently absorbing every word.

I don't interrupt, give her the time alone to reunite with it. Her eyes close for an unknown period of time, before opening again, before the sound of her voice is heard.

"John, chapter eight verses one through twelve. This is the passage that brought me to my knees, surrendering my life to Christ," she reveals. "Such grace, love, mercy and forgiveness, all of it exposing my need for a Savior."

Every word she reads sears into my mind. I am eager to explore every mystery tucked away beneath the surface, every word of wisdom, especially after seeing the profound effects it has had on her, encouraging me to further explore the power it contains. Craving more. I don't say anything, noticing her adrift, consciously someplace else, somewhere only she can go.

"Thank you, Lord, thank you," she whispers, eyes directing skyward. Then turning to me, "We should be going now."

I carefully wrap it back up, lower it into the sunken hole, cover it and while still squatting, allow my emotions to drive through me a final farewell to this special place, to this special book.

Chapter Eighteen

In route to Rana's, I can't help but find myself distracted by her indecision. A reminder of my need to focus on the persuasive speech required in convincing her to join me, if I possess one. We meander through the refreshed neighborhoods, taking the usual path back to her place.

An unexpected question shakes me free from the capturing thoughts, "Do you think Nayef will find out where you live?" she asks, worrisomely.

"Listen, if this is the determining factor holding you back from leaving, it can be easily resolved. The family never has to know where we live. We can even get two places if that's what it takes."

She returns to face the lives passing by through the window.

"O God, please stir within her heart the desire to come with me. I love her with all my heart. She deserves to be freed from this evil bondage strangling her. But, if this is not your plan, regardless of the anguish that may come upon me, I accept it. Whatever you want, let it be clear to her, please Lord, in Christ's name I pray, amen."

We roll to a stop. The lanes of hurried cars pass by, my countrymen at the wheels. What a change it will be in Italy. Women embracing the freedom they deserve. Lydia's selfless character stands out, how she sacrificed those freedoms to follow where God called her. This must be the reason why she hasn't called yet. Her place is here in the Kingdom to complete all the passions spiritually woven into her soul. Is this a taste of what lies ahead? To be torn between the two cultural elements? Each grasping at an end of my heart? Forced to choose? No matter how strong my feelings are for her, it's been made clear I'm to leave. If she stays behind, it's for me to accept and move on. Mindfully, there's a war being fought over what to do. However, peace dwells somewhere deep down on a narrow path convincing me not to waver.

It doesn't register right away. Takes until the second ring before checking the number glowing against the black background. My pulse immediately doubles, trembling my chest with every beat. Attempting to convince myself I'm prepared to answer, I swipe my finger, "Hello?"

"Good morning. I hope you're not busy?"

"No, I'm on my way dropping Rana off."

"How did everything go?"

"It went good," I say, pondering all of our interaction under the date palm. "I think it was something needed for both of us."

"Glory be to God! Is she going with you?"

I turn my head, her eyes studying me intently. I quickly return in time to cross the intersection, traffic crowding me more by the second.

"I don't know yet, will know within the hour...what about you?" Silence. My heart drowns. "Don't...," I begin before being cut off.

"I've been praying nonstop about it. The many complications make it even more difficult. So, I called to tell you...I will go with you. That is if the offer still stands?"

"Yes, of course, it's all I've been thinking about," I respond, ecstatic at her decision. Surprised by it. "Can I ask what it was? What made you say yes?"

"I prayed all last night, all morning, but received no answer, only mixed emotions, generally pushing me to stay. Then about ten minutes ago, I cried out one final time, hearing the most subtle small voice tell me, 'go.' Then a second time, as I began to doubt the response in my mind. It was from the same source, as when I was called here over a year ago. I called right away realizing the time."

"That's amazing! He must be calling you to the next phase of your life. I'm confident in whatever you touch will flourish, always glorifying Him."

"I get the sense that I must move on as well."

"We're pulling into Rana's right now; I'll be there in about ten minutes."

"I'll be ready," Lydia says.

"See you soon."

I lower the phone, turn the car off, habitually heighten my senses for an unexpected appearance from Nayef, the urgency settling in. "How long will it take you to pack?" I ask.

"Who was that?" she asks, in childish curiosity, dismissing my question.

I admire this look, enjoy it a moment before answering. "Lydia."

Through the brown in her eyes, I see the thoughts forming, making sense of what was discussed. I seize the moment.

"She's coming with us, that is, if you decide to. I never told you because she didn't decide until right now. I have been praying about it since our meeting last night. At the same time, I confessed my feelings for her. Unsure of what's awaiting us. We now possess a hope to cling onto, unlike at any other time in the past. This is where we are tested on whether or not we follow what we are being called to do in our lives. All I can ask for is if you agree to go."

She looks down into her lap, pulls the niqab from her head. Shiny black strands of hair come flowing down over the side of her cheek. Witnessing the struggle within, she will be abandoning her country, her husband, family. When I set my hand upon her shoulder to help her relax, to not feel pressured, the tension resists it. Her eyes close in deep concentration. "I want you to know I love you and whatever you decide to do won't change that," I say softly.

Waiting, time of the essence, I picture myself in her position, her thoughts, worries, all the things still finding ways to attack her. Countless difficulties she faces, but ultimately surrounding one transcending foundation. If she listens, the blessing will be laid upon her. Part of me wishes I could choose for her, at the very least nudge her enough to commit to one or the other. However, who am I to interfere with her free will? Forcing anything will only crumble under the wrath of the storm.

"Umar," gently escapes from her lips.

Opening her eyes, moving to face me. "My prayer was for an answer on whether I should leave. During the call with Lydia, it never crossed my mind until afterward when you revealed what you did. Then it became clear this is what we were seeking, exactly what I needed to hear. Lydia and I grew closer together after mother died. The hospital was a pivotal moment for us. We cried on each other's necks, shared things never before disclosed and prayed together. She means a lot to me. Knowing she will be there with us is the final push I need." She lets out a sigh of relief. "I'm going with you."

I immediately pull her into a loving embrace, joy overwhelming me, feeling the tears crawl down my face onto my lips. Relieved as we hold each other, swiping a tear off her blemished cheek.

"We should grab your things. There's not much time to spare," I emphasize.

She hurriedly pops the door, moving faster than expected. In no time I'm on her heels moving through the sitting room, passing the kitchen, before reaching her bedroom. As soon as we enter, the thought of a surprise visit from Nayef makes me freeze.

"You don't have much to pack do you?"

"No, why? "she asks, already stuffing a bag full of clothes.

"I will wait for you at the front door where I can keep an eye out for Nayef if he randomly decides to show up."

"I'll only be another ten minutes, if that."

I navigate back to the entrance beside a nearby window, taking up post. Eventually, my eyes drift off to the furniture, tables, the meaningless items being left behind. All replaceable. My mind then switches to his reaction when stepping into the empty bedroom. How far his anger will drive him to find her and the boys. Maybe I will request Kamal to keep my signing a secret. That will only last momentarily until someone sees me on TV. I give it to God, to deliver us.

I check the time: seven-twelve. We need to get going. I rehearse the plan in my head if he does show up: Rana runs out the back door, bags in hand, waits for him to enter the front door where I will meet him, distract him, giving her plenty of time to get in the car. Then telling him to have her give me a call, she's using the restroom and something came up. I can't help but running this scenario over and over again in my mind, always trying to control every outcome. Heavy breathing approaches from behind.

"I'm ready," she says, dropping two overloaded bags to the floor. I gather up the heavier one, opening the door with my free hand.

"Ready?" I ask, glancing back at her.

"Yeah."

I step out first, leading the way with a quickened pace, scanning for the slightest movement, the last thing wanting is for Nayef to arrive right now. Adrenaline exciting my awareness causing an uneasy nervousness bred from fear. I reach the trunk, open it, swivel from left to right along the entrance keeping my eyes peeled, finish throwing the bag inside as Rana follows my lead, ushering the boys into the back seat. On the way out making sure the doors are securely shut. Once we make the first right off her street, the comfort begins loosening the tightness clenching my body.

"He won't know I'm gone until tomorrow night," she says, seeming undisturbed by the potential consequences. For some reason through the immediate mission to safety, an interest in a statement Rana made earlier competes for my attention. Has been hovering there ever since. I look over at her sensitive face in admiration, before presenting the question.

"How long before the hospital did you and Lydia know each other?" She reads no selfish motives out of the question.

"About three months," she answers, nonchalantly.

"Why?"

"Were you a believer?"

"Yes, for a month at that time. It's amazing isn't it?" she says, now watching me. "After such a heartless affliction, she sacrificially endured, God used you with the wrong intentions to deliver me right into her room." All I'm left with is a slow cower of my head in shame at the role I played, but left in awe for His unlimited reach of love and compassion to His children.

"Remember how long I was in there...the entire time holding her hand, praying with her, whispering in her ear, listening to the graceful words fighting their way from her bandaged mouth with Aditi sitting beside us. Seeing her in such brutal condition, I felt a hint of guilt deep down. Responsible in some unexplainable way because I'm your sister. But before I got up to leave, she requested to say a final prayer. That prayer was specifically for you to come to Christ.

I refuse to speak. I can't escape the disgust I feel looking back inside that moment in my life. There's only one other woman who would willingly show me a love like this after explicitly degrading her over and over again. This helps explain the shift in Rana's character that day - the same kind found in our mother. All those obscure questions I shook free as mere over-analyzing, transformed into fear. Still facing me, what is she expecting from me? An apology for taking advantage of her love for me? How do I express the regret?

"I hope you can forgive me for involving you in everything. My pride and blindness of the truth consumed me. Only now am I barely touching the gratefulness I should have for you, for Lydia. I am undeserving of your untampered love for me."

"I forgive you...God used it for good though, answering my prayer for fellowship. I must also ask you for your forgiveness."

"You don't require forgiveness from me," I say, sternly.

"I do though, for lying to you about what happened in the hospital room with Lydia," she meekly admits.

This explains her reaction during our discussion. There's something else, something deeper, more difficult to confess. I can tell by the heaviness still draping over her. "And...for the anger I've harbored against you."

"Anger for what?" I ask, in effort to know exactly what caused it, however, not ignorant to the fact she has a list to choose from.

"For," she hesitates a split second, "not helping me that day."

She begins tearing up. The images instantly invading my mind, confirming with words what my conscience has been feeling since I walked out on her, always acknowledging the incident, but hiding it behind the veil of Islam until now. How am I to respond? Admit I'm a coward for what I did? I will have to answer for it one day. This is far more complicated than I anticipated. I'm unaware of anything acceptable to say.

At the next red light, I reach out gathering up the wet, loose strands of hair hanging down beside her flushed cheek, tucking them behind her ear. Her young face so vulnerable, precious. I can't resist the pressure any longer. The tears come again. Then the words.

"I forgive you," I say, understanding her desire to hear it. "The way you looked at me when hugging the floor, will forever be inscribed into my memory. I wanted to help, could feel it in the pit of my being, until my wicked heart watched the opportunity slip by. I still haven't forgiven myself for that day, will need God's help to do so if ever able to. I'm the one who should be asking for forgiveness. Maybe my pride has kept me from bringing this up, not knowing what to say. Even though it happened when I was blind, a slave in bondage, that small voice inside was there urging me to intervene. And I ignored it, will have to face that for the rest of my life," I confess, then break eye contact, can't bear to look at her. The green light calls my attention back to the road ahead. I wipe my cheeks dry, take a sharp left into the compound.

"I will always forgive you Akhi," she says, as we're pulling into Lydia's.

I lean across the console taking Rana in my arms, a release overcoming me, one I never knew lived so deep inside my soul. The warmth of her face on my shoulder, the reconciliation that is real, uniting my best friend back to me. What joy in the midst of all this pain and suffering!

The moment we release each other, Lydia's walking out the front door hands full of baggage. The familiar, unique rush of elicit joy she makes me feel every time I see her pushes me out of my seat to help her.

"I'll take those," I say, grabbing them out of her hands.

"I have one more," she says, running back inside, the traditional black abaya flowing over her body. I've always admired her intelligence, staying one step ahead. The last thing we need is unwanted attention because of an uncovered foreign female.

I fit the bags in the trunk next to Rana's and mine. When I glance back at the doorway, there she stands, bag placed on the ground beside her, while hugging an Indian woman. They let go, exchanging words, then the woman embraces Rana who's now joining them. All I can think of is God's great love. The bond they share with one another. The fellowship. A glistening sheen can be seen on all three of their faces, as they attempt at wiping them dry. None are covered with niqab. I now realize Rana's hasn't been on since the date palm. I'm glad we made it all the way without any hassle. I'll have to address the issue before we depart. I sympathize with the Indian woman losing her best friends. Just beginning to understand the significance of fellowship. An idea evolves, breaking into these thoughts. I swiftly make my way to join them. Their attention stolen by my unexpected intrusion.

"Do you know of any man nearby who can ride with us to drive the car back to Aditi?" I ask Lydia.

Their expressions remain shocked, before Lydia turns to her for a moment, then back to me. "Actually, I do."

The phone is already ringing, Aditi speaks up. "No, I can't accept it."

"God put this on my heart. Please do not deny me the privilege of giving you this gift."

Her chin lowers in embarrassment, rises with the softest words. "Thank you," humbly stepping into me with a startling warm hug, radiating a sincere gratefulness.

Although touching women who are not related has been forbidden my entire life, it seems more natural, more significant, in stepping outside those boundaries. I can feel the longing as if this is that which I've been missing for so long.

"Amare will be right over," Lydia says, ending the call.

They say their final goodbye. I'm saved until last. "Keep your eyes on Christ. He is faithful in guiding us on His narrow path, if we choose to pursue it. And if you ever want to leave the Kingdom to get away for a while, you're always welcome at our place. We'll be praying for you."

"Thank you, that means a lot. I will be praying for all of you as well," she says, emotions breaking through the surface barrier.

We slowly make our way back to the car and as we do, Amare arrives. My heart begins fluttering. The same dark-skinned man, short, fluffy hair, set with a slim, but muscular build that I will never forget punching at the conclusion of a long chase. Lydia greets him with a comfortable embrace and introduces him.

"Amare, this is Umar."

"Nice to meet you, Umar," he says through a genuine smile, yet with an acknowledgment of our previous encounter.

I firmly shake his extended hand. "It's nice to meet you too. We appreciate your help."

"It's my pleasure."

A warning sparks in me. Why am I not more cautious about being here, outside, mingling with foreigners and women? I initiate our need for departure by getting into the car. Rana and Lydia follow, getting in the back, wrapping their niqabs over their faces as I expected, Amare sitting next to me in the passenger seat.

I find Aditi leaning against the doorway watching us pull away. I feel for her losing two sisters.

The ride is quiet. I double-check the time of our departure then mentally scroll through the checklist. "Rana," I say, finding her in the rear-view mirror, "Do you have your passport?"

"Yes," she answers, confused by the question. "Why?"

"I don't remember you ever applying for one."

"Kamal took me and mother about a year ago."

I welcome the inner smile, the wonder at how God has orchestrated every event each step of my life. Checking everything else off, I cut my thoughts loose to roam free until arriving at the airport.

Chapter Nineteen

The sheer size of Riyadh King Khaled International Airport is overwhelming to take in. Its modern design decorated with transparent glass all throughout the structures leaves a classy, yet comfortable element to it. We pull up to the entrance, bodies racing in every direction, getting dropped off, being picked up, creating an atmosphere of urgency complementing the rumbling thunder of jet engines on the runway. We all step out, meeting at the rear of the car. Before lifting out the bags, I feel for the phone and passport, confirming their proper place. We quickly give our farewells, knowing time is limited.

"Thank you for doing this," I say to Amare. Then, suddenly the urging comes forth. I try to fight it at first, but wisely give in knowing it will haunt me if I reject it. "I...will you forgive me?"

He looks at me strangely for a moment, Rana and Lydia confused about such a question from me to this supposed stranger. "I already have, praying for your salvation this entire time, glory be to God!" he says, a joyful smile beaming at me. "I'm also glad to help out Aditi with this car; what a blessing it will be for her."

"God be with you, Amare," Lydia says. "I will call you once we arrive."

He turns to Rana. "God bless you," she says.

Recognizing the need to move on from his stalled body language, I bend down, taking up my bag, including one of Lydia's, making my way toward the entrance. The girls join me, hands full of luggage, the boys shuffling close behind. I refuse to look back, focusing on completing this final stage. Entering the busy airport, we approach the congregation of kiosks to receive our boarding passes. A familiar, but unexpected nervousness rattles me, warping into fear. I attempt rejecting it knowing there is no place for it to exist if God is with me. We then separate into our own gender-separated security lines.

After what seems forever, it's my turn at the small desk. The middle-aged Saudi stares at me as I pass him my passport. His neatly lined mustache centers his jovial plump face. Leaning forward with a strict expressionless look residing contently on his face, he returns my passport and I step forward. Being my first time inside an airport, it seems relatively serene inside. Mostly men filling the place. I consciously find myself scanning the men's faces for familiarity. There are two in particular who can pose a threat; neither found to pay me any attention though. My turn comes quickly, forcing me away from my wandering thoughts. I place my bags on the x-ray belt now in the security line, everything else required to be placed in the plastic bins, then walk inside the body scan area. I observe the actions of the man before me, copying his movements.

After gathering my bags, I enter the terminal, maneuvering in pursuit of the two girls who should be entering the terminal from the women's side. Yet, for some reason, they're nowhere to be found. Maybe they're waiting at the gate? I check the gate on the boarding pass, finding which direction I need to go.

Person after person pass by, rushing to board an announced flight. The gate area is filled, a line already formed boarding the plane when I arrive. I intentionally direct my attention to the right, as some Westerners gather together, tourists probably. Their laughing and cheerful faces are what draws me to them. Blond curls spiraling down alongside the young woman's tanned skin as she intently focuses on the clean-cut, sharply featured man next to her. Lydia comes to mind, evolving into an unanswerable question. "Will she ever look at me with that kind of passion, with a love so deep?" It lingers, suspending in a cloud of doubt before turning away.

In an instant, I'm forced to stop, preventing a head-on collision with another man in a rush. The grip of both my hands clenches tighter around the handles of each bag, keeping them from slamming into his legs. Then my body locks up from the shock. Adrenaline pumping through me. Heart is throbbing. Blood no longer welcome inside my face. How did this happen so fast? Still trying to catch my breath, his cold stare won't allow it. Only terrifying scenarios of his merciless intentions transpire. Our eyes in a standoff, maybe half a meter between us, his dry lips finally part. "You planning on leaving without saying goodbye?"

"Didn't think you wanted to see me," I respond, refusing to skirt around the seriousness of the question. "We both know that's not why you came here."

His gray eyes glisten intensely. "I still refuse to accept my blood flowing through your veins. Every time I look at you, I see her face staring back at me. That's why during all those cool, dark nights, I'd walk out the door leaving behind two bloody faces instead of one, both yearning to save the other, how pitiful the sight."

The painful memories cut me deeply without relief. A combination of submission, fear, anger, are all stirring at once. However, I feel a peace fighting back now, reminding me of Christ's forgiveness for all the wickedness I've committed and the unconditional love and grace He has given me. All causing my head to bow in a kind of humility. Then, the words come forth naturally from somewhere within. "I've held onto one particular question since mother was killed, one question I've been meaning to ask you, but could never gather up enough courage to do so." His expression doesn't waver, I don't wait for it to. "Why didn't you kill her yourself? You would've been praised for an honor killing. A most noble act it would have been on your part."

The world freezes. Everything stops moving except for the slow-motion flickering of his eyelashes. All the surrounding noise becomes muffled, a secondary sense. The anticipation for an answer is the only concern for concentration. Then, I catch it. His countenance changes in the most subtle way. Perhaps cracking. A tinge of mystery through the hardened exterior. "I wanted to give her as many opportunities as possible to repent, to revert to Islam, to save this family from the shame she would surely bring." The air remains motionless, only capturing the space between us.

"I did it for you. I know how much you loved her, needed her and the devastation you were prone to face in losing her that way. I prayed you wouldn't turn to terrorism in dealing with the pain and grief when moving forward with your life without her. My hope was for you to follow in my footsteps in becoming a prominent sheikh in the Kingdom. Yet, this is not the path you have chosen though. You inherited that weakness from her. Guess you'll be doing what you've always dreamed of. I should be grateful for Kamal and all the time he has dedicated in teaching you this game, in pushing you to play at the highest level. You owe him more than you know. As for me, I've not only lost a wife but a son also." The sudden movement startles me, causing me to flinch enough for him to notice. His arm rises revealing a book in his hand, escaping my sight this entire time till now. Why is he offering it to me?

"It's the only one I could find. It must be yours. This is what you needed the most, yet you left it unopened night after night. I want you to have it back as a reminder of her shameful death and to read it in hopes of one day receiving the honor to be called my son again, a faithful follower of Islam."

At the end of his hollow wish, Rana and Lydia suddenly appear in the distance camouflaged behind the oncoming crowd. This can't be happening. Fear reverberates through my body, palms moistening as I impatiently accept the book, contemplating on how to warn them of his presence. I try interfering with the thoughts of the heinous acts he will commit if he sees them. For a split second, I want to believe my eyes are deceiving me. Lydia's lighter complexion culminating around that radiating greenness is unmistakable though. Approaching closer by the second, the answer emerges out of nowhere, directing my movements with a steady precision.

My vision chases a man to my right, following his every stride, as if he's come here with me. Luring my father's attention, he whips his head in that direction with an evil curiosity to find something to hurt me. The fervent passion burning inside causes him to over-pursue with his focus, allowing me the window to subtly wave the girls away using my left arm without him noticing. They're not paying attention... look at me, come on. Finally, Lydia makes contact. I don't change my position until I begin to see the full onset of confusion in his eyes. Facing each other once again, I can see the back of the two black figures heading away from us. An inner rejoicing screams within.

"Flight 217 group 9 is now boarding," the piercing PA alerts me for departure, stirring the last of the people to join the line. "I must go now. Thank you for the Qur'an," I say, walking past him toward another gate, refusing to glance back.

More concerned about Rana, the boys and Lydia's safety, about getting them on this plane without him seeing us together, I turn when I finally reach the other gate, finding his absence and my urgency to find the girls and join the line. Scouring the last area I saw them in, I'm unable to find them anywhere. I check the line one more time focusing harder on each individual. There they are, about to scan their tickets. I swiftly join the short line, as I catch Lydia turning back and spotting me. I struggle to keep my arms at my side, cautious of my father's revengeful appetite.

The short man, with a pervading expression, willingly accepts my ticket, scans it, returns it to me. I don't pay much attention to the transaction, my focus on who's behind me. I hurry into the small rectangle hallway corralling us to the plane. As I step through the door, I see the aisle still packed with people navigating to their seats, placing their bags overhead. I patiently wait, attempting to look around the bodies to find Rana and Lydia. Eventually, everyone finds their seats in front of me, as I make my way to 30A. Once I arrive, I realize all the seats are not together. Lydia and Ali's seats are in the aisle of the next row next to a boyish-looking Saudi, while Rana, Ahmand and I are together next to a heavier set man already swiping away at his phone. I can see the nervousness in Rana's and Lydia's eyes, but with a touch of relief over the previous encounter. If only we can get the heavier set man to trade with Lydia. I recognize the opportunity.

"Excuse me," I say, his neatly trimmed black bush of hair settled around his chin turns to me. "This woman is with me seated here in the aisle," I look over at Lydia, "and this is my sister next to you. Would you be willing to trade her in the aisle?"

The man rises to his feet, introducing a good-natured grin. "That's fine with me." He grabs his bag, as Rana gets up allowing him to squeeze by. Ali takes jos seat by the window, Rana in the middle, Lydia in the aisle and me in the aisle across from her. I put away my bag, still on high alert, before sitting. The book I tuck away at my side between the seats, waiting until sometime in flight, passing above the powdery white clouds, to be explored. We sit quietly, preparing for takeoff, while the flight attendants are explaining the flight safety. I notice the common anxiety in all of us.

Minutes later, the announcement is made for takeoff. The voice comes as faint echoes in my ears, my mind occupied on potential threats from my father. Then, the sudden rumbling, vibrating every bone in my body, startles me. The turbulence flips my stomach upside down, as the wheels lift off the runway, ascending steeply into the heights of rarely disturbed blue sky. Once we begin leveling out, I cast a glance over to Rana first, then Lydia, investigating their reaction. Their expressions reveal the great relief I'm also beginning to feel. Conversation starts between them, as I try taking it all in, the realization that we made it. However, in my attempt to relax, a prompting draws me to the book. I pull it from its hiding, placing it on my lap, debating on whether or not to throw it away or keep it as a reference for the future.

"Umar?" a distinct voice calls, pulling back. I turn to find Lydia's beauty perking toward me. "We meant to ask you earlier, who was that man you were speaking with?"

I delay before answering. Rana now leaning over Lydia closing the distance between us. "It was my father," I grant silence its time, then continue. "We exchanged some words, he gave me this Qur'an, we said our final farewell," tilting the cover in their direction. "He said it belongs to me...it was our mother's." I look to Rana understandably expressing wounds at the mere mention of her, back to Lydia's moist eyes, then retreat to the small oblong window across from me.

I see Riyadh hovering below. This is the land of my tribe, my kindred. I'll miss you. Will forever guard the special place in my heart for you. Even as the grief persists, whatever must be done to reach you with the truth of Jesus may it be so, not by my will but by the Lord's.

Returning my attention to the book, the only other possession I have of hers besides the phone and black niqab, I casually begin flipping through the pages. This must be the Qur'an she personally used before converting. Surahs flash by one after another stirring up life's memories holding it in my hands. About a quarter of the way through it, something catches my attention. The text changes to penned handwritten pages in black ink. My heart begins pounding again. Feeling it inside my throat with each hurried swallow, I now recognize what it is. I grew up seeing this handwriting around the house. The dates settle near the top of the page: nine-seven-twenty.

How long has she been writing in this? Did my father know? How could he not have ever opened it? My mind overloading with questions. I examine the careful construction of the pages precisely integrated into the binding. A sense of anticipation drives me to the first word on the page and as I do, a guilty presence of invasion reveals itself. Should I read her most precious, heartfelt secrets, intended to be seen by her eyes alone? Would she want me to read it? It doesn't take long for an answer, my heart making it known. She would want me to. God has brought it into my hands specifically for this reason.

"Father, I'm doing everything I can short of unveiling You to him with words. What else am I to do? My heart aches every moment of every day knowing he has yet to surrender his life to You. How am I supposed to reach out to him? Please open a door for me. Soften his heart. Call him to Your grace in Christ. To experience the kind of love that reaches far beyond our understanding. Sweeter than anything ever tasted. I badly desire to reveal it to him, aware of the consequences, possibly my death. If this is what it takes for his salvation, let it be. You told me to be patient, I've been waiting, but my flesh is weak. How much longer? I cannot bear to lose him, my only son. Every time I look into his eyes, I see a desperate need for a Savior. For a father to love him unconditionally. To teach him how to be a man after Your own heart. Forgive me for raising him apart from You. I was too caught up rejecting Your every attempt in reaching me. But You remained faithful to Your promises, through one Russian woman. Slowly chipping away at my stony heart. O Lord, let him taste Your grace. Lift the veil blinding him from the truth, just as You uncovered Rana's through much fasting and prayer. Provide for him that same thirst-quenching her soul experienced. The personal relationship with You, the forgiveness of sins, the absolute assurance of salvation. Casting aside the desires of worldly possessions for new spiritual treasures. I cry out to You Lord! I know You hear me. Help me be that light to him, representing Christ's love through the Holy Spirit. There is so much I long to share with him. Feel guilty for not. Now, I can relate to the doubt, the fear Lydia was facing when presenting Christ to me. I will wait on Your timing though. Who am I to question You? You called me when I was wandering in the darkness. Gave me purpose when I had none. Peace where contention was ripe. Love where hypocrisy was manifesting itself. As the days count down, I will stay focused on Your will for me, fervently praying day and night that this will be the day he accepts Your free gift. Only You know how long our secret will be safe. I can feel death's presence closing in. No longer bringing me any fear though. Fading from me as You grow me. The peace You've given me won't permit it. I know in whatever I must face, You will be with me. Glory be to You. In Christ Jesus's precious name, amen."

My eyelids gush with water. Shameful guilt covering me. The thought alone of having her killed at one point in time sickens me. Reading her words awakens me to the reality of my unworthiness to have died in her place. I welcome the anguish from her death to continue ripping through me, haunting me daily. For in her selflessness, she sacrificed her own life for faith in Jesus, while altering my life significantly in the process. I remember seeing her gentle face holding that mysterious look I had come to notice this past year, causing pause in me just long enough for acknowledgment before dismissing it for more urgent matters to me. It was there all along wasn't it? Silently competing for my heart in the subtlest of ways, only to be rejected by my pride.

I don't look at Lydia, can't force myself to. Too overwhelmed by the strings of emotions, intensely preparing me for what's coming next through her tangible words firmly resting within my grasp. They are the very key to unlocking some of her most confidential thoughts, ones I never expected to know about. Once again, I question my father's knowledge of this. My assurance of his incompetence or intentional dismissal. However, his intentions are clear if indeed his unawareness proves true - to humiliate me by exposing my ignorance of the Qur'an as well as reaffirming her deserved death in hopes of dissuading me from following her, all the while alluding to my partaking in it, to my weakness. It's an underlying attack and insult. Yet, through his hateful intentions, God's working His mighty hand in blessing me with a precious jewel. I don't harbor resentment toward him. I can't, because of the forgiveness freely given to me for being far worse. Hoping in some way God will open his eyes, whether it be through her death, through me or by some other means. This new love I feel extends towards all people who are wandering hopelessly, empty inside, without meaning in life.

My curiosity is burning for more of what's contained inside. What other intimate secrets are buried here? Those bringing tears of joy? Shameful ones? All priceless words to me, yet counted as worthless to the next person. I gently close it, firmly squeezing it between my palms, shutting my eyes, bowing my head in prayer.

"Abba, glory be to You. Thank You for everything. What have I done to deserve such blessings? You have been faithfully directing me to this very point in my life. Motherless, yet possessing a Father who loves me. Fleeing everything familiar to me except Rana and the only woman my heart has ever melted for. In no way can I deny Your presence with me in every moment. The peace in my heart confirms it. I do trust my mother's death was in Your will for reasons I don't entirely grasp right now. I could see it in her that morning - a strength unrecognizable. Did she harbor any regrets? Shame? Maybe these were the precise events required for me to come to faith? If it happened any other way would I still be seeking my own desires?" The question presents itself rather bluntly, "If I could go back, would I change it?"

"Only You know the outcome. You are not constrained within time. I will continue trusting in Your will, calling me to serve You in this unknown place. Whether it brings persecution, trials, sufferings, I will cling to Your loving embrace. You have brought us this far. Help me be that godly man she so passionately hoped I would become, not only for her but for Rana and Lydia. I know they will look to me moving forward for spiritual leadership. May I one day be found worthy enough to live a life honorable as hers. I miss her more than I can express."

An intense burst of loss fills me. With all my might I clench my eyes. "I need You more than ever right now. How can I ever forgive myself for leading Tariq to his death? How can I forgive myself for what I put my mother through? The comfort of knowing she's with You, for some reason has no effect on healing my wounds. The blade only cutting me deeper knowing I will never be with Tariq again. I've lost him forever. Please draw nearer to me. Comfort me. Don't leave me all alone in the desolate darkness where I once walked. I want to be obedient to Your will."

Suddenly I see my father handing me the Qur'an in his evil motives. "And Lord, touch my father's heart. No one is outside of Your reach. Pierce Kamal's heart, the hearts of my people, that they may know the truth. You are the only thing in existence capable of fulfilling their inner hunger. May I keep you first all the days of my life, for You have shown me that without You our lives are but a hopeless journey gasping for a breath, which will never be granted. Thank You for Your grace freely given to me, Your mercy upon me and Your love filling me. I love You. In Christ's precious name, amen."

My final conversation with Tariq arises, my promise to him. I'm ripped in two between the joy I know he would have experienced honoring my word and achieving our dream, yet at the same time grief that he's not here to see it, his blood being on my hands. I suppress it, not entirely ready to confront the depth of what it entails.

All the announcements are merely insignificant vibrations passing by. My eyes open to the deceiving title cradling a treasure residing within. I hold it in my hands like I did the first soccer ball she bought me. Cherishing it, I turn, finding Lydia holding a satisfying, joyful smile, a joy unable to be ripped away by anything or anyone. Her look is a rare glimpse of how we should look at every living soul. I study her as she's concentrating on something in front of us; such a precious gift from God she is. She feels my stare, searches my damp eyes for a reason. She finds it in my silence...we made it. Our new life together begins with Christ as the foundation. We stepped out in faith, excited for what the future will bring. Our smiles meet simultaneously. I pull a black cloth from my pocket, the one wrapping the book's nakedness under the date palm, which captures the special night, the beginning of my new life. Before tucking it away, I take one final glance at the book, thinking of her in the blinding white light falling so gracefully over her presence. Her perfect smile. Her penetrating voice singing praises to God.

I cover the book with the black cloth, tilting my head skyward, my lips moving, void of any sound. "See you soon Amy."

Acknowledgments

First, I give thanks to God for placing this gift and calling within my heart. This has been a very long journey and many have supported and encouraged me along the way. I thank my beautiful and God-fearing wife for all of who she is and how she has loved me through this process. Thanks to my mother for always believing in me, loving me and encouraging me. To my brother and his wife for their love, support and help. To my stepmother for her love, generosity and encouragement. Thanks to my sister for her constant undercover excitement. To my aunt for her love and devoted time scrutinizing each page. To my grandparents for their love and support. To my two best friends and who supported me and encouraged me day after day. To all my friends and family who invested in me, believed in me and supported me through this journey in different ways. Love you.

About the Author

Writer, researcher and creative entrepreneur G.C.Bloodman is quickly rising on many platforms. His passion and desire in reaching the world is inspiring to say the least. Don't miss out on being a part of this transformation. Engage and follow him online and through social media at www.underthedatepalm.com

CPSIA information can be obtained
at www.ICGtesting.com
Printed in the USA
BVHW041710030321
601620BV00012B/86